THE FREAK SHOW

Other books edited by Peter Haining

THE FREAK SHOW

Freaks,
Monsters,
Ghouls,
etc.

Edited by
Peter Haining

THOMAS NELSON INC.
Nashville / New York

SC
HAI

Second printing, September 1973

Library of Congress Cataloging in Publication Data

Haining, Peter, comp.
    The freak show.

    CONTENTS: The magician, by D. Defoe.—Hop frog, by E. A. Poe.—Spurs, by T. Robbins. [etc.]
    1. Horror tales. I. Title.
PZ1.H1255Fr 3 [PR1309.H6]   823'.0872   72-1436
ISBN 0-8407-6244-5

Manufactured in the United States of America

CONTENTS

INTRODUCTION

The Truth about the Bearded Lady

I remember "The Incredible Bearded Lady" as if it was only yesterday that I stood before her booth, my shoes squelching in the fairground mud and my eyes wide open in wonder. Perhaps I should say I remember her showplace, rather than the lady herself, for I was not allowed to spend one of my carefully hoarded sixpences on admission, though I would dearly hav. ...ved to do so.

Still, my childish disappointment has led to an adult's abiding interest in freaks and freak shows which goes far deeper, I hasten to add, than just a morbid interest in people who are different because of a strange quirk of nature. I am fascinated by the showmanship which surrounds most of them—and their amazing ability to use what might well be considered a drawback as the very means whereby they can earn a good living. Of the genuine freaks I have met, I have yet to come across one who was either sorry for himself or would have willingly changed places with me.

They are, in fact, following in an ancient profession that dates back almost to pre-history; a profession which capitalises on the inherent curiosity in mankind for the odd, the strange and the unusual—not to mention the gruesome. For those of us who consider ourselves normal physically (as against mentally, and in that area who can say what is truly normal?) we are vastly intrigued by giant men and women, dwarfs, midgets, bearded ladies, fat men, alligator boys, two-headed children and strangely mutated animals and rodents. We are not often too bothered whether the freak is entirely genuine or not (showmen must have their licence after all), although we do object to being taken too obviously for a ride by what is patently a fraud.

This, then, is the freak show. A world of the unusual, the never-before-seen, the maybe-real and the maybe-not. No fairground is complete without one or two such booths—and no trip there

7

can ever be ended without a visit to at least one of them. Young or old, the fascination is just the same—and often just as strong.

Over the years, apart from my fascination with freak shows, I have also developed a great interest in fantasy and horror stories (no doubt a psychiatrist could make a lot of *that* combination!). And in my reading I have found that my interest in the world of the fairground believe-it-or-not booth is also shared by many of the top writers in this genre. This eventually led to the idea of the anthology you now have in your hands.

I invite you, therefore, to step through the curtains of my booth and view the exhibits I have to offer. They are representative, I think, of the many stories which have been created around the theme and only repetitive in the most minor background details.

Finally, I would like to thank the various people who have made this book possible—my friend and publisher, Ronald Whiting for his enthusiasm, Ray Bradbury and August Derleth for their great generosity with information and suggestions, the various literary agents and publishers who were unstintingly helpful through the labyrinth of copyright problems and, of course, the authors themselves for allowing their stories to appear. To them all, and my wife, Philippa, who again came to my rescue time and time again when the project looked like faltering, my most sincere thanks.

Fortune Telling

Freak shows, as I indicated in the Introduction, have been with us since time immemorial, so it is only right, therefore, to begin this collection with a tale from the past. It is not about a freak as such—although the events it describes on a fairground could certainly be called "freakish"—but it is unquestionably authentic in atmosphere and storyline. Daniel Defoe remains to this day one of the great men of English letters and his story sets a standard for all those which follow.

1

THE MAGICIAN

By DANIEL DEFOE

A magician giving out his bills, and boasting of his mighty performances, went down in the way of his calling, as other tradesmen do, to Bristol Fair, and there he did wonders, told fortunes, calculated nativities, looked in the girls' hands, peeped in their eyes, talked broad things to them to make them blush; and then guessing from their colour how things stood with them, and by a thousand cross questions, first crept into their cases, and then told them for a mighty discovery, what they had revealed to him with their own foolish tongues that very minute.

Among the rest of the young lasses that came to him with their grievances, there comes one with that laudable question; if in love, whether I shall marry the man or no? She was so modest that she could not tell the doctor her case herself, but she brings it him in writing; and instead of stating the question as above, if in love, she had written, if courted.

The doctor (for they are all doctors) looks upon the paper, and seeing it a woman's hand, "It is your own writing, child," says he. "I suppose you would not trust anybody else with it?" She curtsied and said yes.

So he reads it out, "If in love, whether the man will marry me or no?"

The girl coloured, and said, " 'Tis not so, you don't read it right, sir."

"Well, child," says he, "I'll read it right by and by; come hither sweetheart, pull off thy glove, let me see thy hand."

So he takes her by the hand, looks in the palm, cries. "Hum, very well, all's right there." Then he feels her pulse. "Ho!" says he, with a kind of start, "Is it so? Well, come child," says he, "sit down in this chair; I'll tell thee a story."

So, the girl, after a few curtsies and slight refuses, sits down, and the doctor begins his story.

"There was," says he, "a young woman, a very pretty clever girl, as you are, my dear" (and with that he feels her pulse again), "came to me t'other day, just with such a question as this, and after I had a little talk with her, and feeling her pulse, as I do yours, my dear" (and then felt her pulse again, and started again. "Ha," says he, "it is so indeed," and then goes on), "I, by the help of my art, which is the most certain line for the discovery of hidden truth directed by nature, and by the intercourse of invisible beings, which inform me of everything proper to be known, and for the service of those who come to be assisted with my exalted genius, I say, by my infallible judgment, I found the poor girl had concealed something from me, which indeed she ought not to have done.

"For by giving me a wrong account of her case, how should I give a direct answer?—Were it not that I, who am assisted by the good spirits, the inhabitants of the superior world, am not to be deceived.

"So I said to her, 'Sweetheart, thou hast concealed the chief part of thy case: is there not something more in this question than thou hast acknowledged?' She made me no answer at first, till I, being illuminated by the bright spirit of the fifth region of Alahamed Irwishah, and by all the assisting lights of the high exalted atmosphere" (here the doctor ran over a great many Greek words, which almost frighted the poor girl, whom he held fast by the hand or wrist all the while), "I," said he, "that could not be deceived, told her in plain words, 'Why, thou hast concealed from me that thou art with child.' At which," continues he, "the guilty poor girl having nothing to say, and being not able to deny what she found was revealed to me by my never-failing intelligence, confessed to me that it was so; and I having compassion for her circumstances (for she had been deluded) promised her my powerful assistance to bring the knave to marry her, which is now happily done to her infinite satisfaction." All this while he held her by the wrist, and looked frequently in her face.

By the first he discerned an unusual fluttering and sudden disorder in her pulse, occasioned by the story being well enough told, and the first girls' behaviour mimicked to the life; by looking in her face, he saw her colour come and go; and when he talked of his knowing everything from the superior beings and the invisible world, he saw she was in the utmost confusion.

"Now, my dear," says the doctor, raising her by the hand out of the chair, "give me leave to look a little further." So leading her to the window, he gently lifted up one of her eyelids, then he gave two hums, and said, "Pretty well there." The girl all the while blushed and coloured, and changed now red, and then pale; a little conjuration indeed would tell the doctor how it was with her.

"Now, my dear," says he to the girl, "you would do well to be so free with me as let me know your whole case, if you think fit to trust me with it, and for that, I am as secret as death; you need not be under the least concern about that, for it is my business; I am trusted with the secret of princes, and am a counsellor of counsellors; and if I should betray anybody, it would be a double offence, neither would the invisible spirits communicate the secrets of people's affairs to me if they did not judge me faithful. Therefore you may trust me with the utmost safety, child." adds he. "I shall never divulge anything that you commit to me."

The girl was as mute as a fish, and said not one word to him, but blushed and coloured as red as the gills of a turkey-cock when he is angry.

"Come, my dear," says he, "perhaps you can't express yourself freely, so I won't press you any further; but sit down till I consult the good spirits again, who, as I told thee, are always ready to assist distressed innocence; and who will not fail to give me a full information of your case, and directions also for your good; so that I do not need you should make any kind of confession of your case to me. I shall be able presently to tell it you directly without your help; so pray sit but two or three minutes, and I'll come to you again."

Having said this to her, he offered to go away, at which the girl fell to crying vehemently; and the doctor, too cunning not to take hold of it, and satisfied that he had hit the mark, stopped, and came back to her: "Well, my dear," says he, "I see how it is, and I had partly intelligence of it before, as you may easily perceive; but, come, child," adds he, "let's see, what is to be done for thee?"

She cried all the while; but when he said, "What's to be done," she said, but could not speak it plain for crying, "That Thomas would——" and there she stopped.

"I understand thee, child," says he, "that I should make Thomas marry thee, is it not?"

12

"Yes," says she, and blubbered most sadly.

"Well," says the doctor, "but how far are you gone with child? Let me know that, and then I'll tell thee whether I can bring it to pass or no." With that he laid his hand gently upon her belly. "I doubt thou art far gone," says he.

"About four months," says the girl.

"Well, child," says he, "come to me again tomorrow in the afternoon, and I'll tell thee what is resolved in thy case by the powers who assist my never-failing art." So taking a crown off the poor girl for letting him pump the truth out of her own mouth, and getting the reputation of a most eminent magician and man of art, he dismissed her for that time, letting her know that if he undertook to bring Thomas to marry her, he should expect a more considerable acknowledgment.

In a word, he took Thomas's name, and where he lived, and found ways to manage Thomas so well, that Thomas came to him in two or three days to get rid of a ghost, that haunted him. The case was this: the doctor had an implement which he carried with him upon the occasion of his business; a subtle, oily-tongued young fellow, who was a jack-of-all-trades; here was a juggler, there a tumbler, today a conjurer, at one time a ghost or apparition, at another a devil or spirit, and so acted all shapes and postures that could be desired.

The doctor having had his intelligence from the girl where Thomas lived, and finding, very happily, that he lodged in a public-house not far off, being servant to a tradesman, who not having room for him in his house, paid for a lodging for him in the alehouse; I say, having gotten this handle, he sends his engineer to lodge in the same house.

This fellow finds an opportunity to come so far acquainted with Thomas, as always to know whither he went, and upon what errands and business: and the first time that Thomas was sent of an errand (very happily for him) was to a village, about a mile out of the city, and in the evening.

As Thomas was going to this village, this subtle rogue gets behind a wall in his way, and with a hollow dead kind of voice calls him three times by his name; and immediately conveyed himself away into a field of corn, where, had Thomas suspected him, he could not have found him; and getting out of the corn, he runs round by another way, and puts himself just in the way that Thomas was to come, and, as if he had been farther that way, and was returning, meets Thomas, full-but, as they call it, one going from the city and the other coming to it.

They salute as usual, and as acquaintance, and fall into a short discourse upon the occasion of the voice that Thomas had heard.

"George," says Thomas, "I am very glad to see you; I wish you would go back with me to yon town there; I'd be much beholden to you for your company."

"I am in great haste," says George; "I can't go now."

"O pray do, if you can, for I am terribly frighted," says Thomas.

"Frighted?" says George. "At what?"

"Why, as I came along by the stone wall there," says Thomas, "at the bottom of the hill, I heard a voice call me three times by name aloud."

"Why, what does that signify?" says George. " 'Twas somebody behind the wall, to be sure, that knew you; what should you be frighted at that for?"

"No, no, it was not behind the wall, it was rather on t'other side of the road," says Thomas; "but the voice was up in the air, to be sure it must be some spirit."

"Nay, if it was up in the air, indeed," says George, "there may be something in it; those voices are sad things; my master now would tell you exactly what it meant."

"Why, ay," says Thomas, "so they say; your master can tell folks all such things, but can't you tell a-body something of it too? Come, do go back with me a little."

"Nay," says George, "since you are so concerned, I will go till I see you safe at the next town, or so, but I must run home then, for it is almost night, and my master will want me."

So, in short, George goes along with him, which was all he wanted.

"But, George," says Thomas, "what can this voice mean?"

"How many times did it call you?" says George.

"Three times," says Thomas.

"And it was very loud and distinct?" says George. "Are you sure you are not deceived? for sometimes people fancy voices when there are none."

"Ay, that may be," says Thomas, "but I ain't so fanciful; I am very sure I heard it three times; it called my Christian name and surname, Thomas first, then Thomas Saunders, and Thomas

14

Saunders again; it was a devil's voice, to be sure, it was harsh and hollow as the Devil."

"Nay, I don't like it, I confess," says George; "it seems to signify death when people are called so, and it may be in three days, three weeks, or three months, or three years."

"Can't you tell me which?" says Thomas.

"Not really," says George, "I can't go so far as that. If my master was to know the case, he would tell you exactly; but I dare say it is death, or something very bad."

They had not gone far after this, but George, watching a convenient place, gives a little start, and stops, looking as if he saw something. "Hold a little," says he to Thomas.

"What's the matter?" says Thomas.

"Matter," says George, "nay, you best know what's the matter. Have you committed murder, Thomas? Have you killed anybody?"

"I killed anybody! mercy upon me!" says Thomas. "What do you mean?"

"Why, do you see nothing," says George, "do you see nothing there?" (He points to a great tree which stood on the common which they were going over.)

"No, not I," says Thomas; "don't fright me; you know, George, I am frighted enough already."

"Nay," says George, "I don't desire to fright you, Thomas; but you would be worse frighted than I if you saw it; I'm glad you don't."

"But what is it?" says Thomas. "Dear George, tell me, is it the Devil?"

"No, no, not the Devil," says George, "but 'tis a spirit, 'tis a ghost to be sure; that made me ask if you had killed anybody."

"Well, I shall die," says Thomas: "I'm e'en dead with fright; why how should you see it and not I, George?"

"O, there's a reason for that," says George; "my master gave me a particular sight: that I can see apparitions when others can't, it belongs to our business; but you'll see it presently, for it will come nearer, I see that."

"O," says Thomas, "what shall I do, George? Will it speak to me?"

"I don't know yet," says George. "It may be not. I'll tell you presently."

They continued going forward all this while, and began to come

15

pretty near the town; when by and by says George, "I don't know what to think of it, Thomas; it threatens and makes signs as if it would come up to you and strike you."

"Strike me!" says Thomas: "nay then, 'twill kill me, to be sure."

"No, no, they never kill anybody; besides, I see you are in such a fright, I'll see if I can speak to it, and keep it off; if my master were here, he'd send it away with a word speaking." With that George goes three steps forward; bids Thomas stand still, draws a circle with his stick upon the ground, and puts Thomas into it. "Stand there," says George, "and you shall be safe, and don't be afraid, I'll see what I can do for thee."

Thomas stands still as he was bid, but quaking and trembling in the utmost confusion; and George goes forward a little out of the way and talks aloud, but so that Thomas could hear only the voice, not understand the words; and George makes a great many motions and crosses in the air, and this he held a good while, when he comes back to Thomas.

"Well, Thomas," says he. "I believe I have delivered you for this time, but something is the matter; this apparition threatens you strangely; I fancy you'll hear of it again."

"But is it gone now?" says Thomas.

"Stand still," says George, "a little, I think 'tis-agoing."

So George and he stand still a little. "Ay, there," says George, "it goes off that way" (pointing north) "and now 'tis gone up in the air," says George; "come, now we'll go on." So away they went to the town, and George tells him he must take his leave of him, and run home as hard as he can drive.

"Dear George," says Thomas, "don't leave me; why, I could not go back in the dark if you would give me a thousand pounds."

"I can't possibly stay," says George. "If you are so frighted, you had best lie there all night, and come home in the morning."

"I dare not do that neither," says Thomas, "my master will be so angry, 'tis as much as my place is worth."

"Why, then, you must get somebody to come with you at the town," says George, "for indeed I can't stay now." So away comes George and leaves him, and sets up a run, as if he was bound to be back again with the utmost expedition.

When George had got away and was out of sight, he altered himself, as he knew very well how to do by his skill in postures

16

and tumbling, which, as before, was a part of his trade; and having a linen habit in his great-coat pocket, dresses himself up in the habit of a ghost or an apparition, not in a shroud like a dead body but all in white, down to the feet, and a woman's headdress upon his head; and in this posture he places himself where he knew Thomas would come. But before this, covering his habit with his great-coat, he placed himself at the village in sight of the door where Thomas went in, that he might be sure to know when he came out, and which way he went, lest he should take some other way; and also to know who and how many he got to come with him.

He soon found Thomas on his way, for he came out of the house and two fellows with him in about an hour: so George followed them at a distance, till he saw them in a little lane leading into the common as before, and when he knew they could go no other way; upon which he ran by another way over the fields, and got into the common before them.

The first thing he did was to get into a little thicket, where lying flat on the ground, and out of sight, he lay and hissed like a serpent most frightfully; this had its immediate effect, for it frighted them all, and he heard one of them say, It was the Devil, and that he was come for Thomas to be sure: and the other said so too, adding that he would go no further; this was enough for George, for by this he knew they were no champions that Thomas had brought along with him; so removing and getting to another place a little behind them, that they might not run back again, there he changed his note, and then growled like a great dog, and that frighted them again. Now having made this beginning, he leaves off a little, and goes into the common, and stands in the middle of the road just where the lane opened into the heath; so that he might be sure to be seen all in white, a little before they came out of the lane.

The night was not very dark, but no moonlight; some stars, not many, were seen; when coming to the lane's end, they saw the spectre, and no sooner saw it, but all three run away and cried out most terribly. George had now his end, for he didn't desire to carry it on any further; so he kept his post till he found by their noise they crossed the common further off and out of sight; then he put off his habit, and made the best of his way to their lodging; where when Thomas came, he found George very sedately standing at the door smoking his pipe.

17

He bade Thomas welcome home, but said no more, not taking the least notice of anything; but found that Thomas went immediately upstairs, and threw himself down upon the bed; and the next morning Thomas was very sick.

George in the meantime went home to his master, and gave him an account of the whole transaction, who finding his engines work to his mind, gave George further instructions; which were in short to haunt the poor fellow night and day, and give him no quiet till he had managed him up to a necessity of coming to him (the doctor) for help.

I should have observed, that the doctor or cunning man finding he should compass his ends upon Thomas, sent now for the poor girl, and told her, that he had employed the utmost of his art and skill in her behalf. "And upon my word," adds he, "my child, I have had a fatherly concern for you; and I have engaged so many of the good spirits of the superior regions in your favour, that they (always ready to do acts of beneficence and kindness to distressed mortals) have assured me that Thomas shall marry you; ay, and shall come and court you to have him too, as much as if he had not gotten this unjust advantage of you, or he shall have no rest in this life; nay, he shall have no rest in this life till he does."

The poor girl smiled, and was mightily pleased, as you may well suppose, and puts her hand in her pocket, and gives the doctor half a guinea for the good news. The doctor took the money, but told her modestly, that if he did her such a great piece of service as this, she must consider, etc. She understood him, and told him, she had not a great deal of money, but yet she had a rich aunt, and other good friends; and Thomas need not ha' used her so; for that if . . . and then she cried again, she would have scorned to have married him, but . . .

"I understand you, child," says the doctor; "now you must not only take him, but must be glad he will take you?"

"Yes, sir," says she.

"Well," says the doctor, "and does your aunt know this unlucky story?"

"Yes, sir," says the girl, "and she bid me tell you she will make a handsome present to you, if you can bring it about."

"Well, child," says the doctor, "tell your aunt, I will undertake to do it, if she will be as good as her word."

"Indeed she will, sir. I will bring it to you," says she, and named the sum, which was no less than twenty pounds; and the doctor, with an unusual modesty, not craving any more, told her generously, that if he failed, he would have nothing more than she had given him already.

This treaty took up two or three days, and in the meantime George haunted Thomas upon several occasions: nay, he could hardly stir out of doors in the night, but he showed himself, sometimes all in white, sometimes all in black; till at last Thomas comes to him one evening: "George," says he, "dear George, if you don't help me, I know not what to do. I am harassed out of my wits. This Devil, if it is the Devil, haunts me so that it gives me no rest. Last night it called me again three times at my chamber window, the very same voice, and three times over, just as it did at the long wall."

(N.B.—George had cunningly got a ladder in the night, and set it up to the fellow's window, and went up, and called him aloud, with the same hollow dead sound as he did before.)

"Well," says George, "I am sorry for it, Thomas; I would have you send for a minister, and prepare for another world, for I doubt you are not very long for this world."

"But did not you tell me," says Thomas, "your master could do something for me?"

"Yes, indeed," says George, "I did so; and I believe he could, if you hadn't let it run too far, and if you hadn't done some sad thing, Thomas; for the spirits of the invisible world, which my master knows and converses with, are all good spirits, Thomas, and they will do nothing for you," adds he, "if you have committed murder or robbery, or any such thing; and therefore if that be your case, do not let me carry you to my master, for he can do you no good."

Thomas stared as if he had been bewitched. "Mercy upon me! what do you mean, brother George," says he, "I am as innocent as the child unborn. I never did any such thing in my life."

"Well, Thomas," says George, "if you speak honestly, I'll let my master know your case, and if you will come to our office tomorrow morning, you shall have his answer."

"Good George," says Thomas, "don't put it off till tomorrow! What shall I do? Why, George, the Devil will murder me to-night."

"What would you have me do?" says George. "I'll go immediately, if you will, but I doubt he is not at home."

19

However, Thomas pressing him, away they go to the doctor together; which was indeed what George wanted. When they came to him, George introduces the young man; and, in a word, tells him the whole story at large, and implores his high superior assistance to the poor distressed young man, who was daily terrified and harassed, to the danger of his wits.

"But," says the doctor (just as George had been taught to do before), "I fear this man has committed some flagrant crime, and so the evil spirits have a right to pursue him. Hark thee, friend, come hither to me, let me see thy hand; hast thou not committed murder, or treason?"

"No, indeed, sir," says Thomas, "never in my life."

"Well, pull off thy glove," says the doctor.

"Here, sir," says Thomas, "you may see I an't burnt in the hand."

"Prythee, young man," says the doctor, "I don't look for that." So he examines his palm. "Well," says the doctor, "all's well here. Nor you have committed no robbery or felony? Don't come to me if you are guilty of any such crimes as you ought to be hanged for."

"No, indeed, I han't, and't please you," says Thomas.

Then the doctor feels his pulse, and looks him full in the face. "Here is some disorder, some guilt here. Look ye, young man, assure yourself, if you have stole anything, or committed any crime, the good spirits, inhabitants of the invisible world, whose sublime influences I shall apply to them for in your behalf, and to deliver you from the power of the evil spirits which haunt you thus, will do nothing for you if you are a criminal; and more than that, they will certainly inform me of it, as soon as I make my application for your relief, and tell it me as the reason why they can do nothing for you; so you had better let me know it beforehand."

"Indeed, sir, and please you," says Thomas, "I have never done any such thing in my life."

"Hast thou ever done any injury," says the doctor, "to any, for which thou canst be thus plagued?"

"No indeed, sir, not I," says Thomas.

"Well, friend," says the doctor, "I inquire for your service only; for I don't care what you have done, nor do I care to know it. But let me ask you one question more, and then I shall be able to speak for you in general, as a very innocent, honest person. Are you willing to make satisfaction, or reparation, to anybody, or to everybody that you have done any injury to?"

"Yes, sir, with all my heart," says Thomas; "and, sir," adds he, "I have never done any hurt in all my life."

All this while the doctor holds him by the hand, and every now and then feels his pulse. "Look you, friend," says he, "here is some little disorder here in your blood, your conscience flutters, and is a little disturbed. Come, don't send me of a fool's errand, for if thou doest, I cannot only do thee no good, but these evil spirits will tear thee to pieces, when they know, as they will do, that I have spoke for thee. Come, I'll ask thee but one question more: has there been no love business between any young girl and you, and she has broke her heart, and is dead for you, and now pays you home for it, and plagues you? for it seems you say the apparition had a woman's headdress on."

"No, indeed, sir," says Thomas, "I ne'er had any fancy, but for one, and she is alive; I am sure I saw her several times since this happened."

Now the doctor had him fast. "Well, is there anything between you; is she your sweetheart still?"

"No, and't please you," says Thomas, "we have done."

"Done!" says the doctor, "what have you done? you han't lain with her, have you? But however, come, Thomas," says the doctor, "I must own that is not a fair question, so I don't press you to answer me. I hope you have done the girl no wrong; if you have, you say you'll make reparation. Come, sit down there, till I go into my study, and if you have been honest, I shall serve you, I don't doubt; but if you han't, I shall come back, and tell you all you have concealed, without giving myself the trouble of asking you."

Here Thomas began to stare and look frighted. "Why, sir, and't please you," says he, "must I confess everything?"

"No, no, Thomas," says the doctor, "I don't ask you to confess anything; I'll come back presently and tell you, as well as if you told me yourself."

"Ay, but then, sir," says Thomas, "you say, if I don't tell you everything first, then I shall get no help afterwards."

"That's very true, Thomas," says the doctor, gravely, "I do say so; and therefore, if you have anything to tell me before I go, let me know it; but I don't oblige you to tell, you may do as you will; if you have anything to say, tell me; if not, tell me."

21

"Why, nothing, sir, but about the girl, a little."

"Why, there now, I thought so, when I felt your pulse; didn't I almost tell you so?" says the doctor. "I warrant you, ye have lain with the poor girl now, and, it may be, got her with child: is that it?"

"I'm afraid so, indeed, sir," says Thomas; "but it was but twice."

"Well," says the doctor, "you drew her in, I dare say, by promising to marry her, didn't you?"

"I think you know everything," says Thomas; "indeed 'tis so, sir."

"And then," says the doctor, "when you found the poor girl was with child, you disappointed her, I suppose."

"Yes, sir," says Thomas; "there's no hiding anything from you, I think."

"Well, Thomas," says the doctor, "but what shall I do for you now? for unless you make this poor girl some satisfaction, there's no saving you. Where is she? you say she's alive, it seems."

"Yes, and't please you, she's alive," says Thomas; "she don't live far off."

"Well, what must be done, Thomas?" says the doctor. "What, would you marry her? will that give her satisfaction, Thomas?"

"Yes, and't please you, I'll marry her; and I'll send for her just now," says Thomas.

"What, and marry her in the dark!" says the doctor; "that won't do, Thomas."

"Why, sir," says Thomas, "I'll marry her over again by daylight."

"No, no, Thomas," says the doctor, "we won't break through the laws neither. I'll tell you what you shall do: send for the girl, and let me hear her story, and what she demands; if marrying her will do, Thomas, and that will satisfy her, you shall sign a bond here to her to marry her tomorrow morning; and then to protect you from the Devil that haunted you, you shall lie here with my other man Will, tonight, and I will answer none of them will dare to haunt you in my house."

"With all my heart, and't please you," says Thomas; "if you will promise me I shall not be haunted any more afterwards."

"Why, Thomas," says the doctor, "to secure you I'll cast a figure for you tonight, and I will know if those voices and spectres were upon her account or no; and if they were, I will answer for

22

it you shall hear no more of them after you have married her; and if they were not, you shan't be obliged to take her: that's a fair proposal, Thomas."

"Nay, master, and't please you," says Thomas, "I think I should take her, that's the truth on't; and I'll e'en have her, I think, whether I am delivered or no, since you say 'tis just, and I should do it. And besides, master," says Thomas, "she is a good honest girl, and loves me too, mainly, and she'll be a good wife: I'll e'en take her, master, for better for worse."

"Now you speak honestly," says the doctor. "Now I like you, Thomas. I warrant you the Devil will haunt you no more if you take her; but you have been but a kind of a rogue to her before, I understand."

Upon the whole the doctor heartens him on, the young fellow is easy, and the young woman is sent for; and in the morning they were married, and had a great wedding-dinner near the doctor's house; so that all was done to the girl's mind, and the conjurer's too: for the doctor had two guineas of Thomas for delivering him from the Devil (who could do it cheaper?), and twenty of the good wife's friends, and the lady that gave the money thought it very well bestowed.

The Jester

Edgar Allan Poe, like Daniel Defoe, has a giant's position in literature and in his chosen field—the macabre—has no peer. This marvellous little story of the vengeance of a poor freak on those who misuse him so cruelly is both apposite and gruesome—it has long been one of my favourite tales by this particular author.

HOP FROG

By Edgar Allan Poe

I never knew any one so keenly alive to a joke as the king was.
He seemed to live only for joking. To tell a good story of the joke
kind, and to tell it well, was the surest road to his favour. Thus
it happened that his seven ministers were all noted for their
accomplishments as jokers. They all took after the king, too, in
being large, corpulent, oily men, as well as inimitable jokers.
Whether people grow fat by joking, or whether there is something
in fat itself which predisposes to a joke, I have never been quite
able to determine; but certain it is that a lean joker is a *rara avis
in terris*.

About the refinements, or, as he called them, the "ghosts" of
wit, the king troubled himself very little. He had an especial
admiration for *breadth* in a jest, and would often put up with
length, for the sake of it. Overniceties wearied him. He would have
preferred Rabelais' "Gargantua" to the "Zadig" of Voltaire: and,
upon the whole, practical jokes suited his taste far better than
verbal ones.

At the date of my narrative, professing jesters had not
altogether gone out of fashion at court. Several of the great con-
tinental "powers" still retained their "fools," who wore motley,
with caps and bells, and who were expected to be always ready
with sharp witticisms, at a moment's notice, in consideration of
the crumbs that fell from the royal table.

Our king, as a matter of course, retained his "fool." The fact
is, he *required* something in the way of folly—if only to counterbalance the heavy wisdom of the seven wise men who were his
ministers—not to mention himself.

His fool, or professional jester, was not *only* a fool, however.
His value was trebled in the eyes of the king, by the fact of his
being also a dwarf and a cripple. Dwarfs were as common at
court, in those days, as fools; and many monarchs would have

found it difficult to get through their days (days are rather longer at court than elsewhere) without both a jester to laugh *with*, and a dwarf to laugh *at*. But, as I have already observed, your jesters, in ninety-nine cases out of a hundred, are fat, round, and unwieldy —so that it was no small source of self-gratulation with our king that, in Hop-Frog (this was the fool's name), he possessed a triplicate treasure in one person.

I believe the name "Hop-Frog" was *not* that given to the dwarf by his sponsors at baptism, but it was conferred upon him, by general consent of the seven ministers, on account of his inability to walk as other men do. In fact, Hop-Frog could only get along by a sort of interjectional gait—something between a leap and a wriggle—a movement that afforded illimitable amusement, and of course consolation, to the king, for (notwithstanding the protuberance of his stomach and a constitutional swelling of the head) the king, by his whole court, was accounted a capital figure.

But although Hop-Frog, through the distortion of his legs, could move only with great pain and difficulty along a road or floor, the prodigious muscular power which nature seemed to have bestowed upon his arms, by way of compensation for deficiency in the lower limbs, enabled him to perform many feats of wonderful dexterity, where trees or ropes were in question, or anything else to climb. At such exercises he certainly much more resembled a squirrel, or a small monkey, than a frog.

I am not able to say, with precision, from what country Hop-Frog originally came. It was from some barbarous region, however, that no person ever heard of—a vast distance from the court of our king. Hop-Frog, and a young girl very little less dwarfish than himself (although of exquisite proportions, and a marvellous dancer), had been forcibly carried off from their respective homes in adjoining provinces, and sent as presents to the king, by one of his ever-victorious generals.

Under these circumstances, it is not to be wondered at that a close intimacy arose between the two little captives. Indeed, they soon became sworn friends. Hop-Frog, who, although he made a great deal of sport, was by no means popular, had it not in his power to render Trippetta many services; but *she*, on account of her grace and exquisite beauty (although a dwarf), was universally admired and petted; so she possessed much influence; and never failed to use it, whenever she could, for the benefit of Hop-Frog.

26

On some grand state occasion—I forget what—the king determined to have a masquerade; and whenever a masquerade, or any thing of that kind, occurred at our court, then the talents both of Hop-Frog and Trippetta were sure to be called into play. Hop-Frog, in especial, was so inventive in the way of getting up pageants, suggesting novel characters, and arranging costume, for masked balls, that nothing could be done, it seems, without his assistance.

The night appointed for the *fête* had arrived. A gorgeous hall had been fitted up, under Trippetta's eye, with every kind of device which could possibly give *éclat* to a masquerade. The whole court was in a fever of expectation. As for costumes and characters, it might well be supposed that everybody had come to a decision on such points. Many had made up their minds (as to what *rôles* they should assume) a week, or even a month in advance; and, in fact, there was not a particle of indecision anywhere—except in the case of the king and his seven ministers. Why *they* hesitated I never could tell, unless they did it by way of a joke. More probably, they found it difficult, on account of being so fat, to make up their minds. At all events, time flew; and, as a last resort, they sent for Trippetta and Hop-Frog.

When the two little friends obeyed the summons of the king, they found him sitting at his wine with the seven members of his cabinet council; but the monarch appeared to be in a very ill humour. He knew that Hop-Frog was not fond of wine; for it excited the poor cripple almost to madness; and madness is no comfortable feeling. But the king loved his practical jokes, and took pleasure in forcing Hop-Frog to drink and (as the king called it) "to be merry."

"Come here, Hop-Frog," said he, as the jester and his friend entered the room; "swallow this bumper to the health of your absent friends [here Hop-Frog sighed] and then let us have the benefit of your invention. We want characters—*characters*, man, —something novel—out of the way. We are wearied with this everlasting sameness. Come, drink! the wine will brighten your wits."

Hop-Frog endeavoured, as usual, to get up a jest in reply to these advances from the king; but the effort was too much. It happened to be the poor dwarf's birthday, and the command to drink to his "absent friends" forced the tears to his eyes. Many large, bitter drops fell into the goblet as he took it, humbly, from the hand of the tyrant.

"Ah! ha! ha! ha!" roared the latter, as the dwarf reluctantly drained the beaker. "See what a glass of good wine can do! Why, your eyes are shining already!"

Poor fellow! his large eyes *gleamed,* rather than shone; for the effect of wine on his excitable brain was not more powerful than instantaneous. He placed the goblet nervously on the table, and looked round upon the company with a half-insane stare. They all seemed highly amused at the success of the king's "*joke.*"

"And now to business," said the prime minister, a *very* fat man.

"Yes," said the king. "Come, Hop-Frog, lend us your assistance. Characters, my fine fellow; we stand in need of characters —all of us—ha! ha! ha!" and as this was seriously meant for a joke, his laugh was chorused by the seven.

Hop-Frog also laughed, although feebly and somewhat vacantly.

"Come, come," said the king, impatiently, "have you nothing to suggest?"

"I am endeavouring to think of something *novel,*" replied the dwarf, abstractedly, for he was quite bewildered by the wine.

"Endeavouring!" cried the tyrant fiercely; "what do you mean by *that*? Ah, I perceive. You are sulky, and want more wine. Here, drink this!" and he poured out another goblet full and offered it to the cripple, who merely gazed at it, gasping for breath.

"Drink, I say!" shouted the monster, "or by the fiends——"

The dwarf hesitated. The king grew purple with rage. The courtiers smirked. Trippetta, pale as a corpse, advanced to the monarch's seat, and, falling on her knees before him, implored him to spare her friend.

The tyrant regarded her, for some moments, in evident wonder at her audacity. He seemed quite at a loss what to do or say— how most becomingly to express his indignation. At last, without uttering a syllable, he pushed her violently from him, and threw the contents of the brimming goblet in her face.

The poor girl got up as best she could, and, not daring even to sigh, resumed her position at the foot of the table.

There was a dead silence for about half a minute, during which the falling of a leaf, or of a feather, might have been heard. It was interrupted by a low, but harsh and protracted *grating* sound which seemed to come at once from every corner of the room.

"What—what—*what* are you making that noise for?" demanded the king, turning furiously to the dwarf.

The latter seemed to have recovered, in great measure, from his intoxication, and looking fixedly but quietly into the tyrant's face, merely ejaculated:

"I—I? How could it have been me?"

"The sound appeared to come from without," observed one of the courtiers. "I fancy it was the parrot at the window, whetting his bill upon his cage-wires."

"True," replied the monarch, as if much relieved by the suggestion; "but, on the honour of a knight, I could have sworn that it was the gritting of this vagabond's teeth."

Hereupon the dwarf laughed (the king was too confirmed a joker to object to any one's laughing), and displayed a set of large, powerful, and very repulsive teeth. Moreover, he avowed his perfect willingness to swallow as much wine as desired. The monarch was pacified; and having drained another bumper with no very perceptible ill effect, Hop-Frog entered at once, and with spirit, into the plans for the masquerade.

"I cannot tell what was the association of ideas," observed he, very tranquilly, and as if he had never tasted wine in his life, "but *just after* your majesty had struck the girl and thrown the wine in her face—*just after* your majesty had done this, and while the parrot was making that odd noise outside the window, there came into my mind a capital diversion—one of my own country frolics—often enacted among us, at our masquerades; but here it will be new altogether. Unfortunately, however, it requires a company of eight persons, and——"

"Here we *are!*" cried the king, laughing at his acute discovery of the coincidence; "eight to a fraction—I and my seven ministers. Come! what is the diversion?"

"We call it," replied the cripple, "the Eight Chained Orang-Outangs, and it really is excellent sport if well enacted."

"*We* will enact it," remarked the king, drawing himself up, and lowering his eyelids.

"The beauty of the game," continued Hop-Frog, "lies in the fright it occasions among the women."

"Capital!" roared in chorus the monarch and his ministry.

"I will equip you as orang-outangs," proceeded the dwarf;

29

"leave all that to me. The resemblance shall be so striking, that the company of masqueraders will take you for real beasts—and of course, they will be as much terrified as astonished."

"Oh, this is exquisite! " exclaimed the king. "Hop-Frog! I will make a man of you."

"The chains are for the purpose of increasing the confusion by their jangling. You are supposed to have escaped, *en masse,* from your keepers. Your majesty cannot conceive the *effect* produced, at a masquerade, by eight chained orang-outangs, imagined to be real ones by most of the company; and rushing in with savage cries, among the crowd of delicately and gorgeously habited men and women. The *contrast* is inimitable."

"It *must* be," said the king: and the council arose hurriedly (as it was growing late), to put in execution the scheme of Hop-Frog.

His mode of equipping the party as orang-outangs was very simple, but effective enough for his purposes. The animals in question had, at the epoch of my story, very rarely been seen in any part of the civilized world; and as the imitations made by the dwarf were sufficiently beast-like and more than sufficiently hideous, their truthfulness to nature was thus thought to be secured.

The king and his ministers were first encased in tight-fitting stockinet shirts and drawers. They were then saturated with tar. At this stage of the process, some one of the party suggested feathers; but the suggestion was at once overruled by the dwarf, who soon convinced the eight, by ocular demonstration, that the hair of such a brute as the orang-outang was much more efficiently represented by *flax.* A thick coating of the latter was accordingly plastered upon the coating of tar. A long chain was now procured. First, it was passed about the waist of the king, *and tied;* then about another of the party, and also tied; then about all successively, in the same manner. When this chaining arrangement was complete, and the party stood as far apart from each other as possible, they formed a circle; and to make all things appear natural, Hop-Frog passed the residue of the chain, in two diameters, at right angles, across the circle, after the fashion adopted, at the present day, by those who capture chimpanzees, or other large apes, in Borneo.

The grand saloon in which the masquerade was to take place, was a circular room, very lofty, and receiving the light of the sun only through a single window at the top. At night (the season for

30

which the apartment was especially designed) it was illuminated principally by a large chandelier, depending by a chain from the centre of the sky-light, and lowered, or elevated, by means of a counterbalance as usual; but (in order not to look unsightly) this latter passed outside the cupola and over the roof.

The arrangements of the room had been left to Trippetta's superintendence; but, in some particulars, it seems, she had been guided by the calmer judgment of her friend the dwarf. At his suggestion it was that, on this occasion, the chandelier was re-moved. Its waxen drippings (which, in weather so warm, it was quite impossible to prevent) would have been seriously detrimental to the rich dresses of the guests, who, on account of the crowded state of the saloon, could not *all* be expected to keep from out its centre—that is to say, from under the chandelier. Additional sconces were set in various parts of the hall, out of the way; and a flambeau, emitting a sweet odour, was placed in the right hand of each of the Caryatids that stood against the wall—some fifty or sixty all together.

The eight orang-outangs, taking Hop-Frog's advice, waited patiently until midnight (when the room was thoroughly filled with masqueraders) before making their appearance. No sooner had the clock ceased striking, however, than they rushed, or rather rolled in, all together—for the impediments of their chains caused most of the party to fall, and all to stumble as they entered.

The excitement among the masqueraders was prodigious, and filled the heart of the king with glee. As had been anticipated, there were not a few of the guests who supposed the ferocious-looking creatures to be beasts of *some* kind in reality, if not pre-cisely orang-outangs. Many of the women swooned with affright; and had not the king taken the precaution to exclude all weapons from the saloon, his party might soon have expiated their frolic in their blood. As it was, a general rush was made for the doors; but the king had ordered them to be locked immediately upon his entrance; and, at the dwarf's suggestion, the keys had been de-posited with *him*.

While the tumult was at its height, and each masquerader attentive only to his own safety (for, in fact, there was much *real* danger from the pressure of the excited crowd), the chain by which the chandelier ordinarily hung, and which had been drawn up on its removal, might have been seen very gradually to descend, until its hooked extremity came within three feet of the floor.

Soon after this, the king and his seven friends having reeled about the hall in all directions, found themselves, at length, in its centre, and, of course, in immediate contact with the chain. While they were thus situated, the dwarf, who had followed noiselessly at their heels, inciting them to keep up the commotion, took hold of their own chain at the intersection of the two portions which crossed the circle diametrically and at right angles. Here, with the rapidity of thought, he inserted the hook from which the chandelier had been wont to depend; and, in an instant, by some unseen agency, the chandelier-chain was drawn so far upward as to take the hook out of reach, and, as an inevitable consequence, to drag the orang-outangs together in close connection, and face to face.

The masqueraders, by this time, had recovered, in some measure, from their alarm; and, beginning to regard the whole matter as a well-contrived pleasantry, set up a loud shout of laughter at the predicament of the apes.

"Leave them to *me*!" now screamed Hop-Frog, his shrill voice making itself easily heard through all the din. "Leave them to *me*. I fancy *I* know them. If I can only get a good look at them, *I* can soon tell who they are."

Here, scrambling over the heads of the crowd, he managed to get to the wall; when, seizing a flambeau from one of the Caryatids, he returned, as he went, to the centre of the room—leaped, with the agility of a monkey, upon the king's head—and thence clambered a few feet up the chain—holding down the torch to examine the group of orang-outangs, and still screaming: "*I* shall soon find out who they are!"

And now, while the whole assembly (the apes included) were convulsed with laughter, the jester suddenly uttered a shrill whistle; when the chain flew violently up for about thirty feet—dragging with it the dismayed and struggling orang-outangs, and leaving them suspended in mid-air between the sky-light and the floor. Hop-Frog, clinging to the chain as it rose, still maintained his relative position in respect to the eight maskers, and still (as if nothing were the matter) continued to thrust his torch down toward them, as though endeavouring to discover who they were.

So thoroughly astonished was the whole company at this ascent, that a dead silence, of about a minute's duration, ensued. It was broken by just such a low, harsh, *grating* sound, as had before attracted the attention of the king and his councillors when the former threw the wine in the face of Trippetta. But, on the present occasion, there could be no question as to *whence* the sound issued. It came from the fang-like teeth of the dwarf, who ground them and gnashed them as he foamed at the mouth, and glared, with an expression of maniacal rage, into the upturned countenances of the king and his seven companions.

"Ah, ha! " said at length the infuriated jester. "Ah, ha! I begin to see who these people *are,* now! " Here, pretending to scrutinize the king more closely, he held the flambeau to the flaxen coat which enveloped him, and which instantly burst into a sheet of vivid flame. In less than half a minute the whole eight orang-outangs were blazing fiercely, amid the shrieks of the multitude who gazed at them from below, horror-stricken, and without the power to render them the slightest assistance.

At length the flames, suddenly increasing in virulence, forced the jester to climb higher up the chain, to be out of their reach; and, as he made this movement, the crowd again sank, for a brief instant, into silence. The dwarf seized his opportunity, and once more spoke:

"I now see *distinctly*," he said, "what manner of people these maskers are. They are a great king and his seven privy-councillors —a king who does not scruple to strike a defenceless girl, and his seven councillors who abet him in the outrage. As for myself, I am simply Hop-Frog, the jester—and *this is my last jest.*"

Owing to the high combustibility of both the flax and the tar to which it adhered, the dwarf had scarcely made an end of his brief speech before the work of vengeance was complete. The eight corpses swung in their chains, a foetid, blackened, hideous, and indistinguishable mass. The cripple hurled his torch at them, clambered leisurely to the ceiling, and disappeared through the sky-light.

It is supposed that Trippetta, stationed on the roof of the saloon, had been the accomplice of her friend in his fiery revenge, and that, together, they effected their escape to their own country; for neither was seen again.

Freaks

High on the list of the best all-time horror films is M.G.M.'s "Freaks" which was produced by Tod Browning in 1932. Browning, who had been a circus man before entering Hollywood, based his picture on this story which is now extremely rare. To play the characters real freaks were employed, and so effective and gruesome was the result that in America the film was extensively cut—while on this side of the Atlantic the censor refused it a certificate for almost thirty years. "Spurs" is a remarkable story and the reader is unlikely to be left in any doubt as to why it inspired such a terrifying film.

SPURS

By Tod Robbins

Jacques Courbé was a romanticist. He measured only twenty-eight inches from the soles of his diminutive feet to the crown of his head; but there were times, as he rode into the arena on his gallant charger, St. Eustache, when he felt himself a doughty knight of old about to do battle for his lady.

What matter that St. Eustache was not a gallant charger except in his master's imagination—not even a pony, indeed, but a large dog of a nondescript breed, with the long snout and upstanding ears of a wolf? What matter that M. Courbé's entrance was invariably greeted with shouts of derisive laughter and bombardments of banana skins and orange peel? What matter that he had no lady, and that his daring deeds were severely curtailed to a mimicry of the bareback riders who preceded him? What mattered all these things to the tiny man who lived in dreams, and who resolutely closed his shoe-button eyes to the drab realities of life?

The dwarf had no friends among the other freaks in Copo's Circus. They considered him ill-tempered and egotistical, and he loathed them for their acceptance of things as they were. Imagination was the armour that protected him from the curious glances of a cruel, gaping world, from the stinging lash of ridicule, from the bombardments of banana skins and orange peel. Without it, he must have shrivelled up and died. But these others? Ah, they had no armour except their own thick hides! The door that opened on the kingdom of imagination was closed and locked to them; and although they did not wish to open this door, although they did not miss what lay beyond it, they resented and mistrusted anyone who possessed the key.

Now it came about, after many humiliating performances in the arena, made palatable only by dreams, that love entered the circus tent and beckoned commandingly to M. Jacques Courbé.

35

In an instant the dwarf was engulfed in a sea of wild, tumultuous passion.

Mlle. Jeanne Marie was a daring bareback rider. It made M. Jacques Courbé's tiny heart stand still to see her that first night of her appearance in the arena, performing brilliantly on the broad back of her aged mare, Sappho. A tall, blonde woman of the amazon type, she had round eyes of baby blue which held no spark of her avaricious peasant's soul, carmine lips and cheeks, large white teeth which flashed continually in a smile, and hands which, when doubled up, were nearly the size of the dwarf's head.

Her partner in the act was Simon Lafleur, the Romeo of the circus tent—a swarthy, herculean young man with bold black eyes and hair that glistened with grease, like the back of Solon, the trained seal.

From the first performance M. Jacques Courbé loved Mlle. Jeanne Marie. All his tiny body was shaken with longing for her. Her buxom charms, so generously revealed in tights and spangles, made him flush and cast down his eyes. The familiarities allowed to Simon Lafleur, the bodily acrobatic contacts of the two performers, made the dwarf's blood boil. Mounted on St. Eustache, awaiting his turn at the entrance, he would grind his teeth in impotent rage to see Simon circling round and round the ring, standing proudly on the back of Sappho and holding Mlle. Jeanne Marie in an ecstatic embrace, while she kicked one shapely, bespangled leg skywards.

"Ah, the dog!" M. Jacques Courbé would mutter. "Some day I shall teach this hulking stable-boy his place! *Ma foi*, I will clip his ears for him!"

St. Eustache did not share his master's admiration for Mlle. Jeanne Marie. From the first he evinced his hearty detestation for her by low growls and a ferocious display of long, sharp fangs. It was little consolation for the dwarf to know that St. Eustache showed still more marked signs of rage when Simon Lafleur approached him. It pained M. Jacques Courbé to think that his gallant charger, his sole companion, his bedfellow, should not also love and admire the splendid giantess who each night risked life and limb before the awed populace. Often, when they were alone together, he would chide St. Eustache on his churlishness.

"Ah, you devil of a dog!" the dwarf would cry. "Why must you always growl and show your ugly teeth when the lovely Jeanne Marie condescends to notice you? Have you no feelings

36

under your tough hide? Cur, she is an angel, and you snarl at her! Do you not remember how I found you, a starving puppy in a Paris gutter? And now you must threaten the hand of my princess! So this is your gratitude, great hairy pig!"

M. Jacques Courbé had one living relative—not a dwarf, like himself, but a fine figure of a man, a prosperous farmer living just outside the town of Roubaix. The elder Courbé had never married; and so one day, when he was found dead from heart failure, his tiny nephew—for whom, it must be confessed, the farmer had always felt an instinctive aversion—fell heir to a comfortable property. When the tidings were brought to him, the dwarf threw both arms about the shaggy neck of St. Eustache and cried out:

"Ah, now we can retire, marry and settle down, old friend! I am worth many times my weight in gold!"

That evening, as Mlle. Jeanne Marie was changing her gaudy costume after the performance, a light tap sounded on the door.

"Enter!" she called, believing it to be Simon Lafleur, who had promised to take her that evening to the Sign of the Wild Boar for a glass of wine to wash the sawdust out of her throat. "Enter, *mon chéri!*"

The door swung slowly open; and in stepped M. Jacques Courbé, very proud and upright, in the silks and laces of a courtier, with a tiny gold-hilted sword swinging at his hip. Up he came, his shoe-button eyes all a-glitter to see the more than partially revealed charms of his robust lady. Up he came to within a yard of where she sat; and down on one knee he went and pressed his lips to her red-slippered foot.

"Oh, most beautiful and daring lady," he cried, in a voice as shrill as a pin scratching on a window-pane, "will you not take mercy on the unfortunate Jacques Courbé? He is hungry for your smiles, he is starving for your lips! All night long he tosses on his couch and dreams of Jeanne Marie!"

"What play-acting is this, my brave little fellow?" she asked, bending down with the smile of an ogress. "Has Simon Lafleur sent you to tease me?"

"May the black plague have Simon!" the dwarf cried, his eyes seeming to flash blue sparks. "I am not play-acting. It is only too true that I love you, mademoiselle; that I wish to make you my lady. And now that I have a fortune, now that——" He broke off suddenly, and his face resembled a withered apple. "What is this mademoiselle?" he said, in the low, droning tone of a hornet

37

about to sting. "Do you laugh at my love? I warn you mademoiselle—do not laugh at Jacques Courbé!"

Mlle. Jeanne Marie's large, florid face had turned purple from suppressed merriment. Her lips twitched at the corners. It was all she could do not to burst out into a roar of laughter.

Why, the ridiculous little manikin was serious in his love-making! This pocket-sized edition of a courtier was proposing marriage to her! He, this splinter of a fellow, wished to make her his wife! Why, she could carry him about on her shoulder like a trained marmoset!

What a joke this was—what a colossal, corset-creaking joke! Wait till she told Simon Lafleur! She could fairly see him throw back his sleek head, open his mouth to its widest dimensions, and shake with silent laughter. But *she* must not laugh—not now. First she must listen to everything the dwarf had to say; draw all the sweetness out of this bonbon of humour before she crushed it under the heel of ridicule.

"I am not laughing," she managed to say. "You have taken me by surprise. I never thought, I never even guessed—"

"That is well, mademoiselle," the dwarf broke in. "I do not tolerate laughter. In the arena I am paid to make laughter; but those others pay to laugh at *me*. I always make people pay to laugh at me!"

"But do I understand you aright, M. Courbé? Are you proposing an honourable marriage?"

The dwarf rested his hand on his heart and bowed. "Yes, mademoiselle, an honourable marriage, and the wherewithal to keep the wolf from the door. A week ago my uncle died and left me a large estate. We shall have a servant to wait on our wants, a horse and carriage, food and wine of the best, and leisure to amuse ourselves. And you? Why, you will be a fine lady! I will clothe that beautiful big body of yours with silks and laces! You will be as happy, mademoiselle, as a cherry tree in June!"

The dark blood slowly receded from Mlle. Jeanne Marie's full cheeks, her lips no longer twitched at the corners, her eyes had narrowed slightly. She had been a bareback rider for years, and she was weary of it. The life of the circus tent had lost its tinsel. She loved the dashing Simon Lafleur; but she knew well enough that this Romeo in tights would never espouse a dowerless girl.

The dwarf's words had woven themselves into a rich mental

38

tapestry. She saw herself a proud lady, ruling over a country estate, and later welcoming Simon Lafleur with all the luxuries that were so near his heart. Simon would be overjoyed to marry into a country estate. These pygmies were a puny lot. They died young! She would do nothing to hasten the end of Jacques Courbé. No, she would be kindness itself to the poor little fellow; but, on the other hand, she would not lose her beauty mourning for him.

"Nothing that you wish shall be withheld from you as long as you love me, mademoiselle," the dwarf continued. "Your answer?"

Mlle. Jeanne Marie bent forward, and, with a single movement of her powerful arms, raised M. Jacques Courbé and placed him on her knee. For an ecstatic instant she held him thus, as if he were a large French doll, with his tiny sword cocked coquettishly out behind. Then she planted on his cheek a huge kiss that covered his entire face from chin to brow.

"I am yours!" she murmured, pressing him to her ample bosom. "From the first I loved you, M. Jacques Courbé!"

*　　*　　*

The wedding of Mlle. Jeanne Marie was celebrated in the town of Roubaix, where Copo's Circus had taken up its temporary quarters. Following the ceremony, a feast was served in one of the tents, which was attended by a whole galaxy of celebrities.

The bridegroom, his dark little face flushed with happiness and wine, sat at the head of the board. His chin was just above the tablecloth, so that his head looked like a large orange that had rolled off the fruit-dish. Immediately beneath his dangling feet, St. Eustache, who had more than once evinced by deep growls his disapproval of the proceedings, now worried a bone with quick, sly glances from time to time at the plump legs of his new mistress. Papa Copo was on the dwarf's right, his large round face as red and benevolent as a harvest moon. Next to him sat Griffo, the giraffe boy, who was covered with spots, and whose neck was so long that he looked down on all the rest, including M. Hercule Hippo, the giant. The rest of the company included Mlle. Lupa, who had sharp white teeth of an incredible length, and who growled when she tried to talk; the tiresome M. Jejongle, who insisted on juggling fruit, plates and knives, although the whole company was heartily sick of his tricks; Mme. Sampson, with her trained boa constrictors coiled about her neck and peeping out timidly, one above each ear; Simon Lafleur and a score of others.

The bareback rider had laughed silently and almost continually ever since Jeanne Marie had told him of her engagement. Now he sat next to her in his crimson tights. His black hair was brushed back from his forehead and so glistened with grease that it reflected the lights overhead, like a burnished helmet. From time to time he tossed off a brimming goblet of Burgundy, nudged the bride in the ribs with his elbow, and threw back his sleek head in another silent outburst of laughter.

"And you are sure that you will not forget me, Simon?" she whispered. "It may be some time before I can get the little ape's money."

"Forget you, Jeanne?" he muttered. "By all the dancing devils in champagne, never! I will wait as patiently as Job till you have fed that mouse some poisoned cheese. But what will you do with him in the meantime, Jeanne? You must allow him no liberties. I grind my teeth to think of you in his arms!"

The bride smiled, and regarded her diminutive husband with an appraising glance. What an atom of a man! And yet life might linger in his bones for a long time to come. M. Jacques Courbé had allowed himself only one glass of wine, and yet he was far gone in intoxication. His tiny face was suffused with blood, and he stared at Simon Lafleur belligerently. Did he suspect the truth?

"Your husband is flushed with wine!" the bareback rider whispered. "*Ma foi*, madame, later he may knock you about! Possibly he is a dangerous fellow in his cups. Should he maltreat you, Jeanne, do not forget that you have a protector in Simon Lafleur."

"You clown!" Jeanne Marie rolled her large eyes roguishly, and laid her hand for an instant on the bareback rider's knee. "Simon, I could crack his skull between my finger and thumb, like this hickory nut!" She paused to illustrate her example, and then added reflectively: "And, perhaps, I shall do that very thing, if he attempts any familiarities. Ugh! The little ape turns my stomach!"

By now the wedding guests were beginning to show the effects of their potations. This was especially marked in the case of M. Jacques Courbé's associates in the side-show.

Griffo, the giraffe boy, had closed his large brown eyes, and

40

was swaying his small head languidly above the assembly, while a slightly supercilious expression drew his lips down at the corners. M. Hercule Hippo, swollen out by his libations to even more colossal proportions, was repeating over and over: "I tell you I am not like other men. When I walk, the earth trembles!" Mlle. Lupa, her hairy upper lip lifted above her long white teeth, was gnawing at a bone, growling unintelligible phrases to herself and shooting savage, suspicious glances at her companions. M. Jejongle's hands had grown unsteady, and, as he insisted on juggling the knives and plates of each new course, broken bits of crockery littered the floor. Mme. Samson, uncoiling her necklace of baby boa constrictors, was feeding them lumps of sugar soaked in rum. M. Jacques Courbé had finished his second glass of wine, and was surveying the whispering Simon Lafleur through narrowed eyes.

There can be no genial companionship among great egotists who have drunk too much. Each one of these human oddities thought that he or she alone was responsible for the crowds that daily gathered at Copo's Circus; so now, heated with the good Burgundy, they were not slow in asserting themselves. Their separate egos rattled angrily together, like so many pebbles in a bag. Here was gunpowder which needed only a spark.

"I am a big—a very big man!" M. Hercule Hippo said sleepily. "Women love me. The pretty little creatures leave their pygmy husbands, so that they may come and stare at Hercule Hippo of Copo's Circus. Ha, and when they return home, they laugh at other men always! 'You may kiss me again when you grow up,' they tell their sweethearts."

"Fat bullock, here is one woman who has no love for you!" cried Mlle. Lupa, glaring sideways at the giant over her bone. "That great carcass of yours is only so much food gone to waste. You have cheated the butcher, my friend. Fool, women do not come to see *you*! As well they might stare at the cattle being led through the street. Ah, no, they come from far and near to see one of their own sex who is not a cat!"

"Quite right," cried Papa Copo in a conciliatory tone, smiling, and rubbing his hands together. "Not a cat mademoiselle, but a wolf. Ah, you have a sense of humour! How droll!"

"I *have* a sense of humour," Mlle. Lupa agreed, returning to her bone, "and also sharp teeth. Let the erring hand not stray too near!"

41

"You, M. Hippo and Mlle. Lupa, are both wrong," said a voice which seemed to come from the roof. "Surely it is none other than me whom the people come to stare at!"

All raised their eyes to the supercilious face of Griffo, the giraffe boy, which swayed slowly from side to side on its long, pipe-stem neck. It was he who had spoken, although his eyes were still closed.

"Of all the colossal impudence!" cried the matronly Mme. Samson. "As if my little dears had nothing to say on the subject!" She picked up the two baby boa constrictors, which lay in drunken slumber on her lap, and shook them like whips at the wedding guests. "Papa Copo knows only too well that it is on account of these little charmers, Mark Antony and Cleopatra, that the side-show is so well attended!"

The circus owner, thus directly appealed to, frowned in perplexity. He felt himself in a quandary. These freaks of his were difficult to handle. Why had he been fool enough to come to M. Jacques Courbé's wedding feast? Whatever he said would be used against him.

As Papa Copo hesitated, his round, red face wreathed in ingratiating smiles, the long deferred spark suddenly alighted in the powder. It all came about on account of the carelessness of M. Jejongle, who had become engrossed in the conversation and wished to put in a word for himself. Absent-mindedly juggling two heavy plates and a spoon, he said in a petulant tone:

"You all appear to forget *me!*"

Scarcely were the words out of his mouth, when one of the heavy plates descended with a crash on the thick skull of M. Hippo; and M. Jejongle was instantly remembered. Indeed he was more than remembered; for the giant, already irritated to boiling point by Mlle. Lupa's insults, at this new affront struck out savagely past her and knocked the juggler head-over-heels under the table.

Mlle. Lupa, always quick-tempered and especially so when her attention was focused on a juicy chicken bone, evidently considered her dinner companion's conduct far from decorous, and promptly inserted her sharp teeth in the offending hand that had administered the blow. M. Hippo, squealing from rage and pain like a wounded elephant, bounded to his feet, overturning the table.

Pandemonium followed. Every freak's hands, teeth, feet, were

42

turned against the others. Above the shouts, screams, growls and hisses of the combat, Papa Copo's voice could be heard bellowing for peace:

"Ah, my children, my children! This is no way to behave! Calm yourselves, I pray you! Mlle. Lupa, remember that you are a lady as well as a wolf!"

There is no doubt that M. Jacques Courbé would have suffered most in this undignified fracas had it not been for St. Eustache, who had stationed himself over his tiny master and who now drove off all would-be assailants. As it was, Griffo, the unfortunate giraffe boy, was the most defenceless and therefore became the victim. His small, round head swayed back and forth to blows like a punching bag. He was bitten by Mlle. Lupa, buffeted by M. Hippo, kicked by M. Jejongle, clawed by Mme. Samson, and nearly strangled by both the baby boa constrictors, which had wound themselves about his neck like hangmen's nooses. Undoubtedly he would have fallen victim to circumstance, had it not been for Simon Lafleur, the bride and half a dozen of her acrobatic friends, who Papa Copo had implored to restore peace. Roaring with laughter, they sprang forward and tore the combatants apart.

M. Jacques Courbé was found sitting grimly under a fold of the tablecloth. He held a broken bottle of wine in one hand. The dwarf was very drunk, and in a towering rage. As Simon Lafleur approached with one of his silent laughs, M. Jacques Courbé hurled the bottle at his head.

"Ah, the little wasp!" the bareback rider cried, picking up the dwarf by his waistband. "Here is your fine husband, Jeanne! Take him away before he does me some mischief. *Parbleu*, he is a bloodthirsty fellow in his cups!"

The bride approached, her blonde face crimson from wine and laughter. Now that she was safely married to a country estate, she took no more pains to conceal her true feelings.

"Oh, *là, là!*" she cried, seizing the struggling dwarf and holding him forcibly on her shoulder. "What a temper the little ape has! Well, we shall spank it out of him before long!"

"Let me down!" M. Jacques Courbé screamed in a paroxysm of fury. "You will regret this, madame! Let me down, I say!"

But the stalwart bride shook her head. "No, no, my little one!" she laughed. "You cannot escape your wife so easily! What, you would fly from my arms before the honeymoon!"

43

"Let me down!" he cried again. "Can't you see that they are laughing at me?"

"And why should they not laugh, my little ape? Let them laugh, if they will; but I will not put you down. No, I will carry you thus, perched on my shoulder, to the farm. It will set a precedent which brides of the future may find a certain difficulty in following!"

"But the farm is quite a distance from here, my Jeanne," said Simon Lafleur. "You are as strong as an ox, and he is only a marmoset; still, I will wager a bottle of Burgundy that you set him down by the roadside."

"Done, Simon!" the bride cried, with a flash of her strong white teeeth. "You shall lose your wager, for I swear that I could carry my little ape from one end of France to the other!"

M. Jacques Courbé no longer struggled. He now sat bolt upright on his bride's broad shoulder. From the flaming peaks of blind passion he had fallen into an abyss of cold fury. His love was dead, but some quite alien emotion was rearing an evil head from its ashes.

"So, madame, you could carry me from one end of France to the other!" he droned in a monotonous undertone. "From one end of France to the other! I will remember that always, madame!"

"Come!" cried the bride suddenly. "I am off. Do you and the others, Simon, follow to see me win my wager."

They all trooped out of the tent. A full moon rode the heavens and showed the road, lying as white and straight through the meadows as the parting in Simon Lafleur's black, oily hair. The bride, still holding the diminutive bridegroom on her shoulder, burst out into song as she strode forward. The wedding guests followed. Some walked none too steadily. Griffo, the giraffe boy, staggered pitifully on his long, thin legs. Papa Copo alone remained behind.

"What a strange world!" he muttered, standing in the tent door and following them with his round blue eyes. "Ah, these children of mine are difficult at times—very difficult!"

*　　　*　　　*

A year had rolled by since the marriage of Mlle. Jeanne Marie and M. Jacques Courbé. Copo's Circus had once more taken up its quarters in the town of Roubaix. For more than a

44

week the country people for miles around had flocked to the side-show to get a peep at Griffo, the giraffe boy; M. Hercule Hippo, the giant; Mlle. Lupa, the wolf lady; Mme. Samson, with her baby boa constrictors; and M. Jejongle, the famous juggler. Each was still firmly convinced that he or she alone was responsible for the popularity of the circus.

Simon Lafleur sat in his lodgings at the Sign of the Wild Boar. He wore nothing but red tights. His powerful torso, stripped to the waist, glistened with oil. He was kneading his biceps tenderly with some strong-smelling fluid.

Suddenly there came the sound of heavy, laborious footsteps on the stairs. Simon Lafleur looked up. His rather gloomy expression lifted, giving place to the brilliant smile that had won for him the hearts of so many lady acrobats.

"Ah, this is Marcelle!" he told himself. "Or perhaps it is Rose, the English girl; or, yet again, little Francesca, although she walks more lightly. Well, no matter—whoever it is, I will welcome her!"

But now the lagging, heavy footfalls were in the hall; and, a moment later, they came to a halt outside the door. There was a timid knock.

Simon Lafleur's brilliant smile hardened. "Perhaps some new admirer who needs encouragement," he told himself. But aloud he said: "Enter, mademoiselle!"

The door swung slowly open and revealed the visitor. She was a tall, gaunt woman dressed like a peasant. The wind had blown her hair into her eyes. Now she raised a large, toil-worn hand, brushed it back across her forehead and looked long and attentively at the bareback rider.

"You do not remember me?" she said at length.

Two lines of perplexity appeared above Simon Lafleur's Roman nose; he slowly shook his head. He, who had known so many women in his time, was now at a loss. Was it a fair question to ask a man who was no longer a boy and who had lived? Women change so in a brief time! Now this bag of bones might at one time have appeared desirable to him.

Parbleu! Fate was a conjurer! She waved her wand; and beautiful women were transformed into hags, jewels into pebbles, silks and laces into hempen cords. The brave fellow, who danced tonight at the prince's ball, might tomorrow dance more lightly on the gallows tree. The thing was to live and die with a full belly. To digest all that one could—that was life!

"You do not remember me?" she said again.

Simon Lafleur once more shook his sleek, black head. "I have a poor memory for faces, madame," he said politely. "It is my misfortune, when there are such beautiful faces."

"Ah, but you should have remembered, Simon!" the woman cried, a sob rising up in her throat. "We were very close together, you and I. Do you not remember Jeanne Marie?"

"Jeanne Marie!" the bareback rider cried. "Jeanne Marie, who married a marmoset and a country estate? Don't tell me, madame, that you——"

He broke off and stared at her, open-mouthed. His sharp black eyes wandered from the wisps of wet, straggling hair down her gaunt person till they rested at last on her thick cowhide boots, encrusted with layer on layer of mud from the country-side.

"It is impossible!" he said at last.

"It is indeed Jeanne Marie," the woman answered, "or what is left of her. Ah, Simon, what a life he has led me! I have been merely a beast of burden! There are no ignominies which he has not made me suffer!"

"To whom do you refer?" Simons Lafleur demanded. "Surely you cannot mean that pocket edition husband of yours—that dwarf, Jacques Courbé?"

"Ah, but I do, Simon! Alas, he has broken me!"

"He—that toothpick of a man?" the bareback rider cried, with one of his silent laughs. "Why, it is impossible! As you once said yourself, Jeanne, you could crack his skull between finger and thumb like a hickory nut!"

"So I thought once. Ah, but I did not know him then, Simon! Because he was small, I thought I could do with him as I liked. It seemed to me that I was marrying a manikin. 'I will play Punch and Judy with this little fellow,' I said to myself. Simon, you may imagine my surprise when he began playing Punch and Judy with me!"

"But I do not understand, Jeanne. Surely at any time you could have slapped him into obedience!"

"Perhaps," she assented wearily, "had it not been for St. Eustache. From the first that wolf dog of his hated me. If I so much as answered his master back, he would show his teeth. Once, at the beginning, when I raised my hand to cuff Jacques Courbé, he sprang at my throat and would have torn me limb

46

from limb, had not the dwarf called him off. I was a strong woman, but even then I was no match for a wolf! "

"There was poison, was there not?" Simon Lafleur suggested.

"Ah, yes, I, too, thought of poison; but it was of no avail. St. Eustache would eat nothing that I gave him; and the dwarf forced me to taste first of all the food that was placed before him and his dog. Unless I myself wished to die, there was no way of poisoning either of them."

"My poor girl! " the bareback rider said, pityingly. "I begin to understand; but sit down and tell me everything. This is a revelation to me, after seeing you stalking homeward so triumphantly with your bridegroom on your shoulder. You must begin at the beginning."

"It was just because I carried him thus on my shoulder that I have had to suffer so cruelly," she said, seating herself on the only other chair the room afforded. "He has never forgiven me the insult which he says I put upon him. Do you remember how I boasted that I could carry him from one end of France to the other?"

"I remember. Well, Jeanne?"

"Well, Simon, the little demon has figured out the exact distance in leagues. Each morning, rain or shine, we sally out of the house—he on my back, the wolf dog at my heels—and I tramp along the dusty roads till my knees tremble beneath me from fatigue. If I so much as slacken my pace, if I falter, he goads me with his cruel little golden spurs; while, at the same time, St. Eustache nips my ankles. When we return home, he strikes so many leagues off a score which he says is the number of leagues from one end of France to the other. Not half that distance has been covered, and I am no longer a strong woman, Simon. Look at these shoes! "

She held up one of her feet for his inspection. The sole of the cowhide boot had worn through; Simon Lafleur caught a glimpse of bruised flesh caked with the mire of the highway.

"This is the third pair that I have had," she continued hoarsely. "Now he tells me that the price of shoe leather is too high, that I shall have to finish my pilgrimage barefooted."

"But why do you put up with all this, Jeanne?" Simon Lafleur asked angrily. "You, who have a carriage and a servant, should not walk at all! "

"At first there was a carriage and a servant," she said, wiping

47

the tears from her eyes with the back of her hand, "but they did not last a week. He sent the servant about his business and sold the carriage at a nearby fair. Now there is no one but me to wait on him and his dog."

"But the neighbours?" Simon Lafleur persisted. "Surely you could appeal to them?"

"We have no near neighbours; the farm is quite isolated. I would have run away many months ago, if I could have escaped unnoticed; but they keep a continual watch on me. Once I tried, but I hadn't travelled more than a league before the wolf dog was snapping at my ankles. He drove me back to the farm, and the following day I was compelled to carry the little fiend till I fell from sheer exhaustion."

"But tonight you got away?"

"Yes," she said, with a quick, frightened glance at the door. "Tonight I slipped out while they were both sleeping, and came here to you. I knew that you would protect me, Simon, because of what we have been to each other. Get Papa Copo to take me back in the circus, and I will work my fingers to the bone! Save me, Simon!"

Jeanne Marie could no longer suppress her sobs. They rose in her throat, choking her, making her incapable of further speech.

"Calm yourself, Jeanne," Simon Lafleur said soothingly. "I will do what I can for you. I shall have a talk with Papa Copo to-morrow. Of course, you are no longer the same woman that you were a year ago. You have aged since then; but perhaps our good Papa Copo could find you something to do."

He broke off and eyed her intently. She had stiffened in the chair; her face, even under its coat of grime, had gone a sickly white.

"What troubles you, Jeanne?" he asked a trifle breathlessly.

"Hush!" she said, with a finger to her lips. "Listen!"

Simon Lafleur could hear nothing but the tapping of the rain on the roof and the sighing of the wind through the trees. An unusual silence seemed to pervade the Sign of the Wild Boar.

"Now don't you hear it?" she cried with an inarticulate gasp. "Simon, it is in the house—it is on the stairs!"

At last the bareback rider's less sensitive ears caught the sound his companion had heard a full minute before. It was a steady

48

pit-pat, pit-pat, on the stairs, hard to dissociate from the drip of the rain from the eaves; but each instant it came nearer, grew more distinct.

"Oh, save me, Simon; save me!" Jeanne Marie cried, throwing herself at his feet and clasping him about the knees. "Save me! It is St. Eustache!"

"Nonsense, woman!" the bareback rider said angrily, but nevertheless he rose. "There are other dogs in the world. On the second landing there is a blind fellow who owns a dog. Perhaps it is he you hear."

"No, no—it is St. Eustache's step! My God, if you had lived with him a year, you would know it, too! Close the door and lock it!"

"That I will not," Simon Lafleur said contemptuously. "Do you think I am frightened so easily? If it is the wolf dog, so much the worse for him. He will not be the first cur I have choked to death with these two hands!"

Pit-pat, pit-pat—it was on the second landing. *Pit-pat, pit-pat* —now it was in the corridor, and coming fast. *Pit-pat*—all at once it stopped.

There was a moment's breathless silence, and then into the room trotted St. Eustache. M. Jacques Courbé sat astride the dog's broad back, as he had so often done in the circus ring. He held a tiny drawn sword; his shoe-button eyes seemed to reflect its steely glitter.

The dwarf brought the dog to a halt in the middle of the room, and took in, at a single glance, the prostrate figure of Jeanne Marie. St. Eustache, too, seemed to take silent note of it. The stiff hair on his back rose up, he showed his long white fangs hungrily, and his eyes glowed like two live coals.

"So I find you *thus,* madame!" M. Jacques Courbé said at last. "It is fortunate that I have a charger here who can scent out my enemies as well as hunt them down in the open. Without him, I might have had some difficulty in discovering you. Well, the little game is up. I find you with your lover!"

"Simon Lafleur is not my lover!" she sobbed. "I have not seen him once since I married you until tonight! I swear it!"

"Once is enough," the dwarf said grimly. "The impudent stable-boy must be chastised!"

"Oh, spare him!" Jeanne Marie implored. "Do not harm him, I beg of you! It is not his fault that I came! I——"

But at this point Simon Lafleur drowned her own in a roar of laughter.

"Ho, ho!" he roared, putting his hands on his hips. "You would chastise me, eh? *Nom d'un chien!* Don't try your circus trick on *me*! Why, hop-o'-my thumb, you who ride on a dog's back like a flea, out of this room before I squash you! Begone, melt, fade away!" He paused, expanded his barrel-like chest, puffed out his cheeks, and blew a great breath at the dwarf. "Blow away, insect," he bellowed, "lest I put my heel on you!"

M. Jacques Courbé was unmoved by this torrent of abuse. He sat very upright on St. Eustache's back, his tiny sword resting on his tiny shoulder.

"Are you done?" he said at last, when the bareback rider had run dry of invectives. "Very well, monsieur! Prepare to receive cavalry!" He paused for an instant, then added in a high, clear voice: "Get him, St. Eustache!"

The dog crouched, and, at almost the same moment, sprang at Simon Lafleur. The bareback rider had no time to avoid him and his tiny rider. Almost instantaneously the three of them had come to death grips. It was a gory business.

Simon Lafleur, strong man as he was, was bowled over by the wolf dog's unexpected leap. St. Eustache's clashing jaws closed on his right arm and crushed it to the bone. A moment later the dwarf, still clinging to his dog's back, thrust the point of his tiny sword into the body of the prostrate bareback rider.

Simon Lafleur struggled valiantly, but to no purpose. Now he felt the foetid breath of the dog fanning his neck, and the wasp-like sting of the dwarf's blade, which this time found a mortal spot. A convulsive tremor shook him and he rolled over on his back. The circus Romeo was dead.

M. Jacques Courbé cleansed his sword on a kerchief of lace, dismounted, and approached Jeanne Marie. She was still crouching on the floor, her eyes closed, her head held tightly between both hands. The dwarf touched her imperiously on the broad shoulder which had so often carried him.

"Madame," he said, "we now can return home. You must be more careful hereafter. *Ma foi*, it is an ungentlemanly business cutting the throats of stable-boys!"

She rose to her feet, like a large trained animal at the word of command.

"You wish to be carried?" she said between livid lips.

"Ah, that is true, madame," he murmured. "I was forgetting our little wager. Ah, yes! Well, you are to be congratulated, madame—you have covered nearly half the distance."

"Nearly half the distance," she repeated in a lifeless voice.

"Yes, madame," M. Jacques Courbé continued. "I fancy that you will be quite a docile wife by the time you have done." He paused, and then added reflectively: "It is truly remarkable how speedily one can ride the devil out of a woman—with spurs!"

*   *   *

Papa Copo had been spending a convivial evening at the Sign of the Wild Boar. As he stepped out into the street he saw three familiar figures preceding him—a tall woman, a tiny man, and a large dog with upstanding ears. The woman carried the man on her shoulder; the dog trotted at her heels.

The circus owner came to a halt and stared after them. His round eyes were full of astonishment.

"Can it be?" he murmured. "Yes, it is! Three old friends! And so Jeanne Marie still carries him! Ah, but she should not poke fun at M. Jacques Courbé! He is so sensitive; but, alas, they are the kind that are always henpecked!"

Giant

No other freak show is more likely to play to capacity crowds than the giant. From the very earliest times showmen have exploited tall men and women in tents, sideshows and circuses across the world. How many of these people are actually genuine—and how many are the result of careful padding and false clothing—it is hard to tell. The tale which follows reveals macabre facts about the growth of one most unusual giant.

THE AMPOI GIANT

By Clark Ashton Smith

A circus had arrived in Auburn. The siding at the station was crowded with long lines of cars from which issued a medley of exotic howls, growls, snarls and trumpetings. Elephants and zebras and dromedaries were led along the main streets; and many of the freaks and performers wandered about the town.

Two bearded ladies passed with the graceful air and walk of women of fashion. Then came a whole troupe of midgets, trudging along with the look of mournful, sophisticated children. And then I saw the giant, who was slightly more than eight feet tall and magnificently built, with no sign of the disproportion which often attends giantism. He was merely a fine physical specimen of the ordinary man, somewhat more than life-size. And even at first glance, there was something about his features and his gait which suggested a seaman.

I am a doctor; and the man provoked my medical curiosity. His abnormal bulk and height, without trace of acromegaly, was something I had never happened to meet before.

He must have felt my interest, for he returned my gaze with a speculative eye; and then, lurching in sailor-like fashion, he came over to me.

"I say, sir, could a chap buy a drink in this 'ere town?" He queried cautiously.

I made a quick decision.

"Come with me," I replied. "I'm an allopath; and I can tell without asking that you're a sick man."

We were only a block from my office. I steered the giant up the stairs and into my private sanctum. He almost filled the place, even when he sat down at my urging. I brought out a bottle of rye and poured a liberal glassful for him. He downed it with manifest appreciation. He had worn an air of mild depression when I first met him; now he began to brighten.

"You wouldn't think, to look at me, that I wasn't always a bloomin' giant," he soliloquized.

"Have another drink," I suggested.

After the second glass, he resumed a little mournfully: "No, sir, Jim Knox wasn't always a damn circus freak."

Then, with little urging on my part, he told me his story.

Knox, an adventurous Cockney, had followed half the seas of the world as a common sailor and boatswain in his younger years. He had visited many strange places, had known many bizarre experiences. Before he had reached the age of thirty, his restless and daring disposition led him to undertake an incredibly fantastic quest.

The events preceding this quest were somewhat unusual in themselves. Ship-wrecked by a wild typhoon in the Banda Sea, and apparently the one survivor, Knox had drifted for two days on a hatch torn from the battered and sinking vessel. Then, rescued by a native-fishing-proa, he had been carried to Salawatti.

The Rajah of Salawatti, an old and monkey-like Malay, was very nice to Knox. The Rajah was a teller of voluminous tales; and the boatswain was a patient listener. On this basis of congeniality, Knox became an honoured guest for a month or more in the Rajah's palace. Here, among other wonders retailed by his host, he heard for the first time the rumour of a most remarkable Papuan tribe.

This unique tribe dwelt on a well-nigh inaccessible plateau of the Arfak Mountains. The women were nine feet tall and white as milk; but the men, strangely, were of normal stature and darker hue. They were friendly to the rare travellers who reached their domains; and they would trade for glass beads and mirrors the pigeon's blood rubies in which their mountain-slopes abounded. As proof of the latter statement, the Rajah showed Knox a large, flawless, uncut ruby, which he claimed had come from this region.

Knox was hardly inclined to credit the item about the giant women; but the rubies sounded far less improbable. It was characteristic of him that, with little thought of danger, difficulty, or the sheer absurdity of such a venture, he made up his mind at once to visit the Arfak Mountains.

Bidding farewell to his host who mourned the loss of a good listener, he continued his odyssey. By means that he failed to specify in history, Knox procured two sackfuls of mirrors and glass beads, and managed to reach the coast of northwestern New

Guinea. At Andai, in Arfak, he hired a guide who purported to know the whereabouts of the giant Amazons, and struck boldly inland towards the mountains.

The guide, who was half Malay and half Papuan, bore one of the sacks of baubles on his shoulders; and Knox carried the other. He fondly hoped to return with the two sacks full of smouldering dark red rubies.

It was a little known land. Some of the peoples were reputed to be head-hunters and cannibals; but Knox found them friendly enough. But somehow, as they went on, the guide began to exhibit a growing haziness in his geography. When they reached the middle slopes of the Arfak range, Knox realized that the guide knew little more than he himself regarding the location of the fabulous ruby-strewn plateau.

They went on through the steepening forest. Before them, above trees that were still tall and semi-tropical, arose the granite scarps and crags of a high mountain wall, behind which the afternoon sun had disappeared. It the early twilight, they camped at the foot of a seemingly insuperable cliff.

Knox awoke in a blazing yellow dawn, to discover that his guide had departed, taking one of the sacks of trinkets—which, from a savage viewpoint, would contribute enough capital to set the fellow up in business for life. Knox shrugged his shoulders and swore a little. The guide wasn't much of a loss; but he didn't like having his jewel-purchasing power diminished by half.

He looked at the cliffs above. Tier on tier they towered in the glow of dawn, with tops scarce distinguishable from the clouds about them. Somehow, the more he looked the surer he became that they were the cliffs which guarded the hidden plateau. With their silence and inaccessible solitude, their air of eternal reserve and remoteness, they couldn't be anything else but the ramparts of a realm of titan women and pigeon's blood rubies.

He shouldered his pack and followed the granite wall in search of a likely starting-place for the climb he had determined to attempt. The upright rock was smooth as a metal sheet, and didn't offer a toehold for a spider monkey. But at last he came to a deep chasm which formed the bed of a summer-dried cataract. He began to ascend the chasm, which was no mean feat in itself, for the stream bed was a series of high shelves, like a giant stairway.

Half the time he dangled by his fingers without a toehold, or

55

stretched on tiptoe and felt precariously for a finger-grip. The climb was a ticklish business, with death on the pointed rocks below as the penalty of the least miscalculation.

He dared not look back on the way he had climbed in that giddy chasm. Towards noon, he saw above him the menacing overhang of a huge crag, where the straightening gully ceased in a black-mouthed cavern.

He scrambled up the final shelf into the cave, hoping that it led, as was likely, to an upper entrance made by the mountain torrent. By the light of struck matches, he scaled a slippery incline. The cave soon narrowed; and Knox could often brace himself between the walls, as if in a chimney's interior.

After long upward groping, he discerned a tiny glimmering ahead, like a pin-prick in the solid gloom. Knox, nearly worn out with his efforts, was immensely heartened. But again the cave narrowed, till he could squeeze no farther with the pack on his back. He slid back a little distance and removed the sack, which he then proceeded to push before him up a declivity of forty-five degrees. In those days, Knox was of average height and somewhat slender; but even so, he could barely wriggle through the last ten feet of the cavern.

He gave the sack a final heave and landed it on the surface without. Then he squirmed through the opening and fell exhausted in the sunlight. He lay almost at the fountain-head of the dried stream, in a saucer-like hollow at the foot of a gentle slope of granite beyond whose bare ridge the clouds were white and near.

Knox congratulated himself on his gift as an alpine climber. He felt no doubt whatever that he had reached the threshold of the hidden realm of rubies and giant women.

Suddenly, as he lay there, several men appeared against the clouds, on the ridge above. Striding like mountaineers, they came towards him with excited jabberings and gestures of amazement; and he rose and stood awaiting them.

Knox must have been a singular spectacle. His clothing and face were bestreaked with dirt and with the stains of parti-coloured ores acquired in his passage through the cavern. The approaching men seemed to regard him with a sort of awe.

They were dressed in short reddish-purple tunics, and wore leather sandals. They did not belong to any of the lowland types: their skin was a light sienna, and their features were good even according to European standards. All were armed with long javelins but seemed friendly. Wide-eyed, and apparently somewhat timorous, they addressed Knox in a language which bore no likeness to any Melanesian tongue he had ever heard.

He replied in all the languages of which he had the least smattering: but plainly they could not understand him. Then he untied his sack, took out a double handful of beads, and tried to convey by pantomime the information that he was a trader from remote lands.

The men nodded their heads. Beckoning to him to follow them, they returned towards the cloud-rimmed ridge. Knox trudged along behind them, feeling quite sure that he had found the people of the Rajah's tale.

Topping the ridge, he saw the perspectives of a long plateau, full of woods, streams and cultivated fields. In the mild and slanting sunlight, he and his guides descended a path among flowering willow-herbs and rhododendrons to the plateau. There it soon became a well-trodden road, running through forests of dammar and fields of wheat. Houses of rough-hewn stone with thatched roofs, evincing a higher civilization than the huts of the Papuan seaboard, began to appear at intervals.

Men, garbed in the same style as Knox's guides, were working in the fields. Then Knox perceived several women, standing together in an idle group. Now he was compelled to believe the whole story about the hidden people, for these women were eight feet or more in height and had the proportions of shapely goddesses! Their complexion was not of a milky fairness, as in the Rajah's tale, but was tawny and cream-like and many shades lighter than that of the men. Knox felt a jubilant excitement as they turned their calm gaze upon him and watched him with the air of majestic statues. He had found the legendary realm; and he peered among the pebbles and grasses of the wayside, half expecting to see them intersown with rubies. None was in evidence, however.

A town appeared, circling a sapphire lake with one-storied but well built houses laid out in regular streets. Many people were strolling or standing about; and all the women were tawny giantesses, and all the men were of average stature, with umber or sienna complexions.

A crowd gathered about Knox; and his guides were questioned in a quite peremptory manner by some of the titan females, who

57

eyed the boatswain with embarrasing intentions. He divined at once the respect and obeisance paid these women by the men, and inferred the superior position which they held. They all wore the tranquil and assured look of empresses.

Knox was led to a building near the lake. It was larger and more pretentious than the others. The roomy interior was arrayed with roughly pictured fabrics and furnished with chairs and couches of ebony. The general effect was rudely sybaritic and palatial, and much enhanced by the unusual height of the ceilings.

In a sort of audience-room, a woman sat enthroned on a broad dais. Several others stood about her like a bodyguard. She wore no crown, no jewels, and her dress differed in no wise from the short kilts of the other women. But Knox knew that he had entered the presence of a queen. The woman was fairer than the rest, with long rippling chestnut hair and fine oval features. The gaze that she turned upon Knox was filled with a feminine mingling of mildness and severity.

The boatswain assumed his most gallant manner, which must have been a little nullified by his dirt-smeared face and apparel. He bowed before the giantess; and she addressed him with a few soft words in which he sensed a courteous welcome. Then he opened his pack and selected a mirror and a string of blue beads which he offered to the queen. She accepted the gifts gravely, showing neither pleasure nor surprise.

After dismissing the men who had brought Knox to her presence, the queen turned and spoke to her female attendants. They came forward and gave Knox to understand that he must accompany them. They led him to an open court, containing a huge bath fed by the waters of the blue lake. Here, in spite of his protests and strugglings, they undressed him as if he had been a little boy. Then they plunged him into the water and scrubbed him thoroughly with scrapers of stiff vegetable fibre. One of them brought him a brown tunic and a pair of sandals in lieu of his former raiment.

Though somewhat discomfited and abashed by his summary treatment, Knox couldn't help feeling like a different man after his renovation. And when the women brought in a meal of taro and millet-cake and roast pigeon, piled on enormous platters, he began to forgive them for his embarrassment.

Two of his fair attendants remained with him during the meal; and afterwards they gave him a lesson in their language by pointing at various objects and naming them. Knox soon acquired a knowledge of much domestic nomenclature.

The queen herself appeared later and proceeded to take a hand in his instruction. Her name, he learned, was Mabousa. Knox was an apt pupil; and the day's lesson was plainly satisfactory to all concerned. Knox realized more clearly than before that the queen was a beautiful woman; but he wished that she was not quite so large and imposing. He felt so juvenile beside her. The queen, on her part, seemed to regard Knox with a far from unfavourable gravity. He saw that she was giving him a good deal of thought and consideration.

Knox almost forgot the rubies of which he had come in search; and when he remembered them, he decided to wait till he had learned more of the language before broaching the subject.

A room in the palace was assigned to him; and he inferred that he could remain indefinitely as Mabousa's guest. He ate at the same table with the queen and half-dozen attendants. It seemed that he was the only man in the establishment. The chairs were all designed for giantesses, with one exception, which resembled the high chair in which a child sits at table amongst its elders. Knox occupied this chair.

Many days went by; and he learned enough of the language for all practical purposes. It was a tranquil but far from unpleasant life. He soon grew familiar with the general conditions of life in the country ruled by Mabousa, which was called Ondoar. It was quite isolated from the world without, for the mountain walls around it could be scaled only at the point which Knox had so fortuitously discovered. Few strangers had ever obtained entrance. The people were prosperous and contented, leading a pastoral existence under the benign but absolute matriarchy of Mabousa. The women governed their husbands by sheer virtue of physical superiority; but there seemed to be fully as much domestic amity as in the households of countries where a reverse dominion prevails.

Knox wondered greatly about the superior stature of the women, which struck him as being a strange provision of nature. Somehow he did not venture to ask any questions; and no one volunteered to tell him the secret.

He kept an eye open for rubies, and was puzzled by the paucity of these gems. A few inferior rubies, as well as small sapphires and emeralds, were worn by some of the men as ear-ring pendants, though none of the women were addicted to such ornaments. Knox wondered if they didn't have a lot of rubies stored away somewhere. He had come there to trade for red corundum and had carried a whole sack-load of the requisite medium of barter up an impossible mountainside; so he was loath to relinquish the idea.

One day he resolved to open the subject with Mabousa. For some reason, he never knew quite why, it was hard to speak of such matters to the dignified and lovely giantess. But business was business.

He was groping for suitable words, when he suddenly noticed that Mabousa too had something on her mind. She had grown uncommonly silent and the way she kept looking at him was disconcerting and even embarrassing. He wondered what was the matter; also, he began to wonder if these people were cannibalistic. Her gaze was so eager and avid.

Before he could speak of the rubies and his willingness to buy them with glass beads, Mabousa startled him by coming out with a flatly phrased proposal of marriage. To say the least, Knox was unprepared. But it seemed uncivil, as well as unpolitic, to refuse. He had never been proposed to before by a queen or a giantess, and he thought it would be hardly the proper etiquette to decline a heart and hand of such capacity. Also, as Mabousa's husband, he would be in a most advantageous position to negotiate for rubies. And Mabousa was undeniably attractive, even though she was built on a grand scale. After a little hemming and hawing, he accepted her proposal, and was literally swept off his feet as the lady gathered him to the gargantuan charms of her bosom.

The wedding proved to be a very simple affair: a mere matter of verbal agreement in the presence of several female witnesses. Knox was amazed by the ease and rapidity with which he assumed the bonds of holy matrimony.

He learned a lot of things from his marriage with Mabousa. He found at the wedding-supper that the high chair he had been occupying at the royal table was usually reserved for the queen's consort. Later, he learned the secret of the women's size and stature. All the children, boys and girls, were of ordinary size at birth; but the girls were fed by their mothers on a certain root which caused them to increase in height and bulk beyond the natural limits.

The root was gathered on the highest mountain slopes. Its

peculiar virtue was mainly due to a mode of preparation whose secret had been carefully guarded by the women and handed down from mother to daughter. Its use had been known for several generations. At one time the men had been the ruling sex; but an accidental discovery of the root by a down-trodden wife named Ampoi had soon led to a reversal of this domination. In consequence the memory of Ampoi was highly venerated by the females, as that of a saviouress.

Knox also acquired much other information, on matters both social and domestic. But nothing was ever said about rubies. He was forced to decide that the plenitude of these jewels in Ondoar must have been sheer fable; a purely decorative addition to the story of the giant Amazons.

His marriage led to other disillusionments. As the queen's consort, he had expected to have a share in the government of Ondoar, and had looked forward to a few kingly prerogatives. But he soon found that he was merely a male adjunct of Mabousa, with no legal rights, no privileges other than those which she, out of wifely affection, might choose to accord him. She was kind and loving, but also strong-minded, not to say bossy; and he learned that he couldn't do anything or go anywhere without first consulting her and obtaining permission.

She would sometimes reprimand him, would often set him right on some point of Ondoarian etiquette, or the general conduct of life, in a sweet but strict manner; and it never occurred to her that he might even wish to dispute any of her mandates. He, however, was irked more and more by this feminine tyranny. His male pride, his manly British spirit, revolted. If the lady had been of suitable size he would, in his own phrase, "have knocked her about a little". But, under the circumstances, any attempt to chasten her by main strength hardly seemed advisable.

Along with all this, he grew quite fond of her in his fashion. There were many things that endeared her to him; and he felt that she would be an exemplary wife, if there were only some way of curbing her deplorable tendency to domineer.

Time went on, as it has a habit of doing. Mabousa seemed to be well enough satisfied with her spouse. But Knox brooded a good deal over the false position in which he felt that she had placed him, and the daily injury to his manhood. He wished that there were some way of correcting matters, and of asserting his natural rights and putting Mabousa in her place.

61

One day he remembered the root on which the women of Ondoar were fed. Why couldn't he get hold of some of it and grow big himself like Mabousa, or bigger? Then he would be able to handle her in the proper style. The more he thought about it, the more this appealed to him as the ideal solution of his marital difficulties.

The main problem, however, was to obtain the root. He questioned some of the other men in a discreet way, but none of them could tell him anything about it. The women never permitted the men to accompany them when they gathered the stuff; and the process of preparing it for consumption was carried on in deep caverns. Several men had dared to steal the food in past years; two of them, indeed, had grown to giant stature in what they had stolen. But all had been punished by the women with life-long exile from Ondoar.

All this was rather discouraging. Also, it served to increase Knox's contempt for the men of Ondoar, whom he looked upon as a spineless, effeminate lot. However, he didn't give up his plan. But, after much deliberation and scheming, he found himself no nearer to a solution of the problem than before.

Perhaps he would have resigned himself, as better men have done, to an inevitable life-long henpecking. But at last, in the birth of a female baby to Mabousa and himself, he found the opportunity he had been seeking.

The child was like any other girl infant, and Knox was no less proud of it, no less imbued with the customary parental sentiments, than other fathers have been. It did not occur to him, till the baby was old enough to be weaned and fed on the special food, that he would now have in his own home a first-rate chance to appropriate some of this food for his personal use.

The simple and artless Mabousa was wholly without suspicion of such unlawful designs. Male obedience to the feministic law of the land was so thoroughly taken for granted that she even showed him the strange foodstuff and often fed the child in his presence. Nor did she conceal from him the large earthen jar in which she kept her reserve supply.

The jar stood in the palace kitchen, among others filled with more ordinary staples of diet. One day, when Mabousa had gone to the country on some political errand, and the waiting women were all preoccupied with other than culinary matters, Knox stole into the kitchen and carried away a small bagful of the stuff, which he then hid in his own room. In his fear of detection, he felt more of an actual thrill than at any time since the boyhood days when he had pilfered apples from London street-barrows behind the backs of the vendors.

The stuff looked like a fine variety of sago, and had an aromatic smell and spicy taste. Knox ate a little of it at once but dared not indulge himself to the extent of a full meal for fear that the consequences would be visible. He had watched the incredible growth of the child, which had gained the proportions of a normal six-year-old girl in a fortnight under the influence of the miraculous nutrient; and he did not wish to have his theft discovered, and the further use of the food prevented, in the first stage of his own development toward gianthood.

He felt that some sort of seclusion would be advisable till he could attain the bulk and stature which would ensure a position as master in his own household. He must somehow remove himself from all female supervision during the period of growth.

This, for one so thoroughly subject to petticoat government, with all his goings and comings minutely regulated, was no mean problem. But again fortune favoured Knox: for the hunting season in Ondoar had now arrived; a season in which many of the men were permitted by their wives to visit the higher mountains and spend days or weeks in tracking down a certain agile species of alpine deer, known as the *oklah*.

Perhaps Mabousa wondered a little at the sudden interest shown by Knox in *oklah*-hunting, and his equally sudden devotion to practice with the javelins used by the hunters. But she saw no reason for denying him permission to make the desired trip; merely stipulating that he should go in company with certain other dutiful husbands, and should be very careful of dangerous cliffs and crevasses.

The company of other husbands was not exactly in accord with Knox's plan; but he knew better than to argue the point. He had contrived to make several more visits to the palace pantry, and had stolen enough of the forbidden food to turn him into a robust and wife-taming titan. Somehow, on that trip among the mountains, in spite of the meek and law-abiding males with whom he was condemned to go, he would find chances to consume all he had stolen. He would return a conquering Anakin, a roaring and swaggering Goliath; and everyone, especially Mabousa, would stand from under.

63

Knox hid the food, disguised as a bag of millet meal, in his private supply of provisions. He also carried some of it in his pockets, and would eat a mouthful or two whenever the other men weren't looking. And at night, when they were all sleeping quietly, he would steal to the bag and devour the aromatic stuff by the handful.

The result was truly phenomenal, for Knox could watch himself swell after the first square meal. He broadened and shot up inch by inch, to the manifest bewilderment of his companions, none of whom, at first, was imaginative enough to suspect the true reason. He saw them eyeing him with a sort of speculative awe and curiosity, such as civilized people would display before a wild man from Borneo. Obviously they regarded his growth as a kind of biological anomaly, or perhaps as part of the queer behaviour that might well be expected from a foreigner of doubtful antecedents.

The hunters were now in the highest mountains, at the northernmost end of Ondoar. Here, among stupendous riven crags and piled pinnacles, they pursued the elusive *oklah*; and Knox began to attain a length of limb that enabled him to leap across chasms over which the others could not follow.

At last one or two of them must have become suspicious. They took to watching Knox, and one night they surprised him in the act of devouring the sacred food. They tried to warn him, with a sort of holy horror in their demeanour, that he was doing a dreadful and forbidden thing, and would bring himself the direst consequences.

Knox, who was beginning to feel as well as look like an actual giant, told them to mind their own business. Moreover, he went on to express his frank and uncensored opinion of the sapless, decadent and effeminate males of Ondoar. After that the men left him alone, but murmured fearfully among themselves and watched his every move with apprehensive glances. Knox despised them so thoroughly, that he failed to attach any special significance to the furtive disappearance of two members of the party. Indeed, at the time, he hardly noticed that they had gone.

After a fortnight of alpine climbing, the hunters had slain their due quota of long-horned and goat-footed *oklah*; and Knox had consumed his entire store of the stolen food and had grown to proportions which, he felt sure, would enable him to subdue his domineering helpmate and show her the proper inferiority of the female sex. It was time to return: Knox's companions would not have dreamt of exceeding the limit set by the women, who had enjoined them to come back at the end of a fortnight; and Knox was eager to demonstrate his new-won superiority of bulk and brawn.

As they came down from the mountains and crossed the cultivated plain, Knox saw that the other men were lagging behind more and more, with a sort of fearfulness and shrinking timidity. He strode on before them, carrying three full-sized *oklah* slung over his shoulders, as a lesser man would have carried so many rabbits.

The fields and roads were deserted, and none of the titan women was in sight anywhere. Knox wondered a little about this; but feeling himself so much the master of the general situation, he did not over-exert his mind in curious conjectures.

However, as they approached the town, the desolation and silence became a trifle ominous. Knox's fellow-hunters were obviously stricken with dire and growing terror. But Knox did not feel that he should lower his dignity by even asking the reason.

They entered the streets, which were also strangely quiet. There was no evidence of life, other than the pale and frightened faces of a few men that peered from windows and furtively opened doors.

At last they came in sight of the palace. Now the mystery was explained, for apparently all the women of Ondoar had gathered in the square before the building! They were drawn up in a massive and appallingly solid formation, like an army of giant Amazons; and their utter stillness was more dreadful than the shouting and tumult of battle-fields. Knox felt an unwilling but irresistible dismay before the swelling thews of their mighty arms, the solemn heaving of gargantuan bosoms, and the awful and austere gaze with which they regarded him in unison.

Suddenly he perceived that he was quite alone—the other men had faded away like shadows, as if they did not even dare to remain and watch his fate. He felt an almost undeniable impulse to flee; but his British valour prevented him from yielding to it. Pace by pace he forced himself to go on towards the embattled women.

They waited for him in stony silence, immovable as caryatids. He saw Mabousa in the front rank, her serving-women about her. She watched him with eyes in which he could read nothing but

65

unutterable reproach. She did not speak; and somehow the jaunty words with which he had intended to greet her were congealed on his lips.

All at once, with a massed and terrible striding movement, the women surrounded Knox. He lost sight of Mabousa in the solid wall of titanesses. Great, brawny hands were grasping him, tearing the spear from his fingers and the *oklah* from his shoulders. He struggled as became a doughty Briton. But one man, even though he had eaten the food of giantesses, could do nothing against the whole tribe of eight-foot females.

Maintaining a silence more formidable than any outcry, they bore him through the town and along the road by which he had entered Ondoar, and up the mountain path to the outmost ramparts of the land. There, from the beetling crag above the gully he had climbed, they lowered him with a tackle of heavy ropes to the dry torrent-bed two hundred feet below, and left him to find his way down the perilous mountainside and back to the outer world that would accept him henceforward only as a circus freak.

Dwarf

Equally popular in their own way as giants are the little men and women variously called dwarfs and midgets. We have already met in earlier stories two ingenious little men, Hop-Frog and M. Courbé, and here Ray Bradbury introduces another tiny human of a very different calibre. Be warned, there are few modern storytellers more capable of sitting you bolt upright than the inventive Mr. Bradbury.

THE DWARF

By RAY BRADBURY

Aimee watched the sky, quietly.

Tonight was one of those motionless hot summer nights. The concrete pier empty, the strung red, white, yellow bulbs burning like insects in the air above the wooden emptiness. The managers of the various carnival pitches stood, like melting wax dummies, eyes staring blindly, not talking, all down the line.

Two customers had passed through an hour before. Those two lonely people were now in the roller coaster, screaming murderously as it plummeted down the blazing night, around one emptiness after another.

Aimee moved slowly across the strand, a few worn wooden hoopla rings sticking to her wet hands. She stopped behind the ticket booth that fronted the MIRROR MAZE. She saw herself grossly misrepresented in three rippled mirrors outside the Maze. A thousand tired replicas of herself dissolved in the corridor beyond, hot images among so much clear coolness.

She stepped inside the ticket booth and stood looking a long while at Ralph Banghart's thin neck. He clenched an unlit cigar between his long uneven yellow teeth as he laid out a battered game of solitaire on the ticket shelf.

When the roller coaster wailed and fell in its terrible avalanche again, she was reminded to speak.

"What kind of people go up in roller coasters?"

Ralph Banghart worked his cigar a full thirty seconds. "People wanna die. That rollie coaster's the handiest thing to dying there is." He sat listening to the faint sound of rifle shots from the shooting gallery. "This whole damn carny business's crazy. For instance, that dwarf. You seen him? Every night, pays his dime, runs in the Mirror Maze all the way back through the Screwy Louie's Room. You should see this little runt head back there. My God!"

"Oh, yes," said Aimee, remembering. "I always wonder what it's like to be a dwarf. I always feel sorry when I see him."

"I could play him like an accordion."

"Don't say that!"

"My Lord." Ralph patted her thigh with a free hand. "The way you carry on about guys you never even met." He shook his head and chuckled. "Him and his secret. Only he don't know I know, see? Boy howdy!"

"It's a hot night." She twitched the large wooden hoops nervously on her damp fingers.

"Don't change the subject. He'll be here, rain or shine."

Aimee shifted her weight.

Ralph seized her elbow. "Hey! You ain't mad? You wanna see that dwarf, don't you? Sh!" Ralph turned. "Here he comes now!"

The Dwarf's hand, hairy and dark, appeared all by itself reaching up into the booth window with a silver dime. An invisible person called, "One!" in a high, child's voice.

Involuntarily, Aimee bent forward.

The Dwarf looked up at her, resembling nothing more than a dark-eyed, dark-haired, ugly man who has been locked in a wine-press, squeezed and wadded down and down, fold on fold, agony on agony, until a bleached, outraged mass is left, the face bloated shapelessly, a face you know must stare wide-eyed and awake at two and three and four o'clock in the morning, lying flat in bed, only the body asleep.

Ralph tore a yellow ticket in half. "One!"

The Dwarf, as if frightened by an approaching storm, pulled his black coat-lapels tightly about his throat and waddled swiftly. A moment later, ten thousand lost and wandering dwarfs wriggled between the mirror flats, like frantic dark beetles, and vanished.

"Quick!"

Ralph squeezed Aimee along a dark passage behind the mirrors. She felt him pat her all the way back through the tunnel to a thin partition with a peekhole.

"This is rich," he chuckled. "Go on—look."

Aimee hesitated, then put her face to the partition.

"You *see* him?" Ralph whispered.

Aimee felt her heart beating. A full minute passed.

There stood the Dwarf in the middle of the small blue room.

His eyes were shut. He wasn't ready to open them yet. Now, he opened his eyelids and looked at a large mirror set before him. And what he saw in the mirror made him smile. He winked, he pirouetted, he stood sidewise, he waved, he bowed, he did a little clumsy dance.

And the mirror repeated each motion with long, thin arms, with a tall, tall body, with a huge wink and an enormous repetition of the dance, ending in a gigantic bow!

"Every night the same thing," whispered Ralph in Aimee's ear. "Ain't that rich?"

Aimee turned her head and looked at Ralph steadily out of her motionless face, for a long time, and she said nothing. Then, as if she could not help herself, she moved her head slowly and very slowly back to stare once more through the opening. She held her breath. She felt her eyes begin to water.

Ralph nudged her, whispering.

"Hey, what's the little gink doin' *now*?"

They were drinking coffee and not looking at each other in the ticket booth half an hour later, when the Dwarf came out of the mirrors. He took his hat off and started to approach the booth, when he saw Aimee and hurried away.

"He wanted something," said Aimee.

"Yeah." Ralph squashed out his cigarette idly. "I know what, too. But he hasn't got the nerve to ask. One night in this squeaky little voice he says, 'I bet those mirrors are expensive.' Well, I played dumb. I said yeah they were. He sort of looked at me, waiting, and when I didn't say any more, he went home, but next night he said, 'I bet those mirrors cost fifty, a hundred bucks.' I bet they do, I said. I laid me out a hand of solitaire."

"Ralph," she said.

He glanced up. "Why you look at me that way?"

"Ralph," she said, "why don't you sell him one of your extra ones?"

"Look, Aimee, do I tell you how to run your hoop circus?"

"How much do those mirrors cost?"

"I can get 'em second-hand for thirty-five bucks."

"Why don't you tell him where he can buy one, then?"

"Aimee, you're not smart." He laid his hand on her knee. She moved her knee away. "Even if I told him where to go, you think he'd buy one? Not on your life. And why? He's self-conscious.

Why, if he even knew I knew he was flirtin' around in front of that mirror in Screwy Louie's Room, he'd never come back. He plays like he's goin' through the Maze to get lost, like everybody else. Pretends like he don't care about that special room. Always waits for business to turn bad, late nights, so he has that room to himself. What he does for entertainment on nights when business is good, God knows. No, sir, he wouldn't dare go buy a mirror anywhere. He ain't got no friends, and even if he did he couldn't ask them to buy him a thing like that. Pride, by God, pride. Only reason he even mentioned it to me is I'm practically the only guy he knows. Besides, look at him—he ain't got enough to buy a mirror like those. He might be savin' up, but where in hell in the world today can a dwarf work? Dime a dozen, drug on the market, outside of circuses."

"I feel awful. I feel sad." Aimee sat staring at the empty boardwalk. "Where does he live?"

"Flytrap down on the waterfront. The Ganghes Arms. Why?"

"I'm madly in love with him, if you must know."

He grinned around his cigar. "Aimee," he said. "You and your very funny jokes."

A warm night, a hot morning, and a blazing noon. The sea was a sheet of burning tinsel and glass.

Aimee came walking, in the locked-up carnival alleys out over the warm sea, keeping in the shade, half a dozen sun-bleached magazines under her arm. She opened a flaking door and called into hot darkness. "Ralph?" She picked her way through the black hall behind the mirrors, her heels tacking the wooden floor. "Ralph?"

Someone stirred sluggishly on the canvas cot. "Aimee?"

He sat up and screwed a dim light bulb into the dressing table socket. He squinted at her, half blinded. "Hey, you look like the cat swallowed a canary."

"Ralph, I came about the midget!"

"Dwarf, Aimee honey, dwarf. A midget is in the cells, born that way. A dwarf is in the glands. . . ."

"Ralph! I just found out the most wonderful thing about him!"

"Honest to God," he said to his hands, holding them out as witnesses to his disbelief. "This woman! Who in hell gives two cents for some ugly little——"

71

"Ralph!" She held out the magazines, her eyes shining. "He's a writer! Think of that!"

"It's a pretty hot day for thinking." He lay back and examined her, smiling faintly.

"I just happened to pass the Ganghes Arms, and saw Mr. Greeley, the manager. He says the typewriter runs all night in Mr. Big's room!"

"Is *that* his name?" Ralph began to roar with laughter.

"Writes just enough pulp detective stories to live. I found one of his stories in the secondhand magazine place, and, Ralph, guess what?"

"I'm tired, Aimee."

"This little guy's got a soul as big as all outdoors; he's got *everything* in his head!"

"Why ain't he writin' for the big magazines, then, I ask you?"

"Because maybe he's afraid—maybe he doesn't know he can do it. That happens. People don't believe in themselves. But if he only tried, I bet he could sell stories anywhere in the world."

"Why ain't he rich, I wonder?"

"Maybe because ideas come slow because he's down in the dumps. Who wouldn't be? So small that way? I bet it's hard to think of anything except being so small and living in a one-room cheap apartment."

"Hell!" snorted Ralph. "You talk like Florence Nightingale's grandma."

She held up the magazine. "I'll read you part of his crime story. It's got all the guns and tough people, but it's told by a dwarf. I bet the editors never guessed the author knew what he was writing about. Oh, please don't sit there like that, Ralph! Listen."

And she began to read aloud.

"I am a dwarf and I am a murderer. The two things cannot be separated. One is the cause of the other.

"The man I murdered used to stop me on the street when I was twenty-one, pick me up in his arms, kiss my brow, croon wildly to me, sing Rock-a-bye Baby, haul me into meat markets, toss me on the scales and cry, 'Watch it. Don't weigh your thumb, there, butcher!'

"Do you *see* how our lives moved toward murder? This fool, this persecutor of my flesh and soul!

"As for my childhood: my parents were small people, not

72

quite dwarfs, not quite. My father's inheritance kept us in a doll's house, an amazing thing like a white-scrolled wedding cake—little rooms, little chairs, miniature paintings, cameos, ambers with insects caught inside, everything tiny, tiny, tiny! The world of Giants far away, an ugly rumour beyond the garden wall. Poor mama, papa! They meant only the best for me. They kept me, like a porcelain vase, small and treasured, to themselves, in our ant world, our beehive rooms, our microscopic library, our land of beetle-sized doors and moth windows. Only now do I see the magnificent size of my parents' psychosis! They must have dreamed they would live forever, keeping me like a butterfly under glass. But first father died, and then fire ate up the little house, the wasp's nest, and every postage-stamp mirror and salt-cellar closet within. Mama, too, gone! And myself alone, watching the fallen embers, tossed out into a world of Monsters and Titans, caught in a landslide of reality, rushed, rolled, and smashed to the bottom of the cliff!

"It took me a year to adjust. A job with a sideshow was unthinkable. There seemed no place for me in the world. And then, a month ago, the Persecutor came into my life, clapped a bonnet on my unsuspecting head, and cried to friends, 'I want you to meet the little woman!' "

Aimee stopped reading. Her eyes were unsteady and the magazine shook as she handed it to Ralph. "You finish it, The rest is a murder story. It's all right. But don't you see? That little man. That little man."

Ralph tossed the magazine aside and lit a cigarette lazily. "I like Westerns better."

"Ralph, you got to read it. He needs someone to tell him how good he is and keep him writing."

Ralph looked at her, his head to one side. "And guess who's going to do it? Well, well, ain't we just the Saviour's right hand?"

"I won't listen!"

"Use your head, damn it! You go busting in on him he'll think you're handing him pity. He'll chase you screamin' outa his room."

She sat down, thinking about it slowly, trying to turn it over and see it from every side. "I don't know. Maybe you're right. Oh, it's not just pity, Ralph, honest. But maybe it'd look like it to him. I've got to be awful careful."

He shook her shoulder back and forth, pinching softly, with

his fingers. "Hell, hell, lay off him, is all I ask; you'll get nothing but trouble for your dough. God, Aimee, I never *seen* you so hepped on anything. Look, you and me, let's make it a day, take a lunch, get us some gas, and just drive on down the coast as far as we can drive; swim, have supper, see a good show in some little town—to hell with the carnival, how about it? A damn nice day and no worries. I been savin' a coupla bucks."

"It's because I know he's different," she said, looking off into darkness. "It's because he's something we can never be—you and me and all the rest of us here on the pier. It's so funny, so funny. Life fixed him so he's good for nothing but carny shows, yet there he is on the land. And life made us so we wouldn't have to work in the carny shows, but here we are, anyway, way out here at sea on the pier. Sometimes it seems a million miles to shore. How come, Ralph, that we got the bodies, but he's got the brains and can think things we'll never even guess?"

"You haven't even been listening to me!" said Ralph.

She sat with him standing over her, his voice far away. Her eyes were half shut and her hands were in her lap, twitching.

"I don't like that shrewd look you're getting on," he said, finally.

She opened her purse slowly and took out a small roll of bills and started couting. "Thirty-five, forty dollars. There. I'm going to phone Billie Fine and have him send out one of those tall-type mirrors to Mr. Bigelow at the Ganghes Arms. Yes, I am!"

"What!"

"Think how wonderful for him, Ralph, having one in his own room any time he wants it. Can I use your phone?"

"Go ahead, *be* nutty."

Ralph turned quickly and walked off down the tunnel. A door slammed.

Aimee waited, then after a while put her hands to the phone and began to dial, with painful slowness. She paused between numbers, holding her breath, shutting her eyes, thinking how it might seem to be small in the world, and then one day someone sends a special mirror by. A mirror for your room where you can hide away with the big reflection of yourself, shining, and write stories and stories, never going out into the world unless you had to. How might it be then, alone, with the wonderful illusion all in one piece in the room. Would it make you happy or sad, would it help your writing or hurt it? She shook her head back and forth, back and forth. At least this way there would be no one to look down at you. Night after night, perhaps rising secretly at three in the cold morning, you could wink and dance around and smile and wave at yourself, so tall, so tall, so very fine and tall in the bright looking glass.

A telephone voice said, "Billie Fine's."

"Oh, *Billie!*" she cried.

Night came in over the pier. The ocean lay dark and loud under the planks. Ralph sat cold and waxen in his glass coffin, laying out the cards, his eyes fixed, his mouth stiff. At his elbow, a growing pyramid of burnt cigarette butts grew larger. When Aimee walked along under the hot red and blue bulbs, smiling, waving, he did not stop setting the cards down slow and very slow. "Hi, Ralph!" she said.

"How's the love affair?" he asked, drinking from a dirty glass of iced water. "How's Charlie Boyer, or is it Cary Grant?"

"I just went and bought me a new hat," she said, smiling. "Gosh, I feel *good!* You know why? Billie Fine's sending a mirror out tomorrow! Can't you just see the nice little guy's face?"

"I'm not so hot at imagining."

"Oh, Lord, you'd think I was going to marry him or something."

"Why not? Carry him around in a suitcase. People say, Where's your husband? all you do is open your bag, well, Here he is! Like a silver cornet. Take him outa his case any old hour, play a tune, stash him away. Keep a little sandbox for him on the back porch."

"I was feeling so good," she said.

"Benevolent is the word." Ralph did not look at her, his mouth tight. "Ben-ev-o-*lent*. I suppose this all comes from me watching him through that knothole, getting my kicks? That why you sent the mirror? People like you run around with tambourines, taking the joy out of my life."

"Remind me not to come to your place for drinks any more. I'd rather go with no people at all than mean people."

Ralph exhaled a deep breath. "Aimee, Aimee. Don't you know you can't help that guy? He's bats. And this crazy thing of yours is like saying, Go ahead, *be* batty, I'll help you, pal."

"Once in a lifetime anyway, it's nice to make a mistake if you think it'll do somebody some good," she said.

"God deliver me from do-gooders, Aimee."

"Shut up, shut up!" she cried, and then said nothing more.

He let the silence lie awhile, and then got up, putting his finger-printed glass aside. "Mind the booth for me?"

"Sure. Why?"

She saw ten thousand cold white images of him stalking down the glassy corridors, between mirrors, his mouth straight and his fingers working themselves.

She sat in the booth for a full minute and then suddenly shivered. A small clock ticked in the booth and she turned the deck of cards over, one by one, waiting. She heard a hammer pounding and knocking and pounding again, far away inside the Maze; a silence, more waiting, and then ten thousand images folding and refolding and dissolving, Ralph striding, looking out at ten thousand images of her in the booth. She heard his quiet laughter as he came down the ramp.

"Well, what's put you in such a good mood?" she asked, suspiciously.

"Aimee," he said, carelessly, "we shouldn't quarrel. You say tomorrow Billie Fine's sending that mirror out to Mr. Big's?"

"You're not going to try anything funny?"

"Me?" He moved her out of the booth and took over the cards, humming, his eyes bright. "Not me, oh no, not me." He did not look at her, but started quickly to slap out the cards. She stood behind him. Her right eye began to twitch a little. She folded and unfolded her arms. A minute ticked by. The only sound was the ocean under the night pier, Ralph breathing in the heat, the soft ruffle of the cards. The sky over the pier was hot and thick with clouds. Out at sea, faint glows of lightning were beginning to show.

"Ralph," she said at last.

"Relax, Aimee," he said.

"About that trip you wanted to take down the coast——"

"Tomorrow," he said. "Maybe next month. Maybe next year. Old Ralph Banghart's a patient guy. I'm not worried, Aimee. Look." He held up a hand. "I'm calm."

She waited for a roll of thunder at sea to fade away.

"I just don't want you mad, is all. I just don't want anything bad to happen, promise me."

The wind, now warm, now cool, blew along the pier. There was a smell of rain in the wind. The clock ticked. Aimee began to perspire heavily, watching the cards move and move. Distantly, you could hear targets being hit and the sound of the pistols at the shooting gallery.

And then, there he was.

Waddling along the lonely concourse, under the insect bulbs, his face twisted and dark, every movement an effort. From a long way down the pier he came, with Aimee watching. She wanted to say to him, This is your last night, the last time you'll have to embarrass yourself by coming here, the last time you'll have to put up with being watched by Ralph, even in secret. She wished she could cry out and laugh and say it right in front of Ralph. But she said nothing.

"Hello, hello!" shouted Ralph. "It's free, on the house, tonight! Special for old customers!"

The Dwarf looked up, startled, his little black eyes darting and swimming in confusion. His mouth formed the word thanks and he turned, one hand to his neck, pulling his tiny lapels tight up about his convulsing throat, the other hand clenching the silver dime secretly. Looking back, he gave a little nod, and then scores of dozens of compressed and tortured faces, burnt a strange dark colour by the lights, wandered in the glass corridors.

"Ralph," Aimee took his elbow. "What's going on?"

He grinned. "I'm going benevolent, Aimee, benevolent."

"Ralph," she said.

"Sh," he said. "*Listen.*"

They waited in the booth in the long warm silence.

Then, a long way off, muffled, there was a scream.

"Ralph!" said Aimee.

"Listen, listen!" he said.

There was another scream, and another and still another, and a threshing and a pounding and a breaking, a rushing around and through the maze. There, there, wildly colliding and ricocheting, from mirror to mirror, shrieking hysterically and sobbing, tears on his face, mouth gasped open, came Mr. Bigelow. He fell out in the blazing night air, glanced about wildly, wailed, and ran off down the pier.

"Ralph, what happened?"

Ralph sat laughing and slapping at his thighs.

She slapped his face. "What'd you *do*?"

He didn't quite stop laughing. "Come on. I'll show you!"

And then she was in the maze, rushed from white-hot mirror

77

to mirror, seeing her lipstick all red fire a thousand times repeated on down a burning silver cavern where strange hysterical women much like herself followed a quick-moving, smiling man. "Come on!" he cried. And they broke free into a dust-smelling tiny room.

"Ralph!" she said.

They both stood on the threshold of the little room where the Dwarf had come every night for a year. They both stood where the Dwarf had stood each night, before opening his eyes to see the miraculous image in front of him.

Aimee shuffled slowly, one hand out, into the dim room.

The mirror had been changed.

This new mirror made even normal people small, small, small; it made even tall people little and dark and twisted smaller as you moved forward.

And Aimee stood before it thinking and thinking that if it made big people small, standing here. God, what would it do to a dwarf, a tiny dwarf, a dark dwarf, a startled and lonely dwarf?

She turned and almost fell. Ralph stood looking at her. "Ralph," she said. "God, why did you do it?"

"Aimee, come back!"

She ran out through the mirrors, crying. Staring with blurred eyes, it was hard to find the way, but she found it. She stood blinking at the empty pier, started to run one way, then another, then still another, then stopped. Ralph came up behind her, talking, but it was like a voice heard behind a wall late at night, remote and foreign.

"Don't talk to me," she said.

Someone came running up the pier. It was Mr. Kelly from the shooting gallery. "Hey, any you see a little guy just now? Little stiff swiped a pistol from my place, loaded, run off before I'd get a hand on him! You help me find him?"

And Kelly was gone, sprinting, turning his head to search between all the canvas sheds, on away under the hot blue and red and yellow strung bulbs.

Aimee rocked back and forth and took a step.

"Aimee, where you going?"

She looked at Ralph as if they had just turned a corner, strangers passing, and bumped into each other. "I guess," she said, "I'm going to help search."

"You won't be able to do nothing."

"I got to try, anyway. Oh God, Ralph, this is all my fault! I shouldn't have phoned Billie Fine! I shouldn't have ordered a mirror and got you so mad you did this! It's *me* should've gone to Mr. Big, not a crazy thing like I bought! I'm going to find him if it's the last thing I ever do in my life."

Swinging about slowly, her cheeks wet, she saw the quivery mirrors that stood in front of the Maze, Ralph's reflection was in one of them. She could not take her eyes away from the image; it held her in a cool and trembling fascination, with her mouth open.

"Aimee, what's wrong? What're you——"

He sensed where she was looking and twisted about to see what was going on. His eyes widened.

He scowled at the blazing mirror.

A horrid, ugly little man, two feet high, with a pale, squashed face under an ancient straw hat, scowled back at him. Ralph stood there glaring at himself, his hands at his sides.

Aimee walked slowly and then began to walk fast and then began to run. She ran down the empty pier and the wind blew warm and it blew large drops of hot rain out of the sky on her all the time she was running.

Ape Man

Here is a marvellous combination of Science Fantasy and Horror. This tale has been widely praised—and several times republished—in the United States, but this marks its first appearance between hardcovers in England. I guarantee you will never look at a sideshow freak in quite the same way after reading the exploits of the Gnarly Man.

THE GNARLY MAN

By L. Sprague de Camp

Dr. Matilda Saddler first saw the gnarly man on the evening of June 14 at Coney Island.

The spring meeting of the Eastern Section of the American Anthropological Association had broken up, and Dr. Saddler had had dinner with two of her professional colleagues, Blue of Columbia and Jeffcott of Yale. She mentioned that she had never visited Coney, and meant to go there that evening. She urged Blue and Jeffcott to come along, but they begged off.

Watching Dr. Saddler's retreating back, Blue of Columbia cackled: "The Wild Woman from Wichita. Wonder if she's hunting another husband?" He was a thin man with a small grey beard and a who-the-hell-are-you-sir expression.

"How many has she had?" asked Jeffcott of Yale.

"Two to date. Don't know why anthropologists lead the most disorderly private lives of any scientists. Must be that they study the customs and morals of all these different peoples, and ask themselves, 'If the Eskimos can do it, why can't we?' I'm old enough to be safe, thank God."

"I'm not afraid of her," said Jeffcott. He was in his early forties and looked like a farmer uneasy in store clothes. "I'm so very thoroughly married."

"Yeah? Ought to have been at Stanford a few years ago, when she was there. Wasn't safe to walk across the campus, with Tuthill chasing all the females and Saddler all the males."

Dr. Saddler had to fight her way off the subway train, as the adolescents who infest the platform of the B. M. T.'s Stillwell Avenue station are probably the worst-mannered people on earth, possibly excepting the Dobu Islanders of the western Pacific. She didn't much mind. She was a tall, strongly built woman in her late thirties, who had been kept in trim by the outdoor rigours of her profession. Besides, some of the inane remarks in Swift's paper on acculturation among the Arapaho Indians had gotten her fighting blood up.

Walking down Surf Avenue towards Brighton Beach, she looked at the concessions without trying them, preferring to watch the human types that did and the other human types that took their money. She did try a shooting gallery, but found knocking tin owls off their perch with a .22 too easy to be much fun. Long-range work with an army rifle was her idea of shooting.

The concession next to the shooting gallery would have been called a side show if there had been a main show for it to be a side show to. The usual lurid banner proclaimed the uniqueness of the two-headed calf, the bearded woman, Arachne the spider girl, and other marvels. The pièce de résistance was Ungo-Bungo, the ferocious ape-man, captured in the Congo at a cost of twenty-seven lives. The picture showed an enormous Ungo-Bungo squeezing a hapless Negro in each hand, while others sought to throw a net over him.

Dr. Saddler knew perfectly well that the ferocious ape-man would turn out to be an ordinary Caucasian with false hair on his chest. But a streak of whimsicality impelled her to go in. Perhaps, she thought, she could have some fun with her colleagues about it.

The spieler went through his leather-lunged harangue. Dr. Saddler guessed from his expression that his feet hurt. The tatooed lady didn't interest her, as her decorations obviously had no cultural significance, as they have among the Polynesians. As for the ancient Mayan, Dr. Saddler thought it in questionable taste to exhibit a poor microcephalic idiot that way. Professor Yoki's legerdemain and fire eating weren't bad.

There was a curtain in front of Ungo-Bungo's cage. At the appropriate moment there were growls and the sound of a length of chain being slapped against a metal plate. The spieler wound up on a high note: "—ladies and gentlemen, the one and only UNGO-BUNGO!" The curtain dropped.

The ape-man was squatting at the back of his cage. He dropped his chain, got up, and shuffled forward. He grasped two of the bars and shook them. They were appropriately loose and rattled alarmingly. Ungo-Bungo snarled at the patrons, showing his even, yellow teeth.

Dr. Saddler stared hard. This was something new in the ape-man line. Ungo-Bungo was about five feet three, but very massive, with enormous hunched shoulders. Above and below his blue swimming trunks thick, grizzled hair covered him from crown to ankle. His short, stout-muscled arms ended in big hands with thick, gnarled fingers. His neck projected slightly forward, so that from the front he seemed to have but little neck at all.

His face—well, thought Dr. Saddler, she knew all the living races of men, and all the types of freak brought about by glandular maladjustment, and none of them had a face like *that*. It was deeply lined. The forehead between the short scalp hair and the brows on the huge supraorbital ridges receded sharply. The nose, although wide, was not apelike; it was a shortened version of the thick, hooked Armenoid nose, so often miscalled Jewish. The face ended in a long upper lip and a retreating chin. And the yellowish skin apparently belonged to Ungo-Bungo.

The curtain was whisked up again.

Dr. Saddler went out with the others, but paid another dime, and soon was back inside. She paid no attention to the spieler, but got a good position in front of Ungo-Bungo's cage before the rest of the crowd arrived.

Ungo-Bungo repeated his performance with mechanical precision. Dr. Saddler noticed that he limped a little as he came forward to rattle the bars, and that the skin under his mat of hair bore several big whitish scars. The last joint of his left ring finger was missing. She noted certain things about the proportions of his shin and thigh, of his forearm and upper arm, and his big splay feet.

Dr. Saddler paid a third dime. An idea was knocking at her mind somewhere. If she let it in, either she was crazy or physical anthropology was haywire or—something. But she knew that if she did the sensible thing, which was to go home, the idea would plague her from now on.

After the third performance she spoke to the spieler. "I think your Mr. Ungo-Bungo used to be a friend of mine. Could you arrange for me to see him after he finishes?"

The spieler checked his sarcasm. His questioner was so obviously not a—not the sort of dame who asks to see guys after they finish.

"Oh, him," he said. "Calls himself Gaffney—Clarence Aloysius Gaffney. That the guy you want?"

"Why, yes."

"I guess you can." He looked at his watch. "He's got four more turns to do before we close. I'll have to ask the boss. He popped through a curtain and called, "Hey, Morrie! " Then he was back. "It's O.K. Morrie says you can wait in his office. First door to the right."

Morrie was stout, bald, and hospitable. "Sure, sure," he said, waving his cigar. "Glad to be of soivice, Miss Saddler. Chust a min while I talk to Gaffey's manager." He stuck his head out. "Hey, Pappas! Lady wants to talk to your ape-man later. I meant *lady*. O.K." He returned to orate on the difficulties besetting the freak business. "You take this Gaffney, now. He's the best damn ape-man in the business; all that hair rilly grows outa him. And the poor guy rilly has a face like that. But do people believe it? No! I hear 'em going out, saying about how the hair is pasted on, and the whole thing is a fake. It's mawtifying." He cocked his head, listening. "That rumble wasn't no rolly-coaster; it's gonna rain. Hope it's over by tomorrow. You wouldn't believe the way a rain can knock ya receipts off. If you drew a coive, it would be like this." He drew a finger horizontally through space, jerking it down sharply to indicate the effect of rain. "But, as I said, people don't appreciate what you try to do for 'em. It's not just the money; I think of myself as an ottist. A creative ottist. A show like this got to have balance and propawtion, like any other ott—"

It must have been an hour later when a slow, deep voice at the door said: "Did somebody want to see me?"

The gnarly man was in the doorway. In street clothes, with the collar of his raincoat turned up and his hat brim pulled down, he looked more or less human, though the coat fitted his great, sloping shoulders badly. He had a thick, nobbly walking stick with a leather loop near the top end. A small, dark man fidgeted behind him.

"Yeah," said Morrie, interrupting his lecture. "Clarence, this is Miss Saddler. Miss Saddler, this is Mr. Gaffney, one of our outstanding creative artists."

"Pleased to meetcha," said the gnarly man. "This is my manager, Mr. Pappas."

Dr. Saddler explained, and said she'd like to talk to Mr. Gaffney if she might. She was tactful; you had to be to pry into the private affairs of Naga headhunters, for instance. The gnarly man said he'd be glad to have a cup of coffee with Miss Saddler;

84

there was a place around the corner that they could reach without getting wet.

As they started out, Pappas followed, fidgeting more and more.

The gnarly man said: "Oh, go home to bed, John. Don't worry about me." He grinned at Dr. Saddler. The effect would have been unnerving to anyone but an anthropologist. "Every time he sees me talking to anybody, he thinks it's some other manager trying to steal me." He spoke general American, with a suggestion of Irish brogue in the lowering of the vowels in words like "man" and "talk." "I made the lawyer who drew up our contract fix it so it can be ended on short notice."

Pappas departed, still looking suspicious. The rain had practically ceased. The gnarly man stepped along smartly despite his limp.

A woman passed with a fox terrier on a leash. The dog sniffed in the direction of the gnarly man, and then to all appearances went crazy, yelping and slavering. The gnarly man shifted his grip on the massive stick and said quietly, "Better hang on to him, ma'am." The woman departed hastily. "They just don't like me," commented Gaffney. "Dogs, that is."

They found a table and ordered their coffee. When the gnarly man took off his raincoat, Dr. Saddler became aware of a strong smell of cheap perfume. He got out a pipe with a big knobby bowl. It suited him, just as the walking stick did. Dr. Saddler noticed that the deep-sunk eyes under the beetling arches were light hazel.

"Well?" he said in his rumbling drawl.

She began her questions.

"My parents were Irish," he answered. "But I was born in South Boston . . . let's see . . . forty-six years ago. I can get you a copy of my birth certificate. Clarence Aloysius Gaffney, May 2, 1900." He seemed to get some secret amusement out of that statement.

"Were either of your parents of your somewhat unusual physical type?"

He paused before answering. He always did, it seemed. "Uh-huh. Both of 'em. Glands, I suppose."

"Were they both born in Ireland?"

"Yep. County Sligo." Again that mysterious twinkle.

She thought. "Mr. Gaffney, you wouldn't mind having some

85

photographs and measurements made, would you? You could use the photographs in your business."

"Maybe." He took a sip. "Ouch! Gazooks, that's hot!"

"*What?*"

"I said the coffee's hot."

"I mean, before that."

The gnarly man looked a little embarrassed. "Oh, you mean the 'gazooks'? Well, I . . . uh . . . once knew a man who used to say that."

"Mr. Gaffney, I'm a scientist, and I'm not trying to get anything out of you for my own sake. You can be frank with me."

There was something remote and impersonal in his stare that gave her a slight spinal chill. "Meaning that I haven't been so far?"

"Yes. When I saw you I decided that there was something extraordinary in your background. I still think there is. Now, if you think I'm crazy, say so and we'll drop the subject. But I want to get to the bottom of this."

He took his time about answering. "That would depend." There was another pause. Then he said: "With your connections, do you know any really first-class surgeons?"

"But . . . yes, I know Dunbar."

"The guy who wears a purple gown when he operates? The guy who wrote a book on 'God, Man, and the Universe'?"

"Yes. He's a good man, in spite of his theatrical mannerisms. Why? What would you want of him?"

"Not what you're thinking. I'm satisfied with my . . . uh . . . unusual physical type. But I have some old injuries—broken bones that didn't knit properly—that I want fixed up. He'd have to be a good man, though. I have a couple of thousand dollars in the savings bank, but I know the sort of fees those guys charge. If you could make the necessary arrangements—"

"Why, yes, I'm sure I could. In fact, I could guarantee it. Then I *was* right? And you'll—" She hesitated.

"Come clean? Uh-huh. But remember, I can still prove I'm Clarence Aloysius if I have to."

"Who *are* you, then?"

Again there was a long pause. Then the gnarly man said: "Might as well tell you. As soon as you repeat any of it, you'll have put your professional reputation in my hands, remember.

"First off, I wasn't born in Massachusetts. I was born on the upper Rhine, near Mommenheim. And I was born, as nearly as I can figure out, about the year 50,000 B.C."

Matilda Saddler wondered whether she'd stumbled on the biggest thing in anthropology, or whether this bizarre personality was making Baron Munchausen look like a piker.

He seemed to guess her thoughts. "I can't prove that, of course. But so long as you arrange about that operation, I don't care whether you believe me or not."

"But . . . but . . . *how*?"

"I think the lightning did it. We were out trying to drive some bison into a pit. Well, this big thunderstorm came up, and the bison bolted in the wrong direction. So we gave up and tried to find shelter. And the next thing I knew I was lying on the ground with the rain running over me, and the rest of the clan standing around wailing about what had they done to get the storm god sore at them, so he made a bull's-eye on one of their best hunters. They'd never said *that* about me before. It's funny how you're never appreciated while you're alive.

"But I was alive, all right. My nerves were pretty well shot for a few weeks, but otherwise I was O.K., except for some burns on the soles of my feet. I don't know just what happened, except I was reading a couple of years ago that scientists had located the machinery that controls the replacement of tissue in the medulla oblongata. I think maybe the lightning did something to my medulla to speed it up. Anyway, I never got any older after that. Physically, that is. I was thirty-three at the time, more or less. We didn't keep track of ages. I look older now, because the lines in your face are bound to get sort of set after a few thousand years, and because our hair was always grey at the ends. But I can still tie an ordinary *Homo sapiens* in a knot if I want to."

"Then you're . . . you mean to say you're . . . you're trying to tell me you're—"

"A Neanderthal man? *Homo neanderthalensis?* That's right."

Matilda Saddler's hotel room was a bit crowded, with the gnarly man, the frosty Blue, the rustic Jeffcott, Dr. Saddler herself, and Harold McGannon, the historian. This McGannon was a small man, very neat and pink-skinned. He looked more like a New York Central director than a professor. Just now his expression was one of fascination. Dr. Saddler looked full of pride; Professor Jeffcott looked interested but puzzled; Dr. Blue looked bored—

87

he hadn't wanted to come in the first place. The gnarly man, stretched out in the most comfortable chair and puffing his overgrown pipe, seemed to be enjoying himself.

McGannon was formulating a question. "Well, Mr.—Gaffney? I suppose that's your name as much as any."

"You might say so," said the gnarly man. "My original name meant something like Shining Hawk. But I've gone under hundreds of names since then. If you register in a hotel as 'Shining Hawk,' it's apt to attract attention. And I try to avoid that."

"Why?" asked McGannon.

The gnarly man looked at his audience as one might look at wilfully stupid children. "I don't like trouble. The best way to keep out of trouble is not to attract attention. That's why I have to pull up stakes and move every ten or fifteen years. People might get curious as to why I never got any older."

"Pathological liar," murmured Blue. The words were barely audible, but the gnarly man heard them.

"You're entitled to your opinion, Dr. Blue," he said affably. "Dr. Saddler's doing me a favour, so in return I'm letting you all shoot questions at me. And I'm answering. I don't give a damn whether you believe me or not."

McGannon hastily threw in another question. "How is it that you have a birth certificate, as you say you have?"

"Oh, I knew a man named Clarence Gaffney once. He got killed by an automobile accident, and I took his name."

"Was there any reason for picking this Irish background?"

"Are you Irish, Dr. McGannon?"

"Not enough to matter."

"O.K. I didn't want to hurt any feelings. It's my best bet. There are real Irishmen with upper lips like mine."

Dr. Saddler broke in. "I mean to ask you, Clarence." She put a lot of warmth into his name. "There's an argument as to whether your people interbred with mine, when mine overran Europe at the end of the Mousterian. Some scientists have thought that some modern Europeans, especially along the west coast of Ireland, might have a little Neanderthal blood."

He grinned slightly. "Well—yes and no. There never was any back in the stone age, as far as I know. But these long-lipped Irish are my fault."

"How?"

"Believe it or not, but in the last fifty centuries there have been some women of your species that didn't find me too repulsive. Usually there were no offspring. But in the sixteenth century I went to Ireland to live. They were burning too many people for witchcraft in the rest of Europe to suit me at that time. And there was a woman. The result this time was a flock of hybrids —cute little devils, they were. So the Irishmen who look like me are my descendants."

"What did happen to your people?" asked McGannon. "Were they killed off?"

The gnarly man shrugged. "Some of them. We weren't at all warlike. But then the tall ones, as we called them, weren't either. Some of the tribes of the tall ones looked on us as legitimate prey, but most of them let us severely alone. I guess they were almost as scared of us as we were of them. Savages as primitive as that are really pretty peaceable people. You have to work so hard to keep fed, and there are so few of you, that there's no object in fighting wars. That comes later, when you get agriculture and livestock, so you have something worth stealing.

"I remember that a hundred years after the tall ones had come, there were still Neanderthalers living in my part of the country. But they died out. I think it was that they lost their ambition. The tall ones were pretty crude, but they were so far ahead of us that our things and our customs seemed silly. Finally we just sat around and lived on the scraps we could beg from the tall ones' camps. You might say we died of an inferiority complex."

"What happened to you?" asked McGannon.

"Oh, I was a god among my own people by then, and naturally I represented them in their dealings with the tall ones. I got to know the tall ones pretty well, and they were willing to put up with me after all my own clan were dead. Then in a couple of hundred years they'd forgotten all about my people, and took me for a hunchback or something. I got to be pretty good at flint working, so I could earn my keep. When metal came in, I went into that, and finally into blacksmithing. If you'd put all the horse-shoes I've made in a pile, they'd—well, you'd have a damn big pile of horseshoes, anyway."

"Did you . . . ah . . . limp at that time?" asked McGannon.

"Uh-huh. I busted my leg back in the Neolithic. Fell out of a tree, and had to set it myself, because there wasn't anybody around. Why?"

"Vulcan," said McGannon softly.

"Vulcan?" repeated the gnarly man. "Wasn't he a Greek god or something?"

"Yes. He was the lame blacksmith of the gods."

"You mean you think that maybe somebody got the idea from me? That's an interesting theory. Little late to check up on it, though."

Blue leaned forward and said crisply: "Mr. Gaffney, no real Neanderthal man could talk as fluently and entertainingly as you do. That's shown by the poor development of the frontal lobes of the brain and the attachments of the tongue muscles."

The gnarly man shrugged again. "You can believe what you like. My own clan considered me pretty smart, and then you're bound to learn something in fifty thousand years."

Dr. Saddler beamed. "Tell them about your teeth, Clarence."

The gnarly man grinned. "They're false, of course. My own lasted a long time, but they still wore out somewhere back in the Paleolithic. I grew a third set, and they wore out, too. So I had to invent soup."

"You *what*?" It was the usually taciturn Jeffcott.

"I had to invent soup, to keep alive. You know, the bark-dish-and-hot-stones method. My gums got pretty tough after a while, but they still weren't much good for chewing hard stuff. So after a few thousand years I got pretty sick of soup and mushy foods generally. And when metal came in I began experimenting with false teeth. Bone teeth in copper plates. You might say I invented them, too. I tried often to sell them, but they never really caught on until around 1750 A.D. I was living in Paris then, and I built up quite a little business before I moved on." He pulled the handkerchief out of his breast pocket to wipe his forehead; Blue made a face as the wave of perfume reached him.

"Well, Mr. Shining Hawk," snapped Blue with a trace of sarcasm, "how do you like our machine age?"

The gnarly man ignored the tone of the question. "It's not bad. Lots of interesting things happen. The main trouble is the shirts."

"Shirts?"

"Uh-huh. Just try to buy a shirt with a twenty neck and a twenty-nine sleeve. I have to order 'em special. It's almost as bad with hats and shoes. I wear an eight and one half hat and a thirteen shoe." He looked at his watch. "I've got to get back to Coney to work."

McGannon jumped up. "Where can I get in touch with you again, Mr. Gaffney? There's lots of things I'd like to ask you."

The gnarly man told him. "I'm free mornings. My working hours are two to midnight on weekdays, with a couple of hours off for dinner. Union rules, you know."

"You mean there's a union for you show people?"

"Sure. Only they call it a guild. They think they're artists, you know. Artists don't have unions; they have guilds. But it amounts to the same thing."

Blue and Jeffcott saw the gnarly man and the historian walkink slowly toward the subway together. Blue said: "Poor old Mac! Always thought he had sense. Looks like he's swallowed this Gaffney's ravings, hook, line, and sinker."

"I'm not so sure," said Jeffcott, frowning. "There's something funny about the business."

"What?" barked Blue. "Don't tell me that *you* believe this story of being alive fifty thousand years? A caveman who uses perfume! Good God!"

"N-no," said Jeffcott. "Not the fifty thousand part. But I don't think it's a simple case of paranoia or plain lying, either. And the perfume's quite logical, if he were telling the truth."

"Huh?"

"Body odour. Saddler told us how dogs hate him. He'd have a smell different from ours. We're so used to ours that we don't even know we have one, unless somebody goes without a bath for a month. But we might notice his if he didn't disguise it."

Blue snorted. "You'll be believing him yourself in a minute. It's an obvious glandular case, and he's made up this story to fit. All that talk about not caring whether we believe him or not is just bluff. Come on, let's get some lunch. Say, see the way Saddler looked at him every time she said 'Clarence'? Like a hungry wolf. Wonder what she thinks she's going to do with him?"

Jeffcott thought. "I can guess. And if he *is* telling the truth, I think there's something in Deuteronomy against it."

The great surgeon made a point of looking like a great surgeon, to pince-nez and Vandyke. He waved the X-ray negatives at the gnarly man, pointing out this and that.

"We'd better take the leg first," he said. "Suppose we do that next Thursday. When you've recovered from that we can tackle the shoulder. It'll all take time, you know."

The gnarly man agreed, and shuffled out of the little private hospital to where McGannon awaited him in his car. The gnarly man described the tentative schedule of operations, and mentioned that he had made arrangements to quit his job. "Those two are the main thing," he said. "I'd like to try professional wrestling again some day, and I can't unless I get this shoulder fixed so I can raise my left arm over my head."

"What happened to it?" asked McGannon.

The gnarly man closed his eyes, thinking. "Let me see. I get things mixed up sometimes. People do when they're only fifty years old, so you can imagine what it's like for me.

"In 42 B.C. I was living with the Biturgies in Gaul. You remember that Cæsar shut up in Werkinghetorich—Vercingetorix to you—in Alesia, and the confederacy raised an army of relief under Caswollon."

"Caswollon?"

The gnarly man laughed shortly, "I meant Wercaswollon. Caswollon was a Briton, wasn't he? I'm always getting those two mixed up.

"Anyhow, I got drafted. That's all you can call it; I didn't want to go. It wasn't exactly *my* war. But they wanted me because I could pull twice as heavy a bow as anybody else.

"When the final attack on Cæsar's ring of fortifications came, they sent me forward with some other archers to provide a covering fire for their infantry. At least, that was the plan. Actually, I never saw such a hopeless muddle in my life. And before I even got within bowshot, I fell into one of the Romans' covered pits. I didn't land on the point of the stake, but I fetched up against the side of it and busted my shoulder. There wasn't any help, because the Gauls were too busy running away from Cæsar's German cavalry to bother about wounded men."

The author of "God, Man, and the Universe" gazed after his departing patient. He spoke to his head assistant: "What do you think of him?"

"I think it's so," said the assistant. "I looked over those X-rays pretty closely. That skeleton never belonged to a human being. And it has more healed fractures than you'd think possible."

"Hm-m-m," said Dunbar. "That's right, he wouldn't be human, would he? Hm-m-m. You know, if anything happened to him—"

The assistant grinned understandingly. "Of course, there's the S.P.C.A."

"We needn't worry about *them*. Hm-m-m." He thought, you've been slipping; nothing big in the papers for a year. But if you published a complete anatomical description of a Neanderthal man—or if you found out why his medulla functions the way it does—Hm-m-m. Of course, it would have to be managed properly—

"Let's have lunch at the Natural History Museum," said McGannon. "Some of the people there ought to know you."

"O.K.," drawled the gnarly man. "Only I've still got to get back to Coney afterward. This is my last day. Tomorrow, Pappas and I are going up to see our lawyer about ending our contract. Guy named Robinette. It's a dirty trick on poor old John, but I warned him at the start that this might happen."

"I suppose we can come up to interview you while you're . . . ah . . . convalescing? Fine. Have you ever been to the museum, by the way?"

"Sure," said the gnarly man. "I get around."

"What did you . . . ah . . . think of their stuff in the Hall of the Age of Man?"

"Pretty good. There's a little mistake in one of those big wall paintings. The second horn on the woolly rhinoceros ought to slant forward more. I thought of writing them a letter. But you know how it is. They'd say: 'Were you there?' and I'd say, 'Uh-huh,' and they'd say, 'Another nut.' "

"How about the pictures and busts of Paleolithic men?'

"Pretty good. But they have some funny ideas. They always show us with skins wrapped around our middles. In summer we didn't wear skins, and in winter we hung them around our shoulders, where they'd do some good.

"And then they show those tall ones that you call Cro-Magnon men clean-shaven. As I remember, they all had whiskers. What would they shave with?"

"I think," said McGannon, "that they leave the beards off the busts to . . . ah . . . show the shape of the chins. With the beards they'd all look too much alike."

"Is that the reason? They might say so on the labels." The gnarly man rubbed his own chin, such as it was. "I wish beards would come back into style. I look much more human with a beard. I got along fine in the sixteenth century when everybody had whiskers.

"That's one of the ways I remember when things happened, by the haircuts and whiskers that people had. I remember when a wagon I was driving in Milan lost a wheel and spilled flour bags from hell to breakfast. That must have been in the sixteenth century, before I went to Ireland, because I remember that most of the men in the crowd that collected had beards. Now—wait a minute—maybe that was the fourteenth. There were a lot of beards then, too."

"Why, why didn't you keep a diary?" asked McGannon with a groan of exasperation.

The gnarly man shrugged characteristically. "And pack around six trunks full of paper every time I moved? No, thanks."

"I . . . ah . . . don't suppose you could give me the real story of Richard III and the princes in the tower?"

"Why should I? I was just a poor blacksmith, or farmer, or something most of the time. I didn't go around with the big shots. I gave up all my ideas of ambition a long time before that. I had to, being so different from other people. As far as I can remember, the only real king I ever got a good look at was Charlemagne, when he made a speech in Paris one day. He was just a big, tall man with Santa Claus whiskers and a squeaky voice."

Next morning McGannon and the gnarly man had a session with Svedberg at the museum. Then McGannon drove Gaffney around to the lawyer's office, on the third floor of a seedy office building in the West Fifties. James Robinette looked something like a movie actor and something like a chipmunk. He looked at his watch and said to McGannon: "This won't take long. If you'd like to stick around, I'd be glad to have lunch with you." The fact was that he was feeling just a trifle queasy about being left with this damn queer client, this circus freak or whatever he was, with his barrel body and his funny slow drawl.

When the business had been completed, and the gnarly man had gone off with his manager to wind up his affairs at Coney, Robinette said: "Whew! I thought he was a half-wit, from his looks. But there was nothing half-witted about the way he went

94

over those clauses. You'd have thought the damn contract was for building a subway system. What *is* he, anyhow?"

McGannon told him what he knew.

The lawyer's eyebrows went up. "Do you *believe* his yarn? Oh, I'll take tomato juice and filet of sole with tartar sauce— only without the tartar sauce—on the lunch, please."

"The same for me. Answering your question, Robinette, I do. So does Saddler. So does Svedberg up at the museum. They're both topnotchers in their respective fields. Saddler and I have interviewed him, and Svedberg's examined him physically. But it's just opinion. Fred Blue still swears it's a hoax or . . . ah . . . some sort of dementia. Neither of us can prove anything."

"Why not?"

"Well . . . ah . . . how are you going to prove that he was, or was not, alive a hundred years ago? Take one case: Clarence says he ran a sawmill in Fairbanks, Alaska, in 1906 and '07, under the name of Michael Shawn. How are you going to find out whether there was a sawmill operator in Fairbanks at that time? And if you did stumble on a record of a Michael Shawn, how would you know whether he and Clarence were the same? There's not a chance in a thousand that there'd be a photograph or a detailed description that you could check with. And you'd have an awful time trying to find anybody who remembered him at this late date.

"Then, Svedberg poked around Clarence's face, yesterday, and said that no *Homo sapiens* ever had a pair of zygomatic arches like that. But when I told Blue that, he offered to produce photographs of a human skull that did. I know what'll happen. Blue will say that the arches are practically the same, and Svedberg will say that they're obviously different. So there we'll be."

Robinette mused. "He does seem damned intelligent for an ape-man."

"He's not an ape-man, really. The Neanderthal race was a separate branch of the human stock; they were more primitive in some ways and more advanced in others than we are. Clarence may be slow, but he usually grinds out the right answer. I imagine that he was . . . ah . . . brilliant, for one of his kind, to begin with. And he's had the benefit of so much experience. He knows an incredible lot. He knows us; he sees through us and our motives."

The little pink man puckered up his forehead. "I do hope nothing happens to him. He's carrying around a lot of priceless information in that big head of his. Simply priceless. Not much about war and politics; he kept clear of those as a matter of self-preservation. But little things, about how people lived and how they thought thousands of years ago. He gets his periods mixed up sometimes, but he gets them straightened out if you give him time.

"I'll have to get hold of Pell, the linguist. Clarence knows dozens of ancient languages, such as Gothic and Gaulish. I was able to check him on some of them, like vulgar Latin; that was one of the things that convinced me. And there are archaeologists and psychologists—

"If only something doesn't happen to scare him off. We'd never find him. I don't know. Between a man-crazy female scientist and a publicity-mad surgeon—I wonder how it'll work out."

The gnarly man innocently entered the waiting room of Dunbar's hospital. He, as usual, spotted the most comfortable chair and settled luxuriously into it.

Dunbar stood before him. His keen eyes gleamed with anticipation behind their pince-nez. "There'll be a wait of about half an hour, Mr. Gaffney," he said. "We're all tied up now, you know. I'll send Mahler in; he'll see that you have anything you want." Dunbar's eyes ran lovingly over the gnarly man's stumpy frame. What fascinating secrets mightn't he discover once he got inside it?

Mahler appeared, a healthy-looking youngster. Was there anything Mr. Gaffney would like? The gnarly man paused as usual to let his massive mental machinery grind. A vagrant impulse moved him to ask to see the instruments that were to be used on him.

Mahler had his orders, but this seemed a harmless enough request. He went and returned with a tray full of gleaming steel.

"You see," he said, "these are called scalpels."

Presently the gnarly man asked: "What's this?" He picked up a peculiar-looking instrument.

"Oh, that's the boss's own invention. For getting at the mid-brain."

"Mid-brain? What's that doing here?"

"Why, that's for getting at your— That must be there by mistake—"

Little lines tightened around the queer hazel eyes. "Yeah?"

96

He remembered the look Dunbar had given him, and Dunbar's general reputation. "Say, could I use your phone a minute?"

"Why . . . I suppose . . . what do you want to phone for?"

"I want to call my lawyer. Any objections?"

"No, of course not. But there isn't any phone here."

"What do you call that?" The gnarly man got up and walked towards the instrument in plain sight on a table. But Mahler was there before him, standing in front of it.

"This one doesn't work. It's being fixed."

"Can't I try it?"

"No, not till it's fixed. It doesn't work, I tell you."

The gnarly man studied the young physician for a few seconds. "O.K., then I'll find one that does." He started for the door.

"Hey, you can't go out now!" cried Mahler.

"Can't I? Just watch me!"

"Hey!" It was a full-throated yell. Like magic more men in white coats appeared.

Behind them was the great surgeon. "Be reasonable, Mr. Gaffney," he said. "There's no reason why you should go out now, you know. We'll be ready for you in a little while."

"Any reason why I shouldn't?" The gnarly man's big face swung on his thick neck, and his hazel eyes swivelled. All the exits were blocked. "I'm going."

"Grab him!" said Dunbar.

The white coats moved. The gnarly man got his hands on the back of a chair. The chair whirled, and became a dissolving blur as the men closed on him. Pieces of chair flew about the room, to fall with the dry, sharp *ping* of short lengths of wood. When the gnarly man stopped swinging, having only a short piece of the chair back left in each fist, one assistant was out cold. Another leaned whitely against the wall and nursed a broken arm.

"Go on!" shouted Dunbar when he could make himself heard. The white wave closed over the gnarly man, then broke. The gnarly man was on his feet, and held young Mahler by the ankles. He spread his feet and swung the shrieking Mahler like a club, clearing the way to the door. He turned, whirled Mahler around his head like a hammer thrower, and let the now mercifully unconscious body fly. His assailants went down in a yammering tangle.

One was still up. Under Dunbar's urging he sprang after the gnarly man. The latter had gotten his stick out of the umbrella

stand in the vestibule. The knobby upper end went *whoosh* past
the assistant's nose. The assistant jumped back and fell over one
of the casualties. The front door slammed, and there was a deep
roar of "Taxi!"

"Come on!" shrieked Dunbar. "Get the ambulance out!"

James Robinette was sitting in his office, thinking the thoughts
that lawyers do in moments of relaxation, when there was a
pounding of large feet in the corridor, a startled protest from Miss
Spevak in the outer office, and the strange client of the day before
was at Robinette's desk, breathing hard.

"I'm Gaffney," he growled between gasps. "Remember me?
I think they followed me down here. They'll be up any minute.
I want your help."

"They? Who's they?" Robinette winced at the impact of that
damn perfume.

The gnarly man launched into his misfortunes. He was going
well when there were more protests from Miss Spevak, and Dr.
Dunbar and four assistants burst into the office.

"He's ours," said Dunbar, his glasses agleam.

"He's an ape-man," said the assistant with the black eye.

"He's a dangerous lunatic," said the assistant with the cut lip.

"We've come to take him away," said the assistant with the torn
coat.

The gnarly man spread his feet and gripped his stick like a
baseball bat by the small end.

Robinette opened a desk drawer and got out a large pistol.
"One move towards him and I'll use this. The use of extreme
violence is justified to prevent commission of a felony, to wit:
kidnapping."

The five men backed up a little. Dunbar said: "This isn't
kidnapping. You can only kidnap a person, you know. He isn't
a human being, and I can prove it."

The assistant with the back eye snickered. "If he wants pro-
tection, he better see a game warden instead of a lawyer."

"Maybe that's what *you* think," said Robinette. "You aren't
a lawyer. According to the law, he's human. Even corporations,
idiots, and unborn children are legally persons, and he's a damn
sight more human than they are."

"Then he's a dangerous lunatic," said Dunbar.

"Yeah? Where's your commitment order? The only persons

98

who can apply for one are: (a) close relatives and (b) public officials charged with the maintenance of order. You're neither."

Dunbar continued stubbornly: "He ran amuck in my hospital and nearly killed a couple of my men, you know. I guess that gives us some right."

"Sure," said Robinette. "You can step down to the nearest station and swear out a warrant." He turned to the gnarly man. "Shall we throw the book at 'em, Gaffney?"

"I'm all right," said that individual, his speech returning to its normal slowness. "I just want to make sure these guys don't pester me any more."

"O.K. Now listen, Dunbar. One hostile move out of you and we'll have a warrant out for you for false arrest, assault and battery, attempted kidnapping, criminal conspiracy, and disorderly conduct. *And* we'll slap on a civil suit for damages for sundry torts, to wit: assault, deprivation of civil rights, placing in jeopardy of life and limb, menace, and a few more I may think of later."

"You'll never make that stick," snarled Dunbar. "We have all the witnesses."

"Yeah! And wouldn't the great Evan Dunbar look sweet defending such actions? Some of the ladies who gush over your books might suspect that maybe you weren't such a damn knight in shining armour. We can make a prize monkey of you, and you know it."

"You're destroying the possibility of a great scientific discovery, you know, Robinette."

"To hell with that. My duty is to protect my client. Now beat it, all of you, before I call a cop." His left hand moved suggestively to the telephone.

Dunbar grasped at a last straw. "Hm-m-m. Have you got a permit for that gun?"

"Damn right. Want to see it?"

Dunbar sighed. "Never mind. You *would* have." His greatest opportunity for fame was slipping out of his fingers. He drooped towards the door.

The gnarly man spoke up. "If you don't mind, Dr. Dunbar, I left my hat at your place. I wish you'd send it to Mr. Robinette here. I have a hard time getting hats to fit me."

Dunbar looked at him silently and left with his cohorts.

The gnarly man was giving the lawyer further details when the

99

telephone rang. Robinette answered: "Yes. . . . Saddler? Yes, he's here. . . . Your Dr. Dunbar was going to murder him so he could dissect him. . . . O.K." He turned to the gnarly man. "Your friend Dr. Saddler is looking for you. She's on her way up here."

"Zounds!" said Gaffney. "I'm going."

"Don't you want to see her? She was phoning from around the corner. If you go out now you'll run into her. How did she know where to call?"

"I gave her your number. I suppose she called the hospital and my boardinghouse, and tried you as a last resort. This door goes into the hall, doesn't it? Well, when she comes in the regular door I'm going out this one. And I don't want you saying where I've gone. It's nice to have known you, Mr. Robinette."

"Why? What's the matter? You're not going to run out now, are you? Dunbar's harmless, and you've got friends. I'm your friend."

"You're durn tootin' I'm going to run out. There's too much trouble. I've kept alive all these centuries by staying away from trouble. I let down my guard with Dr. Saddler, and went to the surgeon she recommended. First he plots to take me apart to see what makes me tick. If that brain instrument hadn't made me suspicious, I'd have been on my way to the alcohol jars by now. Then there's a fight, and it's just pure luck I didn't kill a couple of those internes, or whatever they are, and get sent up for manslaughter. Now Matilda's after me with a more-than-friendly interest. I know what it means when a woman looks at you that way and calls you 'dear.' I wouldn't mind if she weren't a prominent person of the kind that's always in some sort of garboil. That would mean more trouble, sooner or later. You don't suppose I *like* trouble, do you?"

"But look here, Gaffney, you're getting steamed up over a lot of damn—"

"*Ssst!*" The gnarly man took his stick and tiptoed over to the private entrance. As Dr. Saddler's clear voice sounded in the outer office, he sneaked out. He was closing the door behind him when the scientist entered the inner office.

Matilda Saddler was a quick thinker. Robinette hardly had time to open his mouth when she flung herself at and through the private door with a cry of "Clarence!"

Robinette heard the clatter of feet on the stairs. Neither the

100

pursued nor the pursuer had waited for the creaky elevator. Looking out the window, he saw Gaffney leap into a taxi. Matilda Saddler sprinted after the cab, calling: "Clarence! Come back!" But the traffic was light and the chase correspondingly hopeless.

They did hear from the gnarly man once more. Three months later Robinette got a letter whose envelope contained, to his vast astonishment, ten ten-dollar bills. The single sheet was typed, even to the signature.

DEAR MR. ROBINETTE:

I do not know what your regular fees are, but I hope that the enclosed will cover your services to me of last June.

Since leaving New York I have had several jobs, I pushed a hack—as we say—in Chicago, and I tried out as pitcher on a bush league baseball team. Once I made my living by knocking over rabbits and things with stones, and I can still throw fairly well. Nor am I bad at swinging a club, such as a baseball bat. But my lameness makes me too slow for a baseball career, and it will be some time before I try any remedial operations again.

I now have a job whose nature I cannot disclose because I do not wish to be traced. You need pay no attention to the postmark; I am not living in Kansas City, but had a friend post this letter there.

Ambition would be foolish for one in my peculiar position. I am satisfied with a job that furnishes me with the essentials, and allows me to go to an occasional movie, and a few friends with whom I can drink beer and talk.

I was sorry to leave New York without saying good-by to Dr. Harold McGannon, who treated me very nicely. I wish you would explain to him why I had to leave as I did. You can get in touch with him through Columbia University.

If Dunbar sent you my hat as I requested, please mail it to me: General Delivery, Kansas City, Mo. My friend will pick it up. There is not a hat store in this town where I live that can fit me. With best wishes, I remain,

Yours sincerely,
SHINING HAWK
Alias CLARENCE ALOYSIUS GAFFNEY.

101

The Entertainer

This tale must certainly qualify as one of the most sinister in the collection—that it comes from the pen of a woman shows you can't be too careful even where ladies are concerned. We've all met somebody like the central character, Papa Frolic, in our childhood: the friendly, funny man in crazy clothes who makes us laugh. But behind the smile lurks a very strange kind of evil.

THE GAY DECEIVER

By Mildred Clingerman

The crowd pressed tightly all along the parade route. Far away down the street Verna could hear the band music, but so faintly she knew the parade was still several blocks away. Skilfully she manoeuvered her thin body through the crowd till at last she stood directly behind the small children who lined the curb. On both sides of the street the children made an animated edging for the empty parade route, bouncing small bottoms up and down on the curbs, twisting, nudging, calling, laughing. A few were already tired with the waiting and excitement, and were roaring their discomfort monotonously, but none of these, Verna noted, were not bothering to produce any real tears, as yet. Their mothers, she saw, were also well aware that the howls were not the all-out, serious kind that had to be dealt with strenuously. A small shaking sufficed, or an admonitory pat, perhaps, with a few shaming words.

In a minute, any minute now, Papa Frolic will come, Verna silently promised the bawling youngsters, *and then you'll hush your ugly racket.* As if on cue, she heard then the high, sweet trilling she'd been waiting for. She leaned far out over the children till she caught sight of him down at the end of the block, advancing along the parade route, the balloons dancing and straining over his head, and Papa Frolic dancing and prancing under them, as if it were the balloons themselves that propelled him. He was wearing his yellow and red outfit today. His hat was high and pointed in the crown and made of sewn-together diamond-shaped pieces of red and yellow leather, as was the jacket he wore. Beside the balloons, which were yellow, red, pink, green, purple, and gold, he carried a fistful of slender red canes with little yellow pennants which waved in the spring breeze.

He was delightful to look at, but oh he was even more

103

wonderful to hear. Now all the children had grown quiet to listen, their eyes round and shining, all turned upon him. Even knowing, as Verna did, all about the cheap little tin whistle that was hidden inside his mouth, she could still imagine that there were small, brilliant birds hidden under his cap, peeking out through his white curls, or else hidden inside the beautiful jacket, and perhaps singing their song through his button-holes.

As he drew nearer though, one stopped wondering where the birds were hidden. It didn't matter *where* they were; it was what the birds were telling in their singing that charmed away one's curiosity. All along the street, Papa Frolic had paused, still whistling, selling his balloons and canes, leaving in small, reaching hands the bobbing and weaving pretties. Sometimes, if the grown-ups asked, he reached into a back pocket and sold one of the whistles, exactly like the one inside his mouth. Verna was scornful when this happened. Silly fools. Did they think they could ever make music like his? They'd find out. A few, wavering, sour-sounding bird noises was all they'd ever produce out of those whistles. Papa Frolic was the only person in the world who could make a whistle sound like sunlight slanting on a green meadow, with baby lambs leaping around and a million flowers bending to a soft wind. He could make it sound like puffy white clouds, too, with pink-winged baby angels sound asleep on top of them. But best of all, when he wanted to, or when Verna begged and nagged him into it, he could turn the whistle into a flowering lane with trees arching overhead, and the lane would beckon, with its leaf shadows and speckled sunlight, toward a dear, green-painted door set in a garden wall. Behind that wall lay, one knew, that long-ago place called home. Not, of course, the home (if you could call it that) that Verna had been born into, or the crowded, dirty places she'd grown up in. What a laugh, to think anybody would want to go back to that. No, the lane and the doorway at the end of it which Papa Frolic conjured up was the secret way that led to Verna's real home, the one she had been born remembering. When she tried to explain it to him, Papa Frolic always laughed and nodded and quoted some old puzzling poetry by a man named Wordsworth, trying to convince her that everybody was born with some miserable homesickness and longing for a place they'd never see.

"The soul," he'd quote, *"... cometh from afar:*
Not in entire forgetfulness,
And not in utter nakedness,
But trailing clouds of glory do we come ..."

It made Verna feel cheated and angry to think other people wanted to find her old home. They had no right there; it was hers alone. She distinctly remembered ... well, not distinctly, maybe, but she could almost remember what it had been like, and she certainly did not recall sharing anything with anybody. Coming from a father-deserted, charity family of seven squalling kids, she'd had enough of sharing to last her the rest of her life.

It was at a parade like this one that Verna had first seen and heard Papa Frolic. The only difference was, it had been held in a big old dingy, smoky city, and the skies then had been overcast, not bright and blue as they were today out here in the west. Verna, with three other waitresses, had stood in front of the greasy-spoon restaurant where they all worked, to watch the parade go by. Big deal. The fat, slobby boss had generously waved them out to see the sights, since nobody obviously was going to eat in his sleazy joint when they could be watching a parade. Papa Frolic had moved into Verna's sight with all the colour and impact of a steam calliope. Then when he stopped right in front of her and began to whistle up the vision of the lane and the door that led home ... and handed her a free balloon, that was enough for Verna. She told him to wait—*begged* him to wait, and while he stood there whistling that calling, calling song, she'd run into the restaurant, dragging off her cap and apron, and flung them at the boss, right in his teeth, and left the place forever.

She'd been travelling with Papa Frolic now for three years. He had been very casual about accepting her. She could come along or she could stay, it didn't matter much to him, he'd said. She was useful, though. She kept his clothes clean and mended. She cooked—not very well—and cleaned the filthy light-housekeeping rooms they rented in every town. Nights she slept beside him in the sagging double beds that were the same in all the towns. Mostly, in his way, he was good to her. He taught her to drive the old station wagon they travelled in. He tried to teach her about food and music and poetry. Sometimes at night when he was restless and edgy he told her stories from history, though Verna privately

105

didn't care much for history. So much of it was dark and bloody. He was good at telling stories, though. He made Verna see the little crooked medieval streets, with the timbered houses jutting out, the tall towers, and the stone bridges humped over the rivers.

She was lucky, she knew, and she ought to have been perfectly happy, but she wasn't. She didn't mind that he was so much older than she was, and knew so much she'd never know. It wasn't that at all, and really, he was exciting to be with. Moreover, Verna loved their life of travelling from town to town, year in and year out. They tried to hit all the major fairs, horseraces, parades, festivals, and town celebrations. In three years they'd been in almost every state in the union. They travelled light and easy, too, without any permanent possessions to speak of except the tin trunk that held Papa Frolic's collection of musical instruments—"pipes," he called them. The trunk was full of every kind of reed, wood, or metal pipes you could imagine. Some of them were very old, real antiques and "collector's items," Papa Frolic said. Sometimes on moonlit nights when the whole world felt hungry and yearning, he selected one and played far into the night, while Verna lay quietly on the bed and walked closer and closer to the door at the end of the lane.

She didn't want to leave him, ever, no matter what. . . . Anyway, she didn't *know* anything, for sure. It could be coincidence —the horrible things that happened in the towns they'd passed through. She'd first noticed it about a year ago. She had tried to tell herself to forget it, to stop reading the newspapers, to comfort herself with the nice new dresses he was always buying her, to stop *thinking*. Lately, though, she hadn't been sleeping well. Twice Papa Frolic had waked to find her pacing the floor, silently wringing her hands. He didn't like it at all, and she was a little frightened of him when he got angry.

And right here he was, pausing right in front of her, studying her face, his clear blue eyes narrowed but smiling. Now he was handing her a pink balloon over the heads of the children on the curb, who gazed up at him with awed, but loving, regard. Verna shivered as if the spring wind had turned suddenly cold. But, as always, she took the balloon from his hand, and managed a gay laugh and even bobbed a little thank-you curtsy to him. Then, without pausing, she presented the pink balloon to the youngest child near her. It was a crowd-pleasing gesture that sold almost the whole stock of balloons and a few more of the canes. When

Papa Frolic moved on down the line, Verna slipped out of the crowd and hurried away just as the leading band in the parade appeared. She wasn't in the mood for a parade today.

She would walk back to their room, leaving the station-wagon in the car park for Papa Frolic, who would return to it from time to time to replenish his supply of balloons and canes. He would not come back to their room till dusk. After the parade was over he would cover the town—certain sections of it—on foot. Sometimes he whistled his way through the nicer parts of the towns, selling his balloons to the kids who wore clean clothes and always had plenty to eat, but he preferred to walk through the slum areas, where the kids swarmed in the streets and alleys and followed him for blocks, dancing to his music. Maybe Papa Frolic really liked kids. In the slum sections he gave away more balloons than he sold.

On her way home Verna paused at a newsstand to buy all the newspapers of all the surrounding towns, including the towns they had just come from. Papa Frolic liked to read about things that had happened after he left a town, as well as the news of fairs and celebrations in the next towns they were going to. Verna, after circling the block twice, finally identified the drab house they had taken rooms in the night before. Sometimes, moving so often, she got confused as to just which house she belonged in. It was funny the way all towns looked alike when you always took rooms on the wrong side of the tracks. Just once, she thought, I wish we could stay in a decent place . . . some place clean and shiny with starched curtains, a good bed, and no bugs to kill. But this was the kind of neighbourhood Papa Frolic liked best. He preferred to stay, he said, right in the centre of a melting pot where there were lots and lots of children of many different racial backgrounds. Well, this was certainly it.

From the dirty kitchen window Verna surveyed several unsavoury backyards while she washed a head of lettuce under the tap. They were all alike, and all drearily familiar. Grey, sagging washing on a line, old cardboard boxes stacked around full of junk, rusted bedsprings leaning against a tumble-down shed, old worn-out automobile tyres, empty bottles, chairs with the stuffing hanging out, old refrigerators with burnt-out motors, rags, paper, weeds, and children everywhere. Only the children and weeds seemed alive, whole, and flourishing. Verna fixed herself a bologna sandwich with lettuce and drank a glass of milk. She put the remainder of the meat, milk, and lettuce back into the big old almost-empty refrigerator that took up most of the kitchen space. In the living-bedroom she shuffled through the newspapers she had laid on the tin trunk and selected two or three to read while she lay down to rest. Her eye was caught once again by the name painted on the tin trunk. *H. P. Froelich.* That's Papa Frolic's real name, she thought again in wonder. Wouldn't it be funny if people called me Mrs. Froelich instead of Mrs. Frolic? I can't even say it right—not to please him. That's why he changed his name, he said. So many people like Verna were too stupid to pronounce it right.

She kicked off her shoes and folded the limp, dank-smelling pillows into a backrest and idly scanned the top newspaper. After a moment she stiffened and threw it on to the floor. There it was again. Almost identical to the headlines she'd read less than a month ago, and had been reading far too frequently in the past year or two: TOTS DIE IN OLD REFRIGERATOR. She wouldn't read the details. They were always the same, more or less. No evidence of foul play. Some silly notion made the little kids crawl inside the old, junked boxes and pull the door to behind them. Verna lay a long while with her eyes closed and her teeth gritted, but it was no use. Finally she had to run to the bathroom to be very sick. When she crawled back on to the sagging bed she fell asleep at last from sheer exhaustion.

She woke as he opened the door. She had slept a long time; dusk now shadowed the room. He turned on the overhead light, and she heard the scratching and scuttling noises made by cockroaches as they scrambled back into hiding. She shuddered to think that some of them may have crawled on to the bed with her.

Papa Frolic came through the door with arms full of paper sacks from the supermarket. He was whistling softly between his teeth, and he kicked the door to behind him with a cheerful finality that told her his day had been a successful one.

"Up, up, Verna, my dear. I've brought rye bread and cheese, onions and liverwurst, pickles and beer. How's that? I remembered your favourite meal, and as soon as I get rid of these wretched cockroaches we'll eat."

He carried the sacks to the tiny kitchen, and Verna heard him unpacking them.

"Think this sack will be big enough?" He stood laughing in the kitchen doorway, while he spread open a large brown paper sack, and folded over the edges so it would stand firm on the floor. "Have we got a garbage can out back?"

"There's a can out by the back step," Verna said, still not moving from the bed.

Papa Frolic left the brown sack standing open in the middle of the kitchen floor. He moved over to the tin trunk, opened it, and selected a small, slender pipe. Back in the kitchen he began to play a thin, thread-like melody. Verna pressed her hands against her ears to keep out the sound of scuttling insect feet, but she didn't really try to shut out the sound of the flute. As always, she loved the way it called and promised and cajoled. To her mind it called up damp, warm forests with dripping green ferns, and just yonder a decaying doorway. . . . But what it said to the cockroaches might not be that at all. In any case, she knew what was happening. All the cockroaches were emerging from the damp, greasy walls and marching up and over the lip of the sack. In a few moments Papa Frolic would twist the neck of the sack, put it in the garbage can outside and set it afire. He had done this in almost every place they'd ever stayed.

Verna joined him at the supper table (now guaranteed free of vermin, as he said), but found she was not at all hungry. While he ate heartily Papa Frolic talked of the parade, the crowds, and of his day's take. Verna remained silent and withdrawn.

"Anything in the papers?" he asked at last.

"There's a three-day square dance festival in Phoenix," Verna said.

"We'll make it," Papa Frolic said. "I like Phoenix. Now, where's the Albuquerque paper?"

"On the floor by the bed. I read something in it that made me sick . . . just . . . sick. Papa Frolic, what do you suppose makes kids crawl into old refrigerators to die?"

He stopped chewing for a moment, then laughed and swallowed and took a big draught of beer. "Why not?" he said. "My dear Verna, I've told you, children are born with a shadowy recollection of a sweet, warm home that's the essence of ease and delight. Show them any old door or opening that looks to their eyes as if it might lead them back there, and in they go, pleased and eager. Who knows what a child sees when he opens the door and crawls in? But I forget—you do know. If you found your lane, wouldn't you want to explore it?"

Verna nodded, her eyes wide and staring. "Yes," she said, "they see *something*. . . . Papa Frolic, do you make them see it, with your piping?"

He raised his eyebrows and finished his beer. "It doesn't concern you, Verna."

"But why do you do it? In Albuquerque there was a little boy five, holding his three-year-old sister's hand. . . . They found them three days later."

"Hush, Verna."

"What did they ever do to you?" Her voice was rising, and the muscles of her face were twisting uncontrollably. "What kind of monster are you, anyway?"

He had stopped eating and drinking and had pushed his chair away from the table.

"Verna, I'm not any kind of monster. I'm simply a man with a job to do. Long ago, I made a vow . . . a bargain, if you like, and I am fulfilling that vow. Did you ever hear of a town called Hamlin? Hamlin, Germany? The city fathers there owed me a debt, which they have never paid. Think. Use your head, you silly child. Yes, I took their children, all of them, but do you think they stopped having children after we went away? These few children you're worrying about are the strays, the descendants of those people. When I finish with them, I'll go back to Hamlin once more. . . ."

"You'll get caught. . . ." Verna was backing towards the door. "They'll kill you for it. The police . . . you'll die. You'll pay. I'll bet you a million, million dollars you'll never get away with it. I'll tell. . . ."

"I'll take that bet," Papa Frolic said, and he moved closer to her, smiling.

Belatedly Verna remembered that he rarely lost a bet, and that he never forgot a debt or forgave a debtor.

Papa Frolic was opening the door of the big old empty refrigerator that took up too much space in the tiny kitchen, and now he was playing the pipe.

Magician

The magic of the magician exerts its own special influence over children and adults alike. We'd all like to cry "fake" and explain away his tricks—but he's always a step ahead of us. The Rabbit Prince who is waiting to take his bow here is indeed a prince among conjurors and his ability borders on witchcraft. Or perhaps it is something more?

THE RABBIT PRINCE

By Davis Grubb

Tom Spoon ate his good hot breakfast that morning and stumped merrily off up Lafayette Avenue. It was a fine blowing spring day with the wind snapping smartly above the town and there was but one thought that sang like a silver bird in Tom Spoon's mind. Today was the last day of school. Today he was through with the third grade forever. The tyranny of Serena Tinkens was ended for him at last.

It was an odd thing—the trouble with Miss Tinkens. It was not that she was old—though it often seemed that she was. Slim, pale, blue-veined, Serena Tinkens lived alone in a house on Water Street that appeared somehow to have been constructed of old grey valentines pasted recklessly together. The parlour of this house was like the breast of Serena Tinkens itself: narrow, tall, inviolate. Magazines were stacked neatly by the oil lamp; dainty lace doilies lay on the spidery polished tables and a crocheted pillow on the seat of the melodeon. On a drop-leaf table lay a crystal paperweight—a scarlet dusty flower imprisoned in a frozen timeless prism: the heart of Serena Tinkens, bloodless, sorrowless and without joy.

The children were laughing and shouting merrily as Tom Spoon, stamping his feet in happy defiance, marched flamboyantly into the third-grade room. He sat down just as Serena Tinkens rapped sharply for silence.

"Good morning, children!" she cried with the bright dry voice of an August sparrow.

"Good morning, Miss Tinkens!" the children chorused.

"And a good morning it is!" cried Serena Tinkens, pressing her pale lips together in a sarcastic smile. "A *very* good morning for those of us who have done our best work this past winter and are going on to the fourth grade next fall! Today we're having

112

a little party here in our pleasant classroom to celebrate our promotion! All of us except——"

Tom Spoon saw then that the blue eyes of Serena Tinkens had fastened upon him malevolently.

"All of us," continued Miss Tinkens, "except for one! And *he*—like Ned in our third reader—has chosen the slothful road and, as a result, will have to remain in Three-A for another semester. Tom Spoon, stand up!"

Tom stood up, burning, depraved—his head bent as Raleigh's must have been before the blade. Glancing sideways at his school-mates, who now stared breathless at this monster in their midst, Tom essayed a foolish frantic smirk.

"Now, Tom Spoon!" cooed Miss Tinkens, her voice soft with violence. "You may go home and play with your toads and your white mice! We wouldn't want to keep you. Good morning, Tom Spoon!"

Tom swaggered laboriously from the room, the giggles of the simple girls hanging like donkey tails on his back. Down the steps, down the mouldering mossy bricks of the sidewalk, down the street walked Tom Spoon into the shattered ruin of the once so perfect season. Wandering at last out the end of Water Street and into the green valley of the river, Tom Spoon sat upon a stump, abandoning his spirit entirely to the ravages of misery.

It was a good long while before Tom Spoon was aware that anything existed in the whole world but himself and his shame. Then for no particular reason he looked up and saw it there in the meadow: a monstrous wooden wagon such as Tom Spoon imagined only gypsies travelled in—a wagon violent with all the colours of creation and with tall elegant letters of scarlet and gold emblazoned across its side. Hitched to the wagon was the oldest horse that Tom Spoon had ever seen, its poor bony back swayed nigh to the tops of the buttercups. Gaping from the rear of the painted wagon was a small stage upon which stood numerous little pedestals, canisters and gilded chests and a small table with a purple star-spangled cloth thrown over it. Gazing upon all this, Tom Spoon felt his sadness snatched from him like the puff of white steam from a showboat whistle. He sat back on his stump, smiling dreamily and nursing his knees, leisurely reading the great gold scarlet words: Professor Alexander Galvani, the Great!! Prestidigitateur Extraordinaire! ! !

" 'Morning'! " cried a harsh but not unpleasant voice.

Tom Spoon saw an amazing white-haired old man walking briskly towards him, mopping his shiny forehead with a scarlet silk handkerchief and mumbling to himself.

"Boy," cried the Great Galvani, getting right down to business, "it's a sad world! Yes, it is! What's your name?"

"Tom Spoon," whispered Tom.

"Tom," said the Great Galvani, looking about first to be sure he was not being overhead, "got two bits?"

Tom remembered bitterly the twenty-five-cent piece his mother had given him to pay his share of the school party.

"Yes," he said, "I have."

"Good!" sniffed the Great Galvani. "I thought you would. Let's have it. That's the admission to my show."

Tom Spoon pulled the coin out of his pocket and blinked at the wondrous way it popped from his own fingers into those of the Great Galvani without his moving a hair.

"It's a sad world! Yes, it is!" reiterated the professor loudly. "Drove all night up the river from New Troy! Beat off three gypsies with the strength of my two hands in the bend just below Cresap's Landing! Got to town just at daybreak——"

Pausing here, he spat on the coin, rubbed it briskly betwixt thumb and forefinger and then held it up to shine like a lover's moon.

"Hit town, as I say," he continued, "just as the sun came up! Sheriff said I couldn't put my show on in the town limits—the varlet! Pulled out of town again and set up here. Have laid eyes on no mortal soul since then—except you! It's a sad penny-ridden world, I tell you. Folks just don't care for fun like they did in the old days!"

And Tom Spoon ruefully agreed.

"However!" cried the Great Galvani, glaring far down the river road for the faintest cloud of dust and then up Water Street for some harbinger of trade from that direction. "However! If there is but one in this whole town who has come to see my show, then—by the shade of the great Houdini—one shall not be disappointed! Come, Tom Spoon!"

And grabbing Tom Spoon's hand, the Great Galvani hustled him impatiently off to the rear of that beauteous flaming palace on wheels. Tom plunged down, rather breathless, in the grass and looked up at the small stage.

114

"La-a-a-dies—and gentlemen!" bawled the Great Galvani, red-faced and magnificent. "You are about to witness the most astounding performance of magic and legerdemain ever to appear before the unbelieving eye of mortal man!"

And it was true. At least to Tom Spoon it was true. Gold coins sprang like mushrooms from nowhere. Rabbits popped, pink-eared and flopping, from the Great Galvani's coat-tails. A purple billiard ball multiplied miraculously into a dozen rainbow globes between the Great Galvani's fingers. Finally, leaping from the stage to the knee-high grass, the professor hurled a towrope high into the morning air and climbed it. When he had reached the very top he half-disappeared into the blue sky, his lower half remaining within the bewitched vision of Tom Spoon for an instant. Then, scrambling a little, as if his trousers had caught on a sharp edge of sky, the Great Galvani disappeared altogether.

"Ho, Tom Spoon!" cried a voice from the blue-nothing to small Tom far below in the grass, "Ho, Tom! Can you see me?"

And Tom gawked and stared until the sun motes swarmed into his eyes like golden bees and then, to his relief, a foot appeared presently and then a leg and then both legs and quite suddenly and quite modestly the Great Galvani slid down the rope to the ground and, seating himself upon the wagon tongue, began perfunctorily to peel an orange.

"Tom," cried the Great Galvani presently. "I'm grateful! Yes, I am."

"Grateful?" said Tom.

"Yes, boy!" said the professor, spitting seeds neatly into the air, "I'm grateful to find that in this misbegotten village of skinflints there is still someone who would come to see my show! And mind you, Tom Spoon, I know how hard two bits is to come by!"

Tom flushed, pleased with the praise though not understanding it, and watched as the Great Galvani finished his orange and wiped each finger daintily on a magic silk.

"And so," said the professor, "it is nothing but equitable—nay, even honest—that I return your kindness with a favour. What do you desire most in this disenchanted world?"

"You mean—" said Tom, "you mean—what do I want?"

"Precisely!" cried the Great Galvani. "Speak out, boy! But don't disappoint me. You're too good for some kinds of wishes, so think well, boy! Think well! This chance may never come down the pike again! "

Tom Spoon shut his eye—the left one—and scratched thoughtfully at the scab on his ankle. And it crept like a wraith into his mind—the dark fairy wish.

"Anything?" Tom Spoon whispered.

"Anything!" cried the Great Galvani.

Then Tom Spoon stood up, frowning, his small fists clenched.

"Then I wish—I wish you'd change Miss Tinkens into a rabbit!" he cried.

"Miss Tinkens?" said the Great Galvani. "Now who in the name of the Great Merlin might that be?"

"My schoolteacher!" cried Tom Spoon. "The meanest, most hateful, most darned——"

"Say no more!" cried the Great Galvani, holding up his hand for silence. "You shall have your wish, Tom Spoon! Just tell me where this spinster can be found."

"Well," said Tom Spoon, shaking with excitement, "Miss Tinkens lives over there in the big grey house on Water Street and she ought to be walking home before long——"

So the Great Galvani and Tom Spoon hid in the snowball bush by Serena Tinken's steps and waited. A mocking bird cried rain down in the willows just as Tom Spoon heard the footsteps on the bricks.

"Listen!" Tom whispered fiercely, snatching the Great Galvani's sleeve. "That's her!"

"Are you sure, Tom Spoon?" whispered the professor. "We don't want to be making any mistakes!"

"I'm positive!" whispered Tom Spoon hoarsely. "She wears high button shoes! Listen!"

And listening, they could hear the tap, tap of Serena Tinkens' austere grey heels upon the stone. In a matter of seconds she was right upon them—Tom could have reached out and touched the hem of her long sad skirt—and just as she lifted her foot to ascend the steps the voice of the Great Galvani cried out sharp and clear:

"Serena Tinkens! Be a rabbit!"

And Tom stared wildly out, sweating and shaking till he was near tears. And in that moment Tom spied it—the poor timid creature of pink and white, hunched there on the bricks by the steps, its long ears twitching and its pink nose a writhing button of agitation.

116

"Take it home, Tom Spoon!" cried the professor, arising and dusting off his knees.

"Wait!" cried Tom Spoon. "Professor Galvani! Wait! Take the rabbit with you. What will I do with it? I didn't mean——"

"Take it home! Feed it carrots!" cried the Great Galvani, striding off down the sidewalk. "Good-bye, Tom Spoon! Good-bye!"

Tom Spoon stared miserably after the disappearing figure of the old magician and then at the rabbit at his feet. For it was mortal, Tom realised with horror, in spite of its pink and white unimportance. The burden of its safety was now clearly his own. So he took it home and when his mother saw the creature hanging by its ears from Tom Spoon's fist, there in the kitchen door, she dropped a pan of hot cinnamon rolls and screamed out loud.

"Not another varmint!" Tom Spoon's mother cried. "Toads in the attic. White mice in the basement. Goldfish in the parlour. Not another varmint, Tom Spoon! Just take that creature right back where you found it!"

"I—I can't, Mom," Tom gasped. "You don't understand. This is a very *important* rabbit! I have to take *very* good care of it!"

"No impudence, thank you!" cried his plump red-faced mother. "Out with you and out with that varmint too!"

So, with a squeak of despair, Tom Spoon put the white rabbit in an egg basket and set off for the river meadow with the sudden wild hope that the Great Galvani would still be there. But there was never a trace of the professor, only the ruts of his bewitched wagon there in the mud. So Tom Spoon ran off to the house of Bob Miller in the hope that Bob would give the poor creature a home. But Bob's mother stood waiting at the back door to announce that she would have no rabbits in her household, either. Nor would the cruel mother of Benny Blankensop. It seemed that all the mothers of the town stood together that afternoon in a phalanx of resistance and the small boys stood behind their skirts, ogling Tom Spoon and his fine white pet with the wildest envy in the world.

It was late when Tom returned home, defeated and weary, to sit down—a small dark figure of woe—beneath the apple tree.

"Tom Spoon!"

"Yes, Pap," Tom answered and the white beast leaped nervously

117

in its basket. Tom walked up and stood by the porch—a sorry sodden sight.

"Tom," said his father. "Your mother tells me you've brought another animal home. Where did you get it?"

"A strange old man with a white moustache and a horse and wagon—he gave it to me and told me it was a very fine rabbit and —and for heaven's sakes not to let anything happen to it and—and he's gone away and I have to do what he said, Pap!" said Tom Spoon, snatching the words from the thin evening air.

Tom's father stroked his chin thoughtfully.

"It would really be kindest," he said softly, "since you cannot keep it, Tom, to fetch my squirrel gun and let me——"

Tom clutched the basket and staggered back, his eyes round with horror. "No, Pap!" he whispered. "That would be— m-murder!"

"Murder?" laughed Tom's father heartlessly. "Killing a rabbit, murder? Well, we won't kill her, then. We'll just set her free. She'll find her way to the woods all right. She looks like she's lean and fast enough in case any dogs——"

"Dogs!" Tom Spoon sobbed.

"Tom," said his father, "I don't want to hear any more about it! Get rid of the rabbit—I don't care how—but get rid of it! Then come in and get washed for supper."

The screen door slammed and Tom was left alone there in the tangled moon-shadow of the old apple tree. Knowing that there was no appeal, he lifted the white rabbit gently from the basket and set it on the grass.

"Go away!" Tom Spoon whispered. "Scat!"

But the creature sat unmoving, perverse as Serena Tinkens had always been, wiggling its nose and nibbling the tender wet grass.

"Go on!" sobbed Tom Spoon picking up an apple and backing slowly away.

"Scoot!" cried Tom Spoon again and threw the apple. With a bound like an arc of snow, the rabbit disappeared into the shadows.

"Supper, Tom!" his mother called from the kitchen. "Tom!"

"I'm not hungry, Mom!" Tom answered and plodded slowly up the narrow staircase to his room, with the ghastly footsteps of his guilt on the creaking boards behind him. It was long after the big house had grown silent that Tom Spoon slept at last with a square of moonlight framing his tear-stained face.

In the morning Tom awoke, not really believing that it all had happened. Gulping down his prunes and cereal, he ran off down Lafayette Avenue to peer with horror through the shutters of Serena Tinken's empty house and watch the dusty sunlight stream through the still and somehow affrighted air. The crystal gleaming heart of Serena Tinkens winked hauntedly from the dust of the drop-leaf table.

And the days passed into weeks and the weeks into tortured months and one night in August—his awful secret burning like a stolen coin in the pocket of his mind—Tom Spoon knew he could stand it no longer. Rising, he stole silently out on to the dark porch roof, down through the honeysuckle into the wet grass, and slipped away to the river meadow. August, he thought to himself, is the month before September. And August is half over. On a day early in September the school bell would ring. But Serena Tinkens would not be there. During the summer no one had missed her—but then no one ever had. Anonymous and friendless, Serena Tinkens had faded into the shadows of the springs of fifteen years, not to emerge till the school bell rang. But now they would know. And the children would run home and tell their mothers and the sheriff would be called and they would search the town for a certain guilty face (which would surely be the square owlish one of Tom Spoon) and off to the penitentiary he would go for his life or worse.

Tom Spoon stumbled on through the moondust of the meadow, thinking these awful thoughts. Then—although for a moment he thought it was some trick of moonlight and cloud shadow—he saw the two rabbits. He dropped to his haunches, squatting among the flat trembling filigree of the Queen Anne's lace, breathless as much with the beauty of the sight as with his joy that he had found the lost Serena at last. They leaped—the white Serena Tinkens and her brown companion—wild free leaps high over the tops of the meadow grass in a dance so full of freedom and joy that for an instant Tom Spoon half wished he were a rabbit himself. The white one, Tom knew unmistakably, was Miss Tinkens; and the other—a little larger, with a fine rich cinnamon coat—he had never seen before. The moments passed and the mists crept up in sweet pale patches between the willows as Tom Spoon squatted silently watching them. And creeping to his bed at last, he lay awake till nearly dawn. She was still alive. And he had found out where she was and there was still time.

At ten the next morning Tom Spoon was in the public library. Miss Leatherby, the librarian, could scarcely believe her eyes, for she knew Tom Spoon hated books. Yet there he sat, nevertheless, with a great pile on the table before him, poring through them until he found what he wanted, a way to capture shy small creatures of the field without harming as much as a hair of their tails.

By supper time he had finished the trap—a wooden box with the stick to prop it up—and he had fixed up a little secret cage in the chicken house to hide the rabbit from his father, once he had caught it. Late that night he stole a sweet crisp carrot from the refrigerator and slipped off once more to the river meadow.

Tom set the box carefully on a flat clear space in the meadow, propped it loosely with the stick, set the carrot beneath it and crept off, trailing the string behind him. He sat so long in the moonlight that he nearly fell asleep. But just as his head was about to drop, he saw them again: the wonderful white Serena Tinkens leaping majestically through the grass and behind her, in brown springing splendour, her companion. Tom watched for what seemed hours as they frolicked—leaping the length of the meadow and springing high over the top of the Queen Anne's lace. Then, sure enough, as the Wise Woodsman had said in the musty book that morning, Serena Tinkens smelled the carrot, thumped over to where it lay, sniffed, nibbled. Tom Spoon pulled the string, the box fell and she was his again.

It was a puzzling thing to Tom Spoon's mother and father—the sudden hunger for green vegetables that seized upon him.

"I don't understand it!" Tom's mother would exclaim. "That boy has turned up his nose at lettuce and carrots since he was no bigger than a bug."

"He's growing!" Tom's father would say proudly. "That's why."

And Tom would appear at the kitchen door at that moment, like as not, asking for another carrot and then he would wander off casually to sit beneath the apple tree until they had gone into the parlour. Then he would pop into the chicken house and poke Serena Tinken's lunch through the mesh of her secret cage. And daily Tom visited the river road to stare wistfully up the meadow for some sign of the Great Galvani's return. As the black numbers on the kitchen calendar inched fatefully forward to that terrible day of discovery, Tom Spoon nearly gave up hope. He decided that when they came to drag him off to prison he would make one short grand speech in the parlour so that his poor parents would remember his courage at least.

Nor was the Great Galvani's return one moment too soon—a bare three days from the first day of school. Tom Spoon, making his daily visit to the meadow, uttered a shriek of joy when he saw the sunlight flash on the garish gold and scarlet letters of the fabulous wagon. As quickly as his stumpy legs would carry him he ran home, fetched Serena Tinkens and pounded off towards the river again.

" 'Mornin'!" cried Professor Galvani. "Hit town at daybreak again. Never seem to learn about this town. A hamlet of skinflints. Come to town tired and hungry but the sheriff said——"

"Professor!" whispered Tom Spoon, trying to remember how prayers went. "Professor——"

Professor Galvani scooped a fried egg out of the sizzling battered lid of a lard can which served as his frying pan and popped it between two heels of bread. He munched thoughtfully and neatly, regarding Tom Spoon's square white face.

"Tom Spoon!" said the Great Galvani softly. "Have you grown tired so soon of your cruel and foolish wish?"

"Yes," whispered Tom Spoon, "yes!" And he handed the professor the white kicking hare.

"Then come along, Tom Spoon," said the Great Galvani not unkindly and, taking Tom by the hand, led him up the dusty August road to the house of Serena Tinkens. Gently Professor Galvani set the white rabbit on the mossy bricks by the front porch steps.

"Rabbit, be Serena Tinkens!"

And when Tom Spoon opened his eyes she was there, blinking and staring about her in the same bright nervous way she always had; for all the world as if she had never stirred an inch from that moment of her transformation. Then, with never so much as a look at Tom Spoon or the Great Galvani, she walked dreamily up the steps and into her house and softly closed the door.

Tom could scarcely believe that the nightmare was over. Even on that morning not long after, when he walked into the third-

121

grade room, it did not seem possible that she was back in the world of small boys—solid and sound and free from the peril of farmers' dogs and open seasons. Tom Spoon crept nervously to his old desk and, folding his hands upon his worn familiar third reader, looked up at her, wondering if she remembered—if she knew. But if she did she didn't show it. And if, remembering, Serena Tinkens blamed Tom Spoon or anyone else she did not show that either. Yet, strangely, she was changed. And when she spoke her voice was softer, somehow—the same voice, but. . . .

"Good morning, children! " she said.

"Good morning, Miss Tinkens! " they cried.

"It's a beautiful day for the first day of school! " said Serena Tinkens. "So let's begin it pleasantly. Shall we sing a song, children?"

"Please," piped a tiny girl from the rear, "please, Miss Tinkens, tell us a story! "

Miss Tinkens smiled, considering it.

"Very well," she said presently and then for a time she was silent as if remembering. She stood there, her hands folded primly —yet at the same time girlishly—staring out the window into the woods, smouldering now with the lambent golden light of Indian summer.

"Once upon a time," she began, a tender puzzled sadness gleaming in her eyes, "once upon a time—in the kingdom of the spring there lived a rabbit prince. And the rabbit prince loved a rabbit princess——"

But then, quite suddenly, she stopped. Tom Spoon sat back in his seat and sighed. That, he supposed, was really all of the story Miss Tinkens could possibly remember.

Flea Circus

The flea circus has always had a special place in my affections —dating back to the time, I suppose, when I knew an old man who had once been both chief trainer and main source of nourishment to a bunch of performing fleas! In the story which follows, Stanley Ellin describes an encounter with a similar sort of character—and in the kind of circumstances which could happen to anyone.

BEIDENBAUER'S FLEA

By STANLEY ELLIN

I was seated on a bench in Central Park, half drowsing in the autumn sunlight, when a strange figure approached—the cadaverous figure of a man who bore himself with the grandeur of an ancient matinée idol. As he walked, he swung a malacca stick with practised ease. His hair was snowy-white and swept back almost to his collar, and on it was cocked with indescribable panache a battered homburg. His tight-waisted, velveteen-collared overcoat was long out of fashion and badly frayed at the cuffs. His narrow-toed, patent-leather shoes were scuffed and down at the heels. Yet, so noble was his demeanour and so profound the sorrow written on his lined face that I found myself pitying his curious garb, rather than being moved to scorn by it.

He sat down beside me, propped his stick between his legs, and said, "It is a beautiful day, is it not?"

"Yes," I said, "it is." Then I felt a sudden apprehension. I am too easy a mark for the wayfarer's sad story, his melting eyes, his extended palm. I have never learned to say no to the humble derelict who stops me with hat in hand and asks for carfare to places he never intends to visit. Now I had the feeling that I knew what was coming, and I drew a tight rein on my susceptibilities. This time, I silently resolved, I would escape before it was too late.

But there was no escape. As I started to rise, my companion placed a hand on my shoulder and gently pressed me back into my seat. "It is a beautiful day," he said, "but what does that matter to one who is doomed to suffer and search, search and suffer through every day of his life, fair or foul?"

I was resigned to my fate, but in a bitter mood. He might tell his story to the end, but when he held out his hand for the expected offering he would get nothing more than a handshake. That much I took my oath on.

124

"Evidently," I said, concealing my true emotions with an effort, "you are spending your life in a search for something. What is that something?"

"A flea."

"A flea?"

The aged curio nodded sombrely. "Yes, strange as it seems, that is the object of my search. But perhaps you will understand more readily if I reveal my name to you. It is Beidenbauer. Thaddeus Beidenbauer. There, does that enlighten you?"

He looked at me eagerly, but the light in his eyes faded when I shook my head. "No," I said. "I'm sorry to say it doesn't."

"It doesn't?'

"I'm afraid not."

Beidenbauer sighed. "Well, such is fame. A bubble—a glittering, weightless thing that one holds briefly in hand, and then— but let me tell you my story. There is pain and heartbreak in it, true, but I am inured to that now. I have lived my tragedy over and over so many times in my waking dreams that I can bear to talk about it freely when the occasion arises. I will tell it all to you just as it happened."

"I am sure you will", I said.

There was a time [Beidenbauer said] when my name was known in every mighty city of the world, when I was petted and sought after by the great, when I was drunk each day with my youth and wealth and the joy of my lot. Ah, I should have thought then how the gods destroy those who are too proud, but I did not. I lived only with the happy realization that I was the proprietor of Beidenbauer's Mighty Mites, the greatest flea circus on earth, the one that did more to honour the vast and unsung talents of the flea than any other before or since.

There have been flea circuses before mine and after mine, but always shabby affairs, dismal two-penny entertainments with none of the true glamour of the stage invested in them. But mine was different. It was superlative theatre. Whether performed before the bumpkins who attend touring carnivals or before a soirée of society's bluest blue bloods, it never failed to stir the audience to its depths, to bring it to its feet shouting for endless encores. And all because as a mere child I had learned the secret of the relationship between the flea and its trainer, and with infinite patience had put the secret to work.

125

I can see you are wondering what the secret is; you will be astonished to learn of its simplicity. There is a strange and wonderful symbiosis between flea and man. The flea feeds from its trainer's arm and thus strengthened goes into the arena to perform. The money earned this way is then used by the trainer to buy him his dinner, to enrich his blood, that the performer may feed and return to his performance. So we have a perfect cycle, flea and man feeding off each other, each contributing to their mutual existence.

That is all there is to it, but I was the one to discover that there must be more than mere food involved in this relationship. There must be a symbiosis of emotions as well. Respect, sympathy, understanding, and love—yes, love—must be there, for the flea, a quivering mass of sensitivity, needs them desperately. And unlike all other trainers, I provided them. Cruelty was the rule elsewhere. The harsh word, the heavy hand—these were all my confrères knew in trying to master and instruct the flea. But kindness was my rule, and for that reason I soared to success while all others remained mired in failure.

But enough of myself; after all, it was not I who entered the spotlighted ring every day to perform, to act the clown so that the crowd roared with laughter, to risk my neck in acrobatics so that it gasped, to woo it with grace so that it sighed in rapture. All this was done by the fleas, and it is they who must get the lion's share of admiration.

There were twenty-four members of the troupe, hand-picked, trained for weary hours on end, and it is impossible to imagine the range of their talents. But the unchallenged star of the show, and, sorrow of sorrows, the star of the tragedy I am unfolding, was a flea named Sebastian. Small, volatile, full of riotous wit and invention, he was our featured clown. And he was a true star in every respect. Tense and withdrawn before a performance, he was at ease the instant the spotlights fell on him and in absolute command of the audience.

I can see him now, waiting behind the scenes as the white silk handkerchief was laid on the table and tacks driven into each of its four corners to moor it securely. Then, as the darning hoop which was our main ring was set on it, Sebastian would fretfully start to pace up and down, his mouth drawn tight, his eyes faraway, fighting the fears reborn in him at every performance. I knew those signs, and I would give him a little nod—just one

126

small nod—to make clear my confidence in him. And he would respond with a little nod of his own to show that he understood. It was our private ritual, those two almost imperceptible gestures, and it was all that was ever needed to assure another sterling performance from him. That, and the knowledge that the prima ballerina of our company, an enchanting, doe-eyed little flea named Selina, had eyes only for him and would stand worshipping from afar while he held the spotlight. For Selina, I think, was the only one on earth other than myself to whom he gave his unquestioning devotion.

But, alas, what he did not know at the time, and what I did not know—such is the cruel deviousness of the female heart —was that Selina worshipped only at the altar of success. She loved him not for himself, but for the glory that was his; the laughter and applause of the crowd, the featured billing given him, and the favoured place on my forearm at feeding time. She was a great dancer, but like so many of her kind she had no true warmth in her heart. Only a fanatic adoration of success.

Had I known that at the time I would have made a different turning somewhere along the road to disaster which lay ahead. But how could I know, how could anyone know, when Selina dissembled so brilliantly? When she looked at Sebastian with melting eyes she almost turned my head as well as his. She clung to him, comforted him in his times of doubt, let him know in a hundred different ways that he was her hero. And he, befuddled by her airs and graces, was completely her slave.

It was an apparently meaningless episode—meaningless at the time it occurred—that brought on the inexorable crisis. Hercules, our flea who performed feats of strength, had become old and stiff-legged, and one night while lifting a grape seed over his head before a hushed and awestruck audience, he suddenly fell to the floor in a writhing agony. The veterinarian who diagnosed the case did not mince words. It was a serious rupture, he said grimly, and Hercules would perform no more.

It was shocking beyond measure to me, that news. Not only because of my warm regard for Hercules, but because it left me without one of my featured acts. I instantly gave orders to agents to scour the world, look high and low, pay any price for a flea who could duplicate Hercules' feats, but I did so with a heavy heart. I had already garnered the best there was in the entire world. What chance was there to find a replacement I had not previously considered and found unworthy?

But miracles can and do happen. I had rejected scores of applicants in despair when suddenly a cable arrived from an agent in Bulgaria. The length of the cable alone suggested his state of emotions, and what it said made them even more vivid. By pure chance he had entered a broken-down café in Sofia where the guests were being entertained by a flea circus. Not even a circus. A few acts badly performed by sullen, half-starved fleas. But one flea there—! Nothing would do, save that I come at once and see for myself.

I did not believe him, because I knew he was inordinately proud of his native fleas who are, at best, temperamental performers; but I went. When a man is desperate he will do anything, even to putting his faith in the potentialities of a Bulgarian flea. So I went. And to paraphrase the saying: I came, I saw, I was conquered.

The flea was named Casimir, and even the unspeakable surroundings in which he performed could not dim his lustre. Barrel-chested, bull-necked, glowing with health, and with a frank, open face that gave clear evidence of an honest nature and willing heart, he dwarfed the fleas around him to insignificance. I saw at a glance that I might be looking at a born star. I waited for his performance in a fever of impatience.

At last the motley acts that preceded his were finished, and the café loungers crowded close around the table, I in their forefront. The trainer, a wizened wretch, placed two small wooden blocks on the table, one of which had a series of steps carved into it. Between the blocks I could see a single strand of dark hair—evidently from the trainer's head since it shone greasily in the dim light around me—which was stretched taut from block to block. The trainer then placed Casimir on the table, and before the flea he placed a gleaming pin two inches long which he drew from his lapel.

I could not believe my eyes. To a flea that pin was as a length of railroad track would be to me, yet Casimir stooped low, got a grip on it, and with bulging muscles suddenly lifted it overhead. I gasped, but I had not yet seen the full capabilities of this magnificent creature. Holding the pin overhead he made his way to the steps of the block, climbed them, and then slowly, cautiously, he stepped on to the hair itself. The hair sagged under the weight

128

on it, and Casimir balanced himself with an effort. Then with precise steps, secure as if he were affixed to that hair, he walked its full length, the pin held high overhead throughout and never wavering in his grip. Only when the other block had been reached and the pin laid down could you detect in the convulsive tremors of his body and the heaving of his chest what the strain must have been.

I knew even before the applause started that my search was over. Six hours later, after passionate bargaining and endless rounds of slivovitz, I paid for Casimir's contract more money than anyone on earth would ever have dreamed of paying for a flea. And at that I felt I was fortunate.

I took my prize home with me. I allowed time for him to become accustomed to our American ways; I filled his starved soul with my affection and trust; and only when I was sure that he was accepted by the rest of the company and felt at ease with them did I put him on the stage. That night was his night. When the final curtain fell he was the unchallenged star of the show. Simple, honest, unassuming, it was clear that he would not permit this honour to inflate him; but there was no question about it, he was the star. And Sebastian, the great Punchinello, the unparalleled clown, was in second place.

What were Sebastian's feelings then? What could they have been but anguish at having to yield his place to another. But whatever the torments he suffered, he was a trouper through and through. To him the show was the thing, and if he were asked to sacrifice himself to it, he would do so like a stoic. The quality of his performances remained superb. If anything, they were better than ever. Each time he entered the spotlight he flung himself into his role with an abandon, a virtuosity, far beyond the powers of most fleas.

No, it was not the loss of his commanding place in the company that finally shattered him; it was the loss of his beloved. Selina had seen his glory transferred to Casimir. She watched with narrowed eyes as a new star rose on the horizon. And with cold-blooded deliberation, never heeding the consequences, she turned from the old to worship the new. She had eyes only for Casimir now, comfort only for him, flattery only for him, and he, poor, simple-minded male, accepted this at first incredulously, then eagerly, then with rapture.

That was what destroyed Sebastian. The sight of the couple

together transfixed him like a needle. And there was no escaping the sight, no turning away from it. Selina was unabashed in her pursuit, and Casimir nakedly revelled in it. The outsider might have seen this as a stirring romance; to Sebastian it would be an obscenity. Selina was his; what right did some burly stranger have to fondle her before his very eyes? He must have brooded himself into a state of madness over this.

The end came with shocking suddenness. It was during an evening performance, and the show had gone well until Casimir undertook his master feat. The audience leaned forward with bated breath as he lifted the pin over his head. It hummed with excitement as he climbed the block and set forth on his journey across the taut hair which stretched no less than a foot above the table. And it cried out in alarm when, as he reached the middle of the hair, it suddenly parted, and he plummeted to the table, the pin following him and crushing his chest.

I had leaped forward wildly when I saw the hair part, but I was too late. All I could do was remove the oppressive weight of the pin and turn my head away to conceal my tears from the expiring Casimir. He had his own pains to bear; I would spare him mine. But when my misted eyes fell on the broken strand of hair my grief turned to blazing rage. The hair had not worn through; it had been deliberately cut part of the way. I was looking, not at an accident, but at a murder!

I knew at once who the murderer was. And I could tell from the shock on Selina's face and the growing comprehension on the face of every flea huddled there that the story was clear to all of them. But before I could wreak vengeance on the criminal my glance fell on Casimir, lying there, breathing his last. He looked at me with lustrous eyes full of pain; he tried to smile—oh, pitiful sight—and with a great effort he shook his head at me. He understood, too, noble soul, and he was telling me that vengeance was not for him. Only pity for the malefactor, and forgiveness. It was his last gesture on earth, and the lesson struck me to my heart. It wiped the thirst for vengeance out of me on the spot. I felt only a great need to find Sebastian, to tell him that I alone was the cause of the sorrows that had befallen us. Obsessed by pride in the show, I had put another in his place, had deprived him of his beloved, had driven him at last to insanity and crime.

But when I looked for him I could not find him. Filled with

horror at his deed he had fled into the night. And with his disappearance, with Casimir's death, with the company's morale destroyed, there was nothing left. I cancelled my bookings, broke up the company, and set forth with only one thought in mind—to find Sebastian, to face him as a penitent, and to win forgiveness from him.

It has been a weary search. I have walked the lonely streets day and night, combed dog shows and zoological parks, looked every place where a wanderer like Sebastian might take refuge. But all to no avail. I am old and poor now. I must rely on alms from strangers to help me on my way, but I will never give up my search until I am successful in it. There is no other way for me. I am doomed to suffer and search, search and suffer until then.

Beidenbauer's voice ceased and his narrative ended on this plaintive note. We sat together in silence for a long while, contemplating the pigeons burbling on the grass beyond, and then I said, "I have heard tell that the life span of the flea is extremely brief. Is it not likely that by now, in some unmarked grave—?"

"I do not allow myself to think of that", said Beidenbauer with deep feeling. "It would be the final blow."

"Yes," I said, "I can see that it would be."

We sat in silence again, and then with resignation I took a coin from my pocket and offered it to him. He only looked at it reproachfully. I sighed, put the coin away, and offered him a dollar bill. This he took.

"You are kind", he said, getting to his feet. "I am only sorry that you never saw my circus in its glory. You would better understand then how far I have fallen."

"Well," I said, "that's life."

"No, my friend," said Beidenbauer gravely, "that's show business."

Puppet Show

A puppet show might seem the most harmless of entertainments—except in the hands of the sinister Fritz Leiber. Here he has taken what appears to be a straightforward situation of rumours getting out of hand (no pun intended) and imbued it with the most awesome possibilities.

THE POWER OF THE PUPPETS

By FRITZ LEIBER

"Look at the ugly little thing for yourself then, and tell me if it's an ordinary puppet! " said Delia, her voice rising.

Curiously I examined the limp figure she had jerked out of her handbag and tossed on my desk. The blue-white doll-face grinned at me, revealing yellowish fangs. A tiny wig of black horse hair hung down as far as the empty eye-sockets. The cheeks were sunken. It was a gruesome piece of workmanship, with a strong flavour of the Middle Ages. The maker had evidently made a close study of stone gargoyles and stained-glass devils.

Attached to the hollow papiermâché head was the black garment that gave the figure its appearance of limpness. Something after the fashion of a monk's robe, it had a little cowl that could be tucked over the head, but now hung down its back.

I know something about puppets, even though my line is a far cry from puppeteering. I am a private detective. But I knew that this was not a marionette, controlled by strings, but a hand puppet. It was made so that the operator's hand could be slipped up through the empty garment until his fingers were in a position to animate the head and arms. During an exhibition the operator would be concealed beneath the stage, which had no floor, and only the puppet would be visible above the footlights.

I drew the robe over my hand and fitted my index finger up into the head, my second finger into the right sleeve, and my thumb into the left sleeve of the puppet. That, as I recalled, was the usual technique. Now the figure was no longer limp. My wrist and forearm filled out the robe.

I wiggled finger and thumb, and the manikin waved his arms wildly, though somewhat awkwardly, for I have seldom manipulated a puppet. I crooked my first finger and the little head gave a vigorous nod.

"Good morning, Jack Ketch", I said, making the manikin bow, as if acknowledging my salutation.

"Don't!" cried Delia, and turned her head away.

Delia was puzzling me. I had always thought her a particularly level-headed woman and, up to three years ago, I had seen a great deal of her and had had a chance to judge.

Three years ago she had married the distinguished puppeteer, Jock Lathrop, with whom I was also acquainted. Then our paths had separated. But I'd had no inkling of anything being amiss until she had appeared this morning in my New York office and poured out a series of vague hints and incredible suspicions so strange that anything resembling them did not often come a private detective's way, though I hear many odd and bizarre stories during the course of a year's work.

I looked at her closely. She was, if anything, more beautiful than ever, and considerably more exotic, as might be expected now that she was moving in artistic circles. Her thick, golden hair fell straight to her shoulders, where it was waved under. Her grey suit was smartly tailored, and her grey suede shoes trim. At her throat was a barbaric-looking brooch of hammered gold. A golden pin kept a sketchy little hat and a handful of veil in place.

But she was still the old Delia, still the "softie Viking", as we sometimes used to call her. Except that her anxiety was twisting her lips, and fear showed in her big grey eyes.

"What really is the matter, Delia?" I said, sitting down beside her. "Has Jock been getting out of hand?"

"Oh, don't be foolish, George!" she replied sharply. "It's nothing like that. I'm not afraid of Jock, and I'm not looking for a detective to get any evidence for me. I've come to you because I'm afraid for him. It's those horrible puppets. They're trying. . . . Oh, how can I explain it! Everything was all right until he accepted that engagement in London you must remember about, and began prying into his family history, his genealogy. Now there are things he won't discuss with me, things he won't let me see. He avoids me. And, George, I'm certain that, deep in his heart, he's afraid too. Terribly afraid."

"Listen, Delia", I said. "I don't know what you mean by all this talk about the puppets, but I do know one thing. You're married to a genius. And geniuses, Delia, are sometimes hard to live with. They're notoriously inconsiderate, without meaning to be. Just read their biographies! Half the time they go around in a state of abstraction, in love with their latest ideas, and fly off the handle at the slightest provocation. Jock's fanatically devoted to his puppets, and he should be! All the critics who know anything about the subject say he's the best in the world, better even than Franetti. And they're raving about his new show as the best of his career!"

Delia's grey suede fist beat her knee.

"I know, George. I know all about that! But it has nothing to do with what I'm trying to tell you. You don't suppose I'm the sort of wife who would whine just because her husband is wrapped up in his work? Why, for a year I was his assistant, helped him make the costumes, even operated some of the less important puppets. Now he won't even let me in his workshop. He won't let me come back-stage. He does everything himself. But I wouldn't mind even that, if it weren't that I'm afraid. It's the puppets themselves, George! They—they're trying to hurt him. They're trying to hurt me too."

I searched for a reply. I felt thoroughly uncomfortable. It is not pleasant to hear an old friend talking like a lunatic. I lifted my head and frowned at the malevolent doll-face of Jack Ketch, blue as that of a drowned man. Jack Ketch is the hangman in the traditional puppet play, "Punch and Judy." He takes his name from a seventeenth-century executioner who officiated with rope and red-hot irons at Tyburn in London.

"But Delia," I said, "I don't see what you're driving at. How can an ordinary puppet—"

"But it isn't an ordinary puppet!" Delia broke in vehemently. "That's why I brought it for you to see. Look at it closely. Look at the details. *Is* it an ordinary puppet?"

Then I saw what she meant.

"There are some superficial differences", I admitted.

"What are they?" she pressed.

"Well, this puppet has no hands. Puppets usually have papier-mâché or stuffed muslin hands attached to the ends of the sleeves."

"That's right. Go on."

"Then the head", I continued unwillingly. "There are no eyes painted on it—just eyeholes. And it's much thinner than most I've seen. More like a—a mask."

Delia gripped my arm, dug her fingers in.

"You've said the word, George!" she cried. "Like a mask!

135

Now do you see what I mean? Jock doesn't operate his own puppets any more. He has some horrible little creatures like rats that do it for him. They wear the puppets' robes and heads. That's why he won't allow me or anyone else to come backstage during a performance. And they're trying to hurt him, kill him! I know. I've heard them threaten him."

"Delia," I said, gently taking hold of her arms, "you don't know what you're saying. You're nervous, over-wrought. Just because your husband invents a new type of puppet—why, it explains itself. It's because of his work on these new-type puppets that he's become secretive."

She jerked away from me.

"Won't you try to understand, George? I know how mad it sounds, but I'm *not* mad. At night, when Jock has thought I was asleep I've heard them threaten him with their high little voices like whistles. 'Let us go—let us go or we'll kill you!' they cry, and I'm so weak with fear I can't move. They're so tiny they can creep about everywhere."

"Have you seen them?" I asked quickly.

"No, but I *know* they're real! Last night one of them tried to scratch my eyes out while I was asleep. Look!"

She swept back the thick hair from her temple, and at that moment I also felt as if the needle-touch of fear had been transmitted to me. There in the creamy skin, an inch from the eye, were five little scratches that looked as if they might have been made by a miniature human hand. For a moment I could almost see the ratlike little creature Delia had described, its clawed hand upraised. . . .

Then the image faded and I was realizing that such grotesque happenings were impossible. But oddly I felt as if I no longer could attribute everything Delia had told me to her neurotic fancies. *I* feared, also—but my fear was that there was a plot afoot, one meant to terrify her, to work on her superstitious fears, and delude her.

"Would you like me to visit Jock?" I asked quietly.

Some of the weight seemed to drop from her shoulders.

"I was hoping you'd say that," she said, with relief. . . .

The exquisitely lettered sign read:

LATHROP'S PUPPETS—2nd Floor

Outside, Forty-second Street muttered and mumbled. Inside, a wooden stair with worn brass fittings led up into a realm of dimness and comparative silence.

"Wait a minute, Delia", I said. "There are a couple of questions I'd like you to answer. I want to get this whole thing straight before I see Jock."

She stopped and nodded, but before I could speak again our attention was attracted by a strange series of sounds from the second floor. Heavy stamping, then what seemed to be an explosion of curses in a foreign language, then rapid pacing up and down, another explosion of curses, and more pacing. It sounded as if a high-class tantrum were in progress.

Suddenly the noises ceased. I could visualize a person "pausing and swelling up in silent rage." With equal suddenness they recommenced, this time ending in a swift and jarring *clump-clump* of footsteps down the stairs. Delia shrank back against the railing as a fattish man with grey eyebrows, glaring eyes, and a mouth that was going through wordless but vituperative contortions neared us. He was wearing an expensive checked suit and a white silk shirt open at the neck. He was crumpling a soft felt hat.

He paused a few steps above us and pointed at Delia dramatically. His other hand was crumpling a soft felt hat.

"You, madam, are the wife of that lunatic, are you not?" he demanded accusingly.

"I'm Jock Lathrop's wife, if that's what you mean, Mr. Franetti", Delia said coolly. "What's the matter?"

I recognized Luigi Franetti then. He was often referred to by the press as the "Dean of Puppeteers." I remembered that Jock had been in his workshop and studied under him several years ago.

"You ask me what is the matter with me?" Franetti ranted. "You ask me that, Madame Lathrop? Bah!" Here he crumpled his hat again. "Very well—I will tell you! Your husband is not only a lunatic. He is also an ingrate! I come here to congratulate him on his recent success, to take him to my arms. After all, he is my pupil. Everything he learned from me. And what is his gratitude? What, I ask you? He will not let me touch him? He will not even shake hands! He will not let me into his workshop! Me! Franetti, who taught him everything!"

He swelled up with silent rage, just as I'd visualized it. But only for a moment. Then he was off again.

"But I tell you he is a madman!" he shouted, shaking his

137

finger at Delia. "Last night I attended, unannounced and un-invited, a performance of his puppets. They do things that are impossible—impossible without Black Magic. I am Luigi Franetti, and I know! Nevertheless, I thought he might be able to explain it to me today. But no, he shuts me out! He has the evil eye and the devil's fingers, I tell you. In Sicily people would understand such things. In Sicily he would be shot! Bah! Never will I so much as touch him with my eyes again. Let me pass!"

He hurried down the rest of the stairs, Delia squeezing back and turning her head. In the doorway he turned for a parting shot.

"And tell me, Madame Lathrop," he cried, "what a puppeteer wants with rats!"

With a final "Bah!" he rushed out.

I didn't stop laughing until I saw Delia's face. Then it occurred to me that Franetti's accusations, ludicrous as they were, might seem to her to fit with her own suspicions.

"You can't take seriously what a man like Franetti says", I remonstrated. "He's jealous because Jock won't bow down to him and make a complete revelation of all his new technical discoveries and inventions."

Delia did not reply. She was staring after Franetti, absent-mindedly pulling at the corner of a tiny handkerchief with her teeth. Watching her, I knew again the fear she felt, as if again she were feeling a little creature gouging at her temple.

"Anything to that last remark of Franetti's?" I asked lightly. "Jock doesn't keep white rats for pets by any chance?"

"I don't know", Delia said abstractedly. "I told you he never lets me in his workroom." Then she looked at me. "You said you wanted to ask me some more questions?"

I nodded. On the way here I had been revolving in my mind an unpleasant hypothesis. If Jock no longer loved Delia and had some reason for wanting to be rid of her he might be responsible for her suspicions. He had every chance to trick her.

"You said the change in Jock began to show while you were in London", I said. "Tell me the precise circumstances."

"He'd always been interested in old books and in genealogy, you see, but never to the same extent", she said, after a thoughtful pause. "In a way it was chance that began it. An accident to his hands. A rather serious one, too. A window fell on them, mashing the fingers badly. Of course a puppeteer's no good without hands, and so Jock had to lay off for three weeks. To help pass the time, he took to visiting the British Museum and the library there. Later he made many visits to other libraries to occupy his time, since he's apt to be very nervous when anything prevents him from working. When we came back he did not work here, either, for quite a long time, but kept up his studies.

"Then when he was finally ready to start work again he told me he'd decided to work the puppets alone. I pointed out that one man couldn't give a puppet show, since he could only manage two characters at a time. He told me that he was going to confine himself to puppet plays like *Punch and Judy*, in which there are almost never more than two characters in sight at one time.

"That was three months ago. From that day he's avoided me. George—" her voice broke "—it's almost driven me crazy. I've had the craziest suspicions. I've even thought that he lost both his hands in the accident and refused to tell!"

"What!" I shouted. "Do you mean to tell me you don't know?"

"Do you begin to see how secretive he is?" she said with a wan and rather pitiful smile.

"No. Seems strange, doesn't it? But I can't swear even to that. He never lets me come near, and he wears gloves, except in the dark."

"But the puppet shows—"

"That's just it. That's the question I keep asking myself when I sit in the audience and watch the puppets. *Who* is manipulating them? What's inside them?"

At that moment I determined to do everything I could to battle Delia's fear.

"You're not crazy", I said harshly. "But Jock is!"

She rubbed her hand across her forehead, as if it itched.

"No," she said softly, "it's the puppets. Just as I told you."

As we went on upstairs then I could tell that Delia was anxious to get my interview with Jock started. She had had to nerve herself up to it, and delays were not improving her state of mind. But apparently we were fated to have a hard time getting up that flight of stairs.

This time the interruption came when a slim man in a blue business suit tried to slip by in the semi-darkness unnoticed. But Delia recognized him.

"Why, hello, Dick!" she said. "Don't you know old friends?"

I made out prim, regular features and a head of thinning, neutral-coloured hair.

"Dick, this is George Clayton", Delia was saying. "George, this is Dick Wilkinson. Dick handles my husband's insurance."

Wilkinson's "Howdya do?" sounded embarrassed and constrained. He wanted to get away.

"What did Jock want to see you about?" asked Delia, and Wilkinson's apparent embarrassment increased. He coughed, then seemed to make a sudden decision.

"Jock's been pretty temperamental lately, hasn't he?" he asked Delia.

She nodded slowly.

"I thought so", he said. "Frankly, I don't know why he wanted to see me this morning. I thought perhaps it was something in connection with the accident to his hands. He has never done anything about collecting any of the five-thousand-dollar insurance he took out on them two years ago. But whether that was it or not I can't tell you. He kept me waiting for the best part of half an hour. I could not help hearing Mr. Franetti's display of temper. Perhaps that upset Jock. Anyhow when Franetti went away, fuming, five minutes later Jock leaned out of his workshop door and curtly informed me that he had changed his mind—he didn't say about what—and told me to leave."

"I'm so sorry, Dick", murmured Delia. "That was rude of him." Then her voice took on a strange eager note. "Did he leave the door of his workshop open?"

Dick Wilkinson wrinkled his brow. "Why yes, I—I believe he did. At least, that was my impression. But, Delia—"

Delia had already slipped on ahead, running swiftly up the steps. Hastily I said good-bye to the perplexed insurance agent and followed her.

When I reached the second floor I went into a short hall. Through an open door I glimpsed the closely-ranked seats of the puppet theatre. Delia was vanishing through another door down the hall. I followed her.

Just as I came into a small reception room, I heard her scream.

"George! George! He's whipping the puppet!"

With that bewildering statement ringing in my ears, I darted into what I took to be Jock Lathrop's workshop, then pulled up short. It too was dim, but not as dim as the hall. I could see tables and racks of various kinds, and other paraphernalia.

Delia was cowering back against a wall, stark fear in her eyes. But my attention was riveted on the small, stocky man in the centre of the room—Delia's husband. On, or *in,* his left hand was a puppet. His gloved right hand held a miniature cat-o'-nine-tails and he was lashing the puppet. And the little manikin was writhing and flailing its arms protectively in a manner so realistic that it took my breath away. In that strange setting I could almost imagine I heard a squeaking, protesting voice. Indeed, the realism was such and the grin on Lathrop's face so malign that I heard myself saying:

"Stop it, Jock! Stop it!"

He looked up, saw me, and burst into peals of laughter. His snub-nosed, sallow face was contorted into a mask of comedy. I had expected anything but that.

"So even the sceptical George Clayton, hard-boiled sleuth, is taken in by my cheap illusions!" he finally managed to say.

Then he stopped chuckling and drew himself up nonchalantly, like a magician about to perform a feat of sleight of hand. He tossed the whip on to a nearby table, seized the puppet with his right hand and, to all appearances, wiggled his left hand out of it. Then he quickly flipped me the limp form, thrust both hands into his pockets, and began to whistle.

Delia gave a low, whimpering cry and ran out of the room. If it had been easy for me to imagine a tiny, nude creature scuttling away behind Jock, half concealed by his left hand, what must it have been for her, in her tortured, superstitious state?

"Examine the thing, George", Lathrop directed coolly. "Is it a puppet, or isn't it?"

I looked down at the bundle of cloth and papiermâché I had caught instinctively. It was a puppet all right, and in general workmanship precisely similar to the one Delia had shown me at my office. Its garments, however, were a gay, motley patchwork. I recognized the nose and sardonic, impudent features of Punch.

I was fascinated by the delicate craftsmanship. The face lacked the brutishness of Jack Ketch, but it had a cunning, hair-trigger villainy all its own. Somehow it looked like a composite of all the famous criminals and murderers I had ever read about. As the murderous hero of Punch and Judy, it was magnificent.

But I had not come here to admire puppets.

"Look here, Jock," I said, "what the devil have you been doing to Delia? The poor girl's frightened to death."

He regarded me quizzically.

"You're taking a lot for granted, aren't you?" he said quietly. "I imagine she hunted you up as a friend, not in your capacity as a detective, but don't you think it would have been wiser to hear both sides of the case before forming judgment? I can imagine what sort of wild stories Delia's been telling you. She says I'm avoiding her, doesn't she? She says there's something queer about the puppets. In fact, she says they're alive, doesn't she?"

I heard a furtive scuffling under the work table, and was startled in spite of myself. Jock Lathrop grinned, then whistled shrilly between his teeth. A white rat crept hesitatingly into view from behind a pile of odds and ends.

"A pet", he announced mockingly. "Is it Delia's belief that I have trained rats to animate my puppets?"

"Forget Delia's beliefs for the present! " I said angrily. "Whatever they are, you're responsible for them! You've no excuse in the world for mystifying her, terrifying her."

"Are you so sure I haven't?" he said enigmatically.

"Good Lord, she's your wife, Jock! " I flung at him.

His face became serious and his words took on a deeper quality.

"I know she's my wife," he said, "and I love her dearly. But George, hasn't the obvious explanation of all this occurred to you? I hate to say it, but the truth is that Delia is bothered by —er—neurotic fancies. For some crazy reason, without the slightest foundation she has become obsessed with some sort of deep-seated—and thoroughly unreasonable—jealousy, and she's directing it at the puppets. I can't tell you why. I wish I knew."

"Even admitting that," I countered quickly, "why do you persist in mystifying her?"

"I don't", he flatly denied. "If sometimes I keep her out of the workshop, it's for her own good."

His argument was beginning to make sense. Jock Lathrop's voice had a compelling matter-of-fact quality. I was beginning to feel slightly ridiculous. Then I remembered something.

"Those scratches on her face—" I began.

"I've seen them," said Jock. "Again I hate to say it, but the only rational explanation I can see is that they were self-inflicted with the idea of bolstering up her accusations, or perhaps she scratched herself in her sleep. At any rate, people with delusions have been known to do drastic things. They'll go to any lengths rather than discard their queer beliefs. That's honestly what I think."

142

Pondering this quiet statement, I was looking around. Here were all the tools of the expert puppet-maker. Moulds, paints, varnishes, clay models of heads, unformed papiermâché, paper clippings, and glue. A sewing machine littered with odds and ends of gay-coloured cloth.

Tacked above a desk were a number of sketches of puppets, some in pencil, some in colours. On a table were two half-painted heads, each atop a stick so that the brush could get at them more easily. Along the opposite wall hung a long array of puppets—princesses and Cinderellas, witches and wizards, peasants, oafs, bearded old men, devils, priests, doctors, kings. It almost made me feel as if a whole doll-world was staring at me and choking back raucous laughter.

"Why haven't you sent Delia to a doctor?" I asked suddenly.

"Because she refuses to go. For some time I've been trying to persuade her to consult a psychoanalyst."

I didn't know what to say. The white rat moved into my line of vision. It occurred to me that a rat could be used to explain the scuffling sounds made by anything else, but I put such an irrational thought out of my mind. More and more I found myself being forced into complete agreement with Lathrop. Delia's suspicions were preposterous. Lathrop must be right.

"Look here," I continued feebly, "Delia keeps talking about something that happened to you in London. A change. A sudden interest in genealogy."

"I'm afraid the change was in Delia," he said bitterly. "As for the genealogy business, that's quite correct. I did find out some startling things about a man whom I believe to be an ancestor of mine."

As he spoke, eagerly now, I was surprised to note how his features lost their tight, hard appearance. The look of impudence was gone.

"I *do* love Delia very much", he said, his voice vibrant, low. "What would she think of me, George, if it turned out that her accusations were partly true? Of course, that's nonsense. But you can see that we are in trouble, George—bad trouble, that is considerably out of the line of work a private detective follows. Your work is concrete, though in your criminal investigations you must have learned that the mind and body of man are sometimes subject to brutal powers. Not supernatural—no. But things—hard to talk about.

143

"George, would you do something for me? Come to the performance tonight. Afterward we can discuss this whole matter more fully. And another thing. See that old pamphlet over there? I have good reason for thinking it concerns an ancestor of mine. Take it with you. Read it. But for heaven's sake don't let Delia see it. You see, George—"

He broke off uncertainly. He seemed about to take me into his confidence about something, but then the hard, self-contained look returned to his face.

"Leave me now", he said abruptly. "This talk, and that business with the old fool, Franetti, has made me nervous."

I walked over to the table, carefully laid down Punch, and picked up the yellow-paged, ancient pamphlet he had indicated.

"I'll see you tonight after the show", I said.

As I closed the door behind me, I thought I saw in Lathrop's eyes that same look of fear I had seen in Delia's. But it was deeper, much deeper. And only then did I remember that not once during our interview had Jock Lathrop taken his hands out of his pockets.

Delia rushed up to me. I could tell she had been crying.

"What will we do, George—what will we do? What did he say to you? What did he tell you?"

I had to admit that her hectic manner was consistent with Jock's theory of neurotic fancies.

"Is it true, Delia," I asked abruptly, "that he's been urging you to see a psychoanalyst?"

"Why, yes." Then I saw her stiffen. "Jock's been telling you it's only my imagination, and you've been believing him", she accused.

"No, that's not it," I lied, "but I want to have time to think it all over. I'm coming to the performance tonight. I'll talk with you then."

"He *has* persuaded you! " she insisted, clinging to my sleeve. "But you mustn't believe him, George. He's afraid of them! He's in worse trouble than I am."

"I agree with you partly", I said, not knowing this time whether I was lying or not, "and after the performance we'll talk it over."

She suddenly drew away. Her face had lost something of its helpless look.

"If you won't help me," she said, breathing heavily, "I know

144

a way of finding out whether I'm right or wrong. A sure way."

"What do you mean, Delia?"

"Tonight," she said huskily, "you may find out."

More than that she wouldn't say, although I pressed her. I took away with me a vision of her distraught grey eyes, contrasted oddly with the thick sweep of golden hair. I hurried through the hall, down the stairs. The measured pandemonium of Forty-second Street was welcome. It was good to see so many people, walk with them, be jostled by them and forget the fantastic fears of Delia and Jock Lathrop.

I glanced at the pamphlet in my hand. The type was ancient and irregular. The paper was crumbly at the edges. I read the lengthy title:

A TRUE ACCOUNT, as related by a Notable Personage to a Trustworthy Gentleman, of the CIRCUMSTANCES attending the Life and DEATH of JOCKEY LOW-THROPE, an Englishman who gave PUPPET SHEWS; telling how many surmised that his Death was encompassed by these same PUPPETS.

Night was sliding in over New York. My office was a mass of shadows. From where I was sitting I could see the mammoth Empire State Building topping the irregular skyline.

I rubbed my eyes wearily. But that did not keep my thoughts from their endless circling. Who was I to believe? Delia or Jock? Was there a disordered mind at work, fabricating monstrous suspicions? And if so, whose mind was it? They were questions outside the usual province of a private detective.

I tilted the pamphlet to catch the failing light and re-read two passages that had particularly impressed me.

At this Time it was rumoured that Jockey Lowthrope had made a Pact with the Devil, with a view to acquiring greater Skill in his Trade. There were many who testified privately that his Puppets acted and moved with a Cunning beyond the ability of Christian Man to accomplish. For Jockey took no assistants and would explain to no one how his Manikins were activated. . . .

Some say that Moll Squires and the French Doctor did not tell all they saw when they first viewed Jockey's Corpse.

Certain it was that a long, thin Needle pierced his Heart and that both Hands were hacked off at the Wrists. Jockey's wife Lucy would have been held for Trial for Murder at the Assizes, only that she was never seen afterwards. Moll Squires averred that the Devil had come to fetch Jockey's hands, to which he had previous granted an unholy Skill. But many maintain that he was slain by his own Puppets, who chose the Needle as being a Weapon suitable to their Size and Dexterity. These recall how the Clergyman Penrose inveighed against Jockey, saying "Those are not Puppets, but Imps of Satan, and whosoever views them is in Danger of Damnation."

I pushed the pamphlet to one side. What could one make of events that had happened one hundred and fifty years ago—faint reverberations from the eighteenth-century fear-world that had underlaid the proud Age of Reason? Especially when one read of them in an account obviously written for the sake of sensation-mongering?

True, the names were oddly similar, Lowthrope and Lathrop were undoubtedly alternate spellings. And from what Jock Lathrop had said he had further evidence of a blood relationship.

The pamphlet angered me, made me feel as if someone were trying to frighten me with nursery tales of ghosts and goblins.

I switched on the light and blinked at the electric clock. It was seven forty-five. . . .

When I reached the puppet theatre it was buzzing with conversation and the hall outside was already blue with cigarette smoke. Just as I was getting my ticket from the sad-eyed girl at the door, someone called my name. I looked up and saw Dr. Grendal. I could tell that the garrulous old man had something on his mind besides his shiny, bald pate. After a few aimless remarks he asked his question.

"Seen Jock recently since he got back from London?"

"Just to say hello to", I answered cautiously.

"How'd he impress you, hey?" The doctor's eyes glanced sharply from behind their silver-rimmed spectacles.

"A little uneasy", I admitted. "Temperamental."

"I thought you might say something like that", he commented, as he led me over to an empty corner. "Fact is," he continued, "I think he's definitely queer. Between ourselves, of course. He

146

called me in. I thought he needed me in a professional capacity. But it turned out he wanted to talk about pygmies."

He couldn't have surprised me more.

"Pygmies?" I repeated.

"Just so. Pygmies. Surprised you, didn't it? Did me, too. Well, Jock was especially curious about the lower limits of possible size of mature human beings. Kept asking if there were any cases in which they were as small as puppets. I told him it was impossible, except for infants and embryos.

"Then he began shifting the conversation. Wanted to know a lot about blood relationship and the inheritance of certain traits. Wanted to know all about identical twins and triplets and so on. Evidently thought I'd be a mine of data because of the monographs I've scribbled about medical oddities. I answered as best I could, but some of his questions were queer. Power of mind over matter, and that sort of stuff. I got the impression his nerves were about to crack. Told him as much. Whereupon he told me to get out. Peculiar, hey?"

I could not answer. Dr. Grendal's information put new life into the disturbing notions I had been trying to get out of my mind. I wondered how much I dared tell the old physician, or whether it would be unwise to confide in him at all.

The people in the hall were moving into the theatre. I made a noncommittal remark to Grendal and we followed. A rotund figure pushed in ahead of us, muttering—Luigi Franetti. Evidently he had not been able to resist the temptation presented by his former student's puppets. He threw down the price of the ticket contemptuously, as if it were the thirty pieces of silver due Judas Iscariot. Then he stamped in, sat down, folded his arms, and glared at the curtain.

There must have been two hundred people present, almost a full house. I noticed quite a splash of evening dresses and dress suits. I didn't see Delia, but I noted the prim features of Dick Wilkinson, the insurance agent.

From behind the curtain came the reedy tinkle of a musical box—tones suggestive of a doll orchestra. The seats Grendal and I had were near the front, but considerably to one side.

The little theatre grew dim. A soft illumination flowed up the square of red silk curtain. The melody from the musical box ended on a note so high it sounded as though something in the mechanism had snapped. A pause. The deep, sombre reverberation

147

of a gong. Another pause. Then a voice, which I recognized as Lathrop's pitched in falsetto.

"Ladies and gentlemen, for your entertainment Lathrop's Puppets present—Punch and Judy!"

From behind me I heard Franetti's "Bah!"

Then the curtain parted and slid rustling to the sides. Punch popped up like a jack-in-the-box, chuckled throatily, and began to antic around the stage and make bitingly witty remarks, some of them at the expense of the spectators.

It was the same puppet Jock had let me examine in the workshop. But was Jock's hand inside? After a few seconds I quit worrying about that. This, I told myself, was only an ordinary puppet show, as clever as the manipulations were. The voice was Jock Lathrop's, pitched in puppeteer's falsetto.

It is ironic that Punch and Judy is associated with children and the nursery, for few plays are more fundamentally sordid. Modern child educators are apt to fling up their hands at mention of it. It is unlike any fairy tale or phantasy, but springs from forthright realistic crime.

Punch is the prototype of the egotistical, brutish criminal—the type who today figures as an axefiend or mad-dog slayer. He kills his squalling baby and nagging wife, Judy, merely because they annoy him. He kills the doctor because he doesn't like the medicine. He kills the policeman who comes to arrest him. Finally, after he is thrown into jail and sentenced to death, he manages to outwit and murder the fearsome executioner Jack Ketch.

Only in the end does the devil come to fetch him, and in some versions Punch kills the devil. During all these crimes Punch seldom loses his grim and trenchant sense of humour.

Punch and Judy has long been one of the most popular puppet plays. Perhaps the reason children like it is that they have fewer moral inhibitions than grown-ups to prevent them from openly sympathizing with Punch's primal selfishness. For Punch is as thoughtlessly selfish and cruel as a spoiled child.

These thoughts passed rapidly through my mind, as they always do when I see or think of Punch and Judy. This time they brought with them a vivid memory of Jock Lathrop whipping the puppet.

I have said that the beginning of the play reassured me. But as it progressed, my thoughts crept back. The movements of the

148

puppets were too smooth and clever for my liking. They handled things too naturally.

There is a great deal of clubbing in Punch and Judy, and the puppets always hold on to their clubs by hugging them between their arms—the thumb and second finger of the puppeteer. But Jock Lathrop had made a startling innovation. His puppets held their weapons as a man normally does. I wondered if this could be due to some special device.

Hurriedly I got out my opera glasses and turned them on the stage. It was some time before I could focus one of the puppets; they jerked about too much. Finally I got a clear view of Punch's arms. As far as I could make out, they ended in tiny hands— hands that could shift on the club, clenching and unclenching in an uncannily natural way.

Grendal mistook my smothered exclamation for one of admiration.

"Pretty clever", he said, nodding.

After that I sat still. Of course the tiny hands were only some sort of mechanical attachment to Lathrop's fingertips. And here, I thought, was the reason for Delia's fears. She had been taken in by the astonishing realism of the puppets.

But then how to explain Jock's actions, the strange questions he had put to Dr. Grendal? Merely an attempt to create publicity?

It was hard for a "hard-boiled sleuth" to admit, even to himself, that he did have an odd feeling that those manikins were alive. But I did, and I fought against this feeling, turning my eyes from the stage.

Then I saw Delia. She was sitting in the row behind and two chairs further to the side. There was nothing of the "softie Viking" about her now, despite the glimmering, curving lines of her silver lamé evening dress. In the ghostly illumination from the stage, her lovely face was cold, stony, with a set determination that made me apprehensive.

I heard a familiar mutter and turned to see Franetti moving down the far aisle as if the stage were drawing him like a magnet. He was glaring at the puppets and talking to himself.

Twice I heard him mutter, "Impossible!" Patrons gave him irritated looks as he passed or murmured complainingly. He took no notice. He reached the end of the aisle and disappeared through the black curtained doorway that led backstage.

Rapidly the play was drawing towards its climax. Punch, in a dark and dismal prison, was whining and wailing in self-pity. Jack Ketch was approaching from one side, his face and black hair hideous in the dim light. In one hand he carried a noose; in the other, a needlelike sword about five inches long. He brandished both dexterously.

I could no longer view the scene in a matter-of-fact way. This was a doll-world, where all the dolls were brutes and murderers. The stage was reality, viewed through the wrong end of a telescope.

Then came an ominous rustle behind me. I turned. Delia had risen to her feet. Something was gleaming in her upraised hand. There was a sharp crack, like a whip. Before anyone could stop her she emptied the chambers of a small revolver at the stage.

On the fourth shot I saw a black hole appear in Punch's mask.

Delia did not struggle against the bewildered men who had risen to pinion her hands. She was staring fixedly at the stage. So was I. For I knew what she hoped to prove by those shots.

Punch had disappeared, but not Jack Ketch. He seemed to be staring back at Delia, as if the shots had been an expected part of the performance. Then the high tuning voice screamed, a reedy scream of hate. And it was not Jock Lathrop's falsetto voice that screamed. Then Jack Ketch raised his needlelike sword and plunged down out of sight.

The scream that followed was a full-voiced cry of desperate agony that silenced and froze the milling audience. And this time it was Jock's voice.

Hurriedly I pushed my way toward the curtained door. Old Grendal was close behind me. The first thing that caught my eye in the backstage confusion was the trembling form of Luigi Franetti. His face was like wax. He was on his knees, murmuring garbled prayers.

Then, sprawled on his back beneath the puppet-stage, I saw Lathrop.

Hysterical questions gave way to shocked whispers, which mounted to a chorus as others swarmed backstage.

"Look! He's dead—the man that works the puppets! "

"She got him all right! Fired through the curtains underneath! "

"I saw her do it myself. She shot him a dozen times."

"Somebody said she's his wife."

"She got him on the last shot. I heard him scream. She's crazy."

I understood the mistake they were making, for I knew that everyone of Delia's shots had hit above stage level. I walked over to Jack Lathrop's body. And it was with the shock of my life that I saw that Jack Ketch's pygmy sword had been driven to the hilt in Lathrop's right eyeball. And on Jock Lathrop's right and left hands were the garments and papiermâché heads of Punch and Jack Ketch.

Grendal hastened forward and knelt at Lathrop's side. The chorus of frightened whispers behind us kept rising and falling in a kind of mob rhythm. The drab insurance agent Wilkinson stepped up and peered over Grendal's shoulders. Indrawn breath whistled between his teeth. He turned around slowly and pointed at Franetti.

"Mr. Lathrop was not shot, but stabbed", he said in a curiously calm voice that caught the crowd's ear. "I saw that man sneak back here. He murdered Mr. Lathrop. He was the only one who could have done it. Get hold of him, some of you, and take him out front."

Franetti offered no resistance. He looked dazed and helpless.

"The rest of you had better wait out front too", Wilkinson continued. "I shall telephone the police. See to it that Mrs. Lathrop is not troubled or annoyed. She is hysterical. Do not allow her to come back here."

There was a rustle of hushed interjections and questions but the crowd flowed back into the theatre. Wilkinson, Grendal, and myself were left alone.

"There's no hope, is there?" I managed to say.

Grendal shook his head.

"He's dead as a nail. The tiny instrument penetrated the eyesocket and deep into the brain. Happened to be driven in exactly the proper direction."

I looked down at Lathrop's twisted body. Even now I could hardly repress a shudder at the sight of the puppets. The vindictive expressions on their masks looked so purposeful. I regarded the bullet hole in Punch's mask. A little blood was welling from it. The bullet must have nicked Lathrop's finger.

At that moment I became aware of a confused surge of footsteps outside, and of the crowd's whispering, muffled by the intervening hangings, rising to a new crescendo.

"Look out, she's getting away!"

"She's running! Stop her."

"Has she still got the gun?"

"She's going back there. Grab her, somebody! "

The black draperies eddied wildly as Delia spun through the door, jerking loose from a hand that had sought to restrain her. In a swirl of golden hair and shimmering silver lamé she came in. I glimpsed her wild grey eyes, white-circled.

"*They* killed him, I tell you, *they* killed him! " she screamed, "Not me. Not Franetti. *They!* I killed one. Oh, Jock, Jock, are you dead?"

She ran towards the corpse. Then came the final nightmare.

The arms of blue-faced Jack Ketch began to writhe, and from the puppet-mask came squealing, malevolent laughter.

Delia, about to fling her arms around her dead husband, slid to the floor on her knees. A sigh of horror issued from her throat. The silver lamé billowed down around her. And still the puppet tittered and squealed, as if mocking her and triumphing over her.

"Pull those blasted things off his hands! " I heard myself crying. "Pull them off! "

It was Wilkinson who did it, not the feebly pawing Dr. Grendal. Wilkinson didn't realize what was happening.

He was still convinced that Franetti was the murderer. He obeyed automatically. He seized the papiermâché heads roughly, and jerked.

Then I knew how Jock Lathrop had died. I knew why he had been so secretive, why the ancient pamphlet had affected him so profoundly. I realized that Delia's suspicions had been correct, though not what she had believed. I knew why Jock Lathrop had asked Grendal those peculiar questions. I knew why the puppets had been so realistic. I knew why Jockey Lowthrope had had his hands hacked off. I knew why Jock Lathrop had never let anyone see his own ungloved hands, after that "change" had begun in London.

The little finger and ring finger on each of his hands were normal. The others—the ones used in motivating a puppet—were not. Replacing the thumb and second finger were tiny muscular arms. The first finger was in each case a tiny, wormlike body, of the general shape of a finger, but with a tiny sphincterlike mouth and two diminutive, malformed eyes that were all black pupil. One was dead by Delia's bullet. The other was not. I crushed it under my heel. . . .

Among Jock Lathrop's papers was found the following note, penned in longhand, and evidently written within a few days of the end:

If I die, *they* have killed me. For I am sure they hate me. I have tried to confide in various people, but have been unable to go through with it. I feel compelled to secrecy. Perhaps that is *their* desire, for *their* power over my actions is growing greater every day. Delia would loathe me if she knew. And she suspects.

I thought I would go mad in London, when my injured fingers began to heal with a *new* growth. A monstrous growth —that were my brothers who were engulfed in my flesh at the time of my birth and did not begin to develop until now! Had they been developed and born at the proper time, we would have been triplets. But the *mode* of that development now!

Human flesh is subject to horrible perversions. Can my thoughts and activities as a puppeteer have had a determining influence? Have I influenced their minds until those minds are really those of Punch and Jack Ketch?

And what I read in that old pamphlet. Hands hacked off. . . . Could my ancestor's pact with the devil have given him his fiendish skill? Given him the monstrous growth which led to his ruin? Could this physical characteristic have been inherited, lying dormant until such time as another Lathrop, another puppeteer, summoned it forth by his ambitious desires?

I don't know. What I do know is that as long as I live I am the world's greatest puppeteer—but at what cost! I hate *them*, and *they* hate me. I can hardly control them. Last night one of them clawed Delia while I slept. Even now, when my mind wondered for a moment, the *one* turned the pen and tried to drive it into my wrist. . . .

I did not scoff at the questions that Jock Lathrop had asked himself. I might have at one time. But I had seen *them*, and I had seen the tiny sword driven into Lathrop's eye. No, I'm not going to spend any more time trying to figure out the black mystery behind the amazing skill of Jock Lathrop. I'm going to spend it trying to make Delia forget.

153

Levitation

Hypnotism remains one of the great puzzles of our times—a mystery that is as widely exploited by frauds as it is studied by genuine believers. What the author of this story's particular feelings are, I cannot say—although we might well form some conclusions from his tale—but he does make it quite clear that you are ill-advised to meddle with things you do not understand.

THE RISING MAN

By Joseph Payne Brennan

Morgan's Wonder Carnival moved into Riverville for an overnight stand, setting up its tents in the big ball park on the edge of the village. It was a warm evening in early October and by seven o'clock a sizeable crowd had made its way to the scene of raucous amusement.

The travelling show was neither large nor particularly impressive of its type, but its appearance was eagerly welcomed in Riverville, an isolated mountain community many miles from the motion picture houses, vaudeville theatres and sports arenas situated in larger towns.

The natives of Riverville did not demand sophisticated entertainment; consequently the inevitable Fat Lady, the Tattooed Man and the Monkey Boy kept them chattering animatedly for many minutes at a time. They crammed peanuts and buttered popcorn into their mouths, drank cup after cup of pink lemonade, and got their fingers all but stuck together trying to scrape the paper wrappers off coloured taffy candies.

Everyone appeared to be in a relaxed and tolerant state of mind when the barker for the Hypnotist began his spiel. The barker, a short stocky man wearing a checkered suit, bellowed through an improvised megaphone, while the Hypnotist himself remained aloof at the rear of the plank platform erected in front of his tent. He appeared disinterested, scornful, and he scarcely deigned to glance at the gathering crowd.

At length, however, when some fifty souls had assembled in front of the platform, he stepped forward into the light. A murmur went up from the crowd.

In the harsh overhead electric glare, the Hypnotist made a striking appearance. His tall figure, thin to the point of emaciation, his pale complexion, and most of all his dark, sunken eyes, enormous and brilliant, compelled immediate attention. His dress, a

155

severe black suit and an archaic black string tie, added a final Mephistophelean touch.

He surveyed the crowd coolly, with an expression betraying resignation and a kind of quiet contempt.

His sonorous voice reached to the far edge of the throng. "I will require one volunteer from among you," he said. "If someone will kindly step up—"

Everyone glanced around, or nudged his neighbour, but nobody advanced towards the platform.

The Hypnotist shrugged. "There can be no demonstration," he said in a weary voice, "unless one of you is kind enough to come up. I assure you, ladies and gentlemen, the demonstration is quite harmless, quite without danger."

He looked around expectantly and presently a young man slowly elbowed through the crowd towards the platform.

The Hypnotist helped him up the steps and seated him in a chair.

"Relax", said the Hypnotist. "Presently you will be asleep and you will do exactly what I tell you to do."

The young man squirmed on the chair, grinning self-consciously towards the crowd.

The Hypnotist caught his attention, fixing his enormous eyes on him, and the young man stopped squirming.

Suddenly someone in the crowd threw a large ball of coloured popcorn towards the platform. The popcorn arced over the lights, landing squarely atop the head of the young man sitting in the chair.

He jerked sideways, almost falling off the chair, and the crowd, quiet a moment before, guffawed boisterously.

The Hypnotist was furious. He turned scarlet and literally shook with rage as he glared at the crowd.

"Who threw that?" he demanded in a choking voice.

The crowd grew silent.

The Hypnotist continued to glare at them. At length the colour left his face and he stopped trembling, but his brilliant eyes remained baleful.

Finally he nodded to the young man seated on the platform, dismissing him with brief thanks, and turned again towards the crowd.

"Due to the interruption," he announced in a low voice, "it will be necessary to recommence the demonstration—with a new subject. Perhaps the person who threw the popcorn would care to come up?"

At least a dozen people in the crowd turned to gaze at someone who stood half in shadow at the rear of the gathering.

The Hypnotist spotted him at once; his dark eyes seemed to smoulder. "Perhaps," he said in a purring, mocking voice, "the one who interrupted is afraid to come up. He prefers to hide in the shadows and throw popcorn!"

The culprit voiced a sudden exclamation and then pushed belligerently towards the platform. His appearance was not in any way remarkable; in fact, he somewhat resembled the first young man, and any casual observer would have placed the two of them in the farm-labourer class, neither was more nor less capable than the average.

The second young man sat down in the platform chair with a distinct air of defiance and for some minutes visibly fought the Hynotist's suggestion to relax. Presently, however, his aggressiveness disappeared and he dutifully stared into the smouldering eyes opposite his own.

In another minute or two he arose at the Hypnotist's command and lay flat on his back on the hard planks of the platform. The crowd gasped.

"You will fall asleep", the Hypnotist told him. "You will fall asleep. You are falling asleep. You are falling asleep. You are asleep and you will do anything which I command you to do. Anything which I command you to do. Anything . . ."

His voice droned on, repeating repetitious phrases, and the crowd grew perfectly silent.

Suddenly a new note entered the Hypnotist's voice and the audience became tense.

"Do not stand up—but *rise from the platform!*" the Hypnotist commanded. *"Rise from the platform!"* His dark eyes became wild and luminous-looking and the crowd shivered.

"Rise!"

Then the crowd drew its collective breath with an audible start.

The young man lying rigid on the platform, without moving a muscle, began to ascend horizontally. He arose slowly, almost imperceptibly at first, but soon with a steady and unmistakable acceleration.

"Rise!" the Hypnotist's voice rang out.

The young man continued to ascend, until he was feet off the platform, and still he did not stop.

The crowd was sure it was some kind of trick, but in spite of themselves they stared open-mouthed. The young man appeared to be suspended and moving in mid-air without any possible means of physical support.

Abruptly the focus of the crowd's attention was shifted; the Hypnotist clasped a hand to his chest, staggered, and crumpled to the platform.

There were calls for a doctor. The barker in the chequered suit appeared out of the tent and bent over the motionless form.

He felt for a pulse, shook his head and straightened up. Some-one offered a bottle of whisky, but he merely shrugged.

Suddenly a woman in the crowd screamed.

Everyone turned to look at her and a second later followed the direction of her gaze.

Immediately there were further cries—for the young man whom the Hypnotist had put to sleep was still ascending. While the crowd's attention had been distracted by the fatal collapse of the Hypnotist, he had continued to rise. He was now a good seven feet above the platform and moving inexorably upwards. Even after the death of the Hypnotist, he continued to obey that final ringing command: *"Rise!"*

The barker, eyes all but popping out of his head, made a frantic upwards leap, but he was too short. His fingers barely brushed the moving figure above and he fell heavily back to the platform.

The rigid form of the young man continued to float upwards, as if he were being hoisted by some kind of invisible pulley.

Women began screaming hysterically; men shouted. But no one knew what to do. A look of terror crept over the face of the barker as he stared up. Once he glanced wildly towards the sprawled shape of the Hypnotist.

"Come down, Frank! Come down!" the crowd shrieked. "Frank! Wake up! Come down! Stop! Frank!"

But the rigid form of Frank moved ever upwards. Up, up, until he was level with the top of the carnival tent, until he reached the height of the tallest trees—until he passed the trees and moved on into the soft moonlit sky of early October.

Many in the crowd threw hands over horror-stricken faces and turned away.

Those who continued to stare saw the floating form ascend into the sky until it was no more than a tiny speck, like a little cinder drifting far up near the moon.

Then it disappeared altogether.

Mind Reader

One might well expect the most unusual story in a collection of the unusual to come from John Wyndham, and that is my estimation of the quality of "Jizzle". Here the master displays his wondrous talents in the strange tale of a side-showman who buys a monkey with the most extraordinary powers. Powers which I think none of us would care to encounter!

JIZZLE

By John Wyndham

The first thing that Ted Torby saw, when his reluctant eyelids had gathered enough strength to raise themselves, seemed to be a monkey, perched on the top of the cupboard, watching him. He sat bolt upright with a jerk that joggled Rosie awake and shook the whole trailer.

"Oh, God!" he said. It was a tone which held more of depressed realization than surprise.

He closed his eyes, and then looked again, hard. The monkey was still there, staring from round, dark eyes.

"What's the matter?" Rosie asked sleepily. Then she saw the direction of his gaze. "Oh, that! Serves you right."

"It's real?" said Ted.

"Of course it's real. And lie down. You've pulled all the bed-clothes off me."

Ted leant back, keeping his eyes fixed warily on the monkey. Slowly, and hindered by a painful throbbing in his head, memories of the evening began to reassemble.

"I'd forgotten", he said.

"I don't wonder—seeing the way you came home", said Rosie, dispassionately. "I expect you've got a lovely head", she added with a slightly sadistic shading.

Ted did not answer. He was remembering about the monkey.

"How much did you give for that?" asked Rosie, nodding at it.

"Couple o' quid", said Ted.

"Two pounds for *that*", she said with disgust. "And you call your customers mugs!"

Ted made no response. In point of fact, it had been ten pounds, but he did not feel equal to meeting the storm that the admission would arouse. And he'd beaten the man down from fifteen, so it was a bargain. A big negro he was, speaking a nautical form of English heavily adulterated with some kind of French. He had made his brief entry into Ted's life while the latter was in the Gate and Goat soothing his hard-worked throat after the evening's toil. Ted had not been greatly interested. He had, in his time, refused to buy all manner of things in bars, from bootlaces to ferrets. But the negro had been quietly persistent. Somehow he had got himself into the position of standing Ted a drink, and after that he had the advantage. Ted's protests that he had nothing to do with the circus proper, and that he was utterly indifferent to its fauna, save for such rats as occasionally ventured into the trailer, made no impression at all. The man's conviction that every person connected with the showground must have an encyclopaedic knowledge of the whole brute creation was unshakable: all protestation was merely a form of sales-resistance. He had then proceeded to talk with such animation across several relays of drinks of the attainments and charming qualities of something he referred to as *ma petite Giselle* that Ted had found it necessary to remind himself from time to time that the subject had not shifted beneath their tongues, and it was still a monkey that was under discussion.

In a way, it was hard luck on the negro that he should have chosen Ted for his approach, since Ted himself had been spending the earlier part of the evening in persuading the reluctant to part with half-crowns of known qualities in exchange for bottles of merely hypothetical virtue. But Ted was not mean-minded. He followed the technique with the attention of a connoisseur, and was prepared to concede that the negro wasn't doing too badly, for an amateur. Nevertheless, it was scarcely to be expected that even the utmost fervour and intensity could win more than his detached, and unprofitable, professional approval. Rosie's crack about mugs had more spite than substance. The matter should have ended there, with the negro butting at the immovable. Indeed, there it would have ended had not the negro added a new accomplishment to the list of his Giselle's remarkable qualities.

Ted had smiled. Sooner or later the amateur always overreaches himself. It was safe enough to say that the creature was clean, attractive, intelligent, for these qualities are conveniently relative. It was not dangerous even to say that it was "educated" —there being no public examination to set a standard of simian learning. But in making a definite claim which could be put to the test, the negro's inexperience was laying him wide open to trouble.

At that point Ted had agreed to go to see the prodigy. The concession was almost altruistic: he did not believe a word of it, but neither did he mean trouble. He was the man of experience showing the promising beginner the kind of trouble he *might* have landed himself in by a simple divergence from the debatable to the disprovable.

It had been quite a shock, therefore, to find that the monkey was fully up to specification.

Ted had watched it, first patronizingly, then incredulously, and finally with an excitement which it required all his skill in deadpanning to disguise. Casually he offered five pounds. The negro asked the ludicrous sum of fifteen. Ted would willingly have given fifty had it been necessary. In the end they compromised on ten and a bottle of whisky that Ted had intended to take home. There had been one or two drinks from the bottle to clinch the deal. After that, nothing was very clear, but evidently he had got back somehow—and with the monkey.

"It's got fleas", said Rosie, wrinkling her nose.

"It's a female", said Ted. "And monkeys don't have fleas. They just do that."

"Well, if it isn't looking for fleas, what is it doing?"

"I read somewhere that it's something to do with perspiration —anyway, they all do it."

"I can't see that that's much better," said Rosie.

The monkey broke away from its interests for a moment, and looked seriously at both of them. Then it gave a kind of snickering noise.

"What's it do that for?" Rosie asked.

"How would I know? They just do."

Ted lay and contemplated the monkey for a while. It was predominantly light brown, shot with occasional silver. Its limbs and tail seemed curiously long for its body. From a black, wrinkled face in a round, low-browed head two large eyes, looking like black glass marbles with sorrowful depths, scrutinized first one and then the other with such directness that one almost expected it to produce some sign of opinion. However, it merely returned to its own interests with an indifference which was in itself vaguely offensive.

Rosie continued to regard it without favour.

"Where are you going to keep it? I'm not going to have it in here."

163

"Why not?" asked Ted. "She's quite clean."

"How do you know? You were tight when you bought it."

"I got tight *after* I'd bought her. And don't keep on calling her *it*. She's a her. You get annoyed with me when I call a baby it, and it's probably a lot more important to monkeys than it is to babies. And her name's Jizzle."

"Jizzle?" repeated Rosie.

"A French name", Ted explained.

Rosie remained unimpressed. "All the same, I don't hold with keeping her here. It's not decent."

Jizzle was at the moment in a complicated and unornamental attitude. She had disposed her right foot round her neck, and was absorbed in an intense study of the back of her right knee.

"She's no ordinary monkey—she's educated", said Ted.

"Educated she may be, but she's not refined. Look at her now."

"What——? Oh, well, monkeys, you know——" Ted said vaguely. "But I'll show you how educated she is. Worth a fortune. You watch."

There could be no doubt whatever: one demonstration was enough to convince the most prejudiced that Jizzle was a gold mine.

"I wonder why he sold it—her?" said Rosie. "He could have made a fortune."

"I guess he just wasn't a showman—or a business man", Ted added.

After breakfast he went out of the trailer and looked at his stand. It had an inscription across the front:

Dr. Steven's
Psychological Stimulator

About the rostrum boldly lettered posters asked:

Is Hesitation Hindering Your Career?
Is Your Mind a Flip-Flap?

or stated:

A Steady Mind is a Ready Mind
Planned Thinking Pays
Snap Beats Flap

164

and advised:

Direct Your Own Destiny
Mobilize Mentally and Make Money
Plan Your Prosperity

For the first time the array failed to please him. Also for the first time he was astonished to think of the number of half-crowns it had helped to draw in exchange for the Omni-potent Famous World-Unique Mental Tonic.

"May as well ditch this lot", he said. "We'll need a tent with benches and a stage."

Then he went back to the trailer, and turned Rosie out.

"I got to think", he explained. "I got to work out the patter and the publicity, and we'll get you a new dress for the act."

The try-out took place a couple of days later before a critical audience drawn from the profession. It included Joe Dindell, more widely known as El Magnifico of Magnifico and His Twenty Man-Eating Lions, Dolly Brag or Gipsy Clara, George Haythorpe from the Rifle-Range, Pearl Verity (*née* Jedd), the Only Authentic Three-Legged Woman in the World, and a sprinkling of others from both the main and side shows.

The tent was not as large as Ted would have liked, and incapable of seating more than sixty persons, but better things would come. Meanwhile, he made his appearance before the curtain and delivered the build-up as though he addressed the rising tiers in a super-cinema. It was in the approved style of superlative, and when it ended with the phrase: "—and now, Ladies and Gentlemen, I present to you the greatest—the unbelievable—the supreme wonder of the animal world—JIZZLE!" the applause had a quality of discriminating appreciation.

As Ted concluded he had moved to the left. Now, as the curtains drew away, he turned, left hand extended towards the centre of the stage. Rosie, having hurriedly fixed the curtain, tripped a few steps on from the other side, stopped with her knees bent in a species of curtsy, projected charm at the audience, and extended her right hand to the centre of the stage. Between them stood an easel bearing a large pad of white paper and beside it, on a square table with a red-fringed top, sat Jizzle. She was clad in a bright yellow dress, and a pill-box hat with a curled red

165

feather: for the moment she had pulled the dress aside, and was searching beneath it with great application.

Both Ted's smile and Rosie's were property affairs which could have deceived no one. A few minutes earlier she had flatly and finally declined to wear the new dress he had designed for her.

"I don't care", she said. "I've told you I won't, and I won't. You can dress your beastly monkey how you like, but you won't make me dress like it. I'm surprised at you asking it. Whoever heard of a man dressing his wife like a monkey?"

It was in vain that Ted protested she had it the wrong way round. Rosie's mind was made up. She would appear in the costume in which she was accustomed to hand out bottles of the Psychological Stimulator, or not at all. To Ted's mind it pettily ruined his whole carefully planned effect. It was unfortunate that her brown hair was of much the same shade as the dominant colour of Jizzle's fur, but merely a coincidence.

Ted, after a few more high commendations of his protégée, moved over to the easel and stood beside it, facing the house. Rosie advanced, shifted the table with Jizzle upon it in front of the easel, and handed something to the monkey. Almost before she was able to bob and beam and resume her place, Jizzle was on her feet with her left hand holding on to the side of the pad, her right hand drawing swiftly. An astonished muttering broke out among the spectators. Her technique would not have met with approval in art-schools, and it gave a certain simian flavour, hitherto unnoticed in her subject by others, but the final likeness to Ted was indisputable. Sheer amazement made the applause a trifle slow in starting, but when it came it was wholehearted.

Ted tore off the sheet and moved away, graciously waving Rosie into his place. She took it with a smile that was resolutely fixed. Ted pinned his picture at the back of the stage while Jizzle drew again. Once again the likeness was remarkable, though perhaps the simian quality was a shade more to the fore. Ted felt that from the domestic angle it was possibly just as well after all that Rosie had not worn the dress. Even so, the audience's laugh put Rosie's professional expression to a test which it only just survived.

"Now, if any lady or gentleman in the audience—?" suggested Ted.

Joe Dindell was the first to oblige. Powerful and massive, he

166

stalked on to the stage to take up one of his best El Magnifico poses beside the easel.

Ted continued to try out his patter while Jizzle drew. She needed no persuasion. The moment one sheet was torn off she started on the next as if the plain paper were an irresistible invitation to doodle between clients. Once or twice Ted let her finish, making it clear that she was able to repeat from memory as well as draw from direct observation. By the end of the show the stage was decorated with portraits of the whole of the small audience who were clustered round, wringing Ted's hand, predicting overwhelming success, and inspecting Jizzle as if they were even yet not quite convinced of what they had seen. The only person who held a little aloof in the celebration which followed was Rosie. She sat sipping her drink and speaking little. From time to time she turned a gloomy, speculative look on the self-occupied Jizzle.

Rosie found it difficult to be clear in her own mind whether she disliked Jizzle because she was unnatural, or because she was too natural. Both were, in her view, sound bases for distaste. Jizzle was abnormal, a freak, and it was natural to feel that way about a freak—except, of course, those like Pearle whom one knew well. On the other hand, certain franknesses which would have been unperturbing in a dog, became embarrassing when displayed by a creature, and particularly a female creature, which providence had privileged to be at least a kind of burlesque of the form divine. There was also Jizzle's attitude. It was true that monkeys often snickered: it was true that by the law of averages some of these snickers must be ill-timed—but still . . .

All the same, Jizzle became the third occupant of the trailer.

"She's going to be worth thousands of pounds to us—and that means she's worth thousands to others, too", Ted pointed out. "We can't risk having her pinched. And we can't risk her getting ill, either. Monkeys need warm places to live in." Which was all quite true; and so Jizzle stayed.

From the first performance of the act, there was not an instant's doubt of its success. Ted raised the admission from one shilling to one-and-six, and then to two shillings, and the price of a Jizzle "original" from half a crown to five shillings without any loss of patronage. He opened negotiations for a larger tent.

Rosie tolerated her position as handmaiden for just one week, and then struck. The audience laughed at each of Jizzle's drawings, but Rosie's sensitive ear detected a different note when they saw the portrait of her. It rankled.

"It—she makes me look more monkey-like every time. I believe she does it on purpose", she said. "I won't stand there and be made a fool of by a monkey."

"Darling, that's sheer imagination. All her drawing is a bit monkeyish—after all, it's only natural", Ted remonstrated.

"It's more so when it's me."

"Now, do be reasonable, darling. What would it matter anyway, even if it were so?"

"So you don't mind your wife being jeered at by a monkey?"

"But that's ridiculous, Rosie. You'll get used to her. She's a nice friendly little thing, really."

"She isn't, not to me. She keeps on watching and spying on me all the time."

"Come now, darling, hang it all——"

"I don't care what you say, she does. She just sits there watching and snickering. I suppose she's got to live in the trailer; I'll have to put up with that, but I've had enough of her in the act. You can do without me. If you must have someone, get Irene from the Hoop-La. *She* won't mind."

Ted was genuinely distressed, and more at the troubled state of the larger partnership than the breaking up of the act. It was indisputable that something had happened, and kept on happening, to it since Jizzle's arrival. It took the gilt off a lot of things. He and Rosie had always got along so well together. He had wanted her to have more pleasures and comforts than the returns from Dr. Steven's Stimulator could provide; and now that the big chance had come, discord had arrived with it. No one acquiring such a valuable property as Jizzle could afford not to exploit her properly. Rosie was perfectly well aware of that—but, well, women got such queer fixed ideas . . . Upon that, he had an idea himself. He made a discreet search to discover if Rosie had been sewing any small garments in secret—apparently she had not.

Business thrived. Ted's show was promoted to mention on the advance bills. Jizzle also thrived, and settled in. She took to Ted's left shoulder as her favourite perch, which was somehow slightly flattering, and also had publicity value, but domestically things went the other way. Little was to be seen of Rosie during the day. She seemed always to be helping, or drinking cups of tea, in some other caravan. If Ted had to go out on business he had to shut

168

Jizzle up in the trailer alone when he felt that both her safety and her well-being demanded someone to look after her. But his single suggestion that Rosie might act as guardian had met with so determined a rebuff that he did not like to repeat it. At night Rosie did her best to ignore Jizzle altogether; the monkey responded with sulky moods which broke on occasion into snickers. At such times Rosie would relinquish indifference, and glare at her angrily. She gave it as her opinion that even lions were more companionable creatures. But Rosie herself was far less companionable than before. Ted was aware of an uninterest and grudgingness in her that had never been there before, and he was puzzled; the money that now rolled in was by no means everything . . .

Had he not been a reasonable, clear-thinking man, he might have begun to feel some resentment against Jizzle himself . . .

The puzzle was to a great extent resolved on a night when Jizzle had already been an established success for six weeks. Ted came back to the trailer later than usual. He had had several drinks, but he was not drunk. He walked into the trailer with a sheet of paper rolled in his hand, and stood looking down at Rosie, who was already in bed.

"You——! " he said. He leaned over and smacked her face hard.

Rosie, startled out of a half-sleep, was as much bewildered as hurt. Ted glared down at her.

"Now I understand quite a lot. Spying on you, you said. God, what a mug I've been! No wonder you didn't want her around."

"What are you talking about?" Rosie demanded, tears in her eyes.

"You know. I expect everyone knows but me."

"But, Ted——"

"You can save your breath. Look at this! "

He unrolled the sheet of paper before her. Rosie stared at it. It was surprising how much obscene suggestion could reside in a few simple lines.

"While I was doing the patter", Ted said. "All sniggering their bloody heads off before I saw what was happening. Damn funny, isn't it?" He looked down at the drawing. There could not be a moment's doubt for any who knew them that the woman and man involved were Rosie and El Magnifico . . .

Rosie flushed to her hair. She jumped from the bed and made

a vicious grab at the top of the cupboard. Jizzle evaded her skilfully.

Ted caught her arm and jerked her back.

"It's too late for that now", he said.

The flush had gone, leaving her face white.

"Ted", she said, "you don't believe . . .?"

"Spying on you! " he repeated.

"But, Ted, I didn't mean . . ."

He slapped her again across the face.

Rosie caught her breath; her eyes narrowed.

"Damn you! *Damn you!*" she said, and went for him like a fury.

Ted reached one hand behind him and unlatched the door. He turned round with her, and thrust her outside. She stumbled down the three steps, tripped on the hem of her nightdress, and fell to the ground.

He slammed the door shut, and snapped the bolt.

Upon the cupboard Jizzle snickered. Ted threw a saucepan at her. She dodged it, and snickered again.

The next morning an air of concern spread outwards from the office where the manager and the ringmaster were considering the problem of finding at short notice a man of presence and intrepid appearance to take charge of the lion act. Quite half the day passed before anyone but Ted knew that Rosie also was missing.

Ted went through the next few days with remorse, putting increasing pressure on righteous anger. He had not realized what Rosie's absence would mean. He had done, as he saw it, the only thing a man could do in the circumstances—but very bitterly was he aware of the craven wish that he had never learnt the circumstances.

Jizzle's constant predilection for his shoulder as a perch became a source of irritation. He took to pushing her off impatiently. But for the damned monkey he never need have known about Rosie . . . He began to hate the sight of Jizzle . . .

For a week he continued to give the show, mechanically, but with increasing distaste; then he approached George Haythorpe of the Rifle-Range. George reckoned it could be done. Muriel, his wife, could easily manage the Range with a girl to help her; he himself was willing to take over Jizzle and run the act with Ted retaining a twenty per cent interest in the gross.

"That is," George added, "if the monkey'll stand for it. She seems mighty attached to you."

For a day or two that appeared to be the most doubtful aspect of the arrangement. Jizzle continued to attach herself to Ted, and to watch him rather than George for instruction. But gradually, by patient and repeated removal, the change in mastery was made plain to her, whereupon she sulked for two days before deciding to accept it.

It was a relief to be free of Jizzle—but it did not bring back Rosie. The trailer seemed emptier than ever . . . After a few days of morbid inactivity Ted took himself in hand. He pulled out his old stock, unrolled some of the old bills for the Psychological Stimulator, and lettered some new ones:

Modernize your Mentality
Confidence Creates Cash
A Keen Mind is a Key Mind

In a short while he was back at the old stand and the mugs were putting up their half-crowns with a will—but it still wasn't the same without Rosie handing out the bottles . . .

Jizzle had now settled in well with George. The act was on it feet again and playing to capacity, but Ted felt no tinge of jealousy or regret as he watched the crowds going in. Even his share of the takings brought him little pleasure; they still linked him with Jizzle. He would have given them all up on the spot just to have Rosie beside him again as he shouted the merits of his elixir. He began to try to trace her, but without success . . .

A month passed before a night on which Ted was awakened by a knock on the trailer door. His heart thumped. Even at that moment he had been dreaming of Rosie. He jumped out of bed to open the door.

But it was not Rosie. It was George, with Jizzle on his shoulder and one of the Range rifles in his hand.

"What——?" began Ted dazedly. He had been so sure it was Rosie.

"I'll show you what, you bastard", said George. "Just look at that!"

He brought forward his other hand with a sheet of paper in it.

Ted looked. Compromising would have been the severest understatement for the attitude in which George's wife, Muriel, was displayed with Ted.

He raised his horrified eyes . . .

George was lifting the rifle. On his shoulder Jizzle snickered.

171

Sideshow

Memories of childhood days on the swings and roundabouts at the fair stay bright in most people's minds all their lives. But were they actually as enjoyable as we remember—or was there fear in our hearts as the swings swept up ever higher and the wooden horses reared and plunged around the carousel? August Derleth, surely one of the most famous horror story writers alive, has his own special contribution to make on this subject . . .

CAROUSEL

By AUGUST DERLETH

The abandoned carnival stood behind a high board fence directly across from the Benjin house at the edge of town, and in one corner of it, under a graceful mulberry tree, stood the merry-go-round. Someone had come in before the legal notices appeared, dismantled the ferris wheel, and made away with it. Otherwise it stood just as it had done on that night of carnage when that poor bewildered lonely fellow, goaded beyond endurance by people who hated him for no other reason than that he was a poor, harmless black man, had exploded into long-suppressed passion and killed the owner of the carnival—torn him literally to pieces before he was fallen upon and lynched by the maddened crowd. The creditors had closed the carnival, hoping to sell it; the ferris wheel had been sold before complications had appeared; then the fence went up. For a little while it was a sort of never-never land for the vilage boys and girls; but even they forgot about it at last, and now it was the sole and exclusive domain of Marcia Benjin.

She spent a large part of each day in the carnival grounds, and haunted the merry-go-round. It was not without reason that she went through the opening the children had made in the fence; she needed the security and escape from her stepmother, for when Marcia's father was away at work, his second wife made no secret of her resentment for the only child of his first.

The child was five, and much alone. Because of her step-mother's malicious hatred, she was far lonelier than she should ever have been. In another year, she would be old enough to go to school, but in that time, too, she would escape her step-mother, and Mrs. Benjin did not know whether she wished that end.

Mrs. Benjin was dark, with a thin mouth and snapping brown eyes. She was jealous of her stepdaughter, who she looked upon as the symbol of John Benjin's first wife. She was jealous of her

173

with a dark, sultry passion, and yet she resented with ill-suppressed fury, the little girl's escape into the carnival grounds.

Unfortunately for the child, she did not always notice the passage of time, and so from time to time came home late to her meals. This only increased her stepmother's rage, but Mrs. Benjin saw in Marcia's laxity a possible way in which the girl could be brought wholly into her power.

"I don't want to speak to Marcia about her habits, John", she said silkily. "You know I hesitate. After all, she is *your* daughter, and I don't want to intrude between you, but I think she ought to learn to come home on time."

"Of course, she should", agreed John Benjin, good-naturedly. He was a large, broad-shouldered man, easy-going and completely unaware of anything in his wife but the aspect she chose for him to see. "I'll talk to her."

Marcia came into the house and brought the evening sunlight with her. She kissed her father, smiled gravely at her stepmother, and sat down.

"I'm sorry I'm late", she said.

"You ought not to be late", said Benjin gently. "It's hard enough to keep supper warm till I get home, and it's twice as hard to keep after that. Your mother works hard all day and she's always glad to get the dishes off the table."

"I just didn't notice", said Marcia.

"Oh, it doesn't really matter about me, I suppose", Mrs. Benjin interjected with a helpless air.

"I didn't notice, really", persisted Marcia earnestly. "We were playing, and before I knew it I heard the six o'clock bell."

"With whom were you playing?" asked John Benjin casually, feeling that now he had done his duty.

"With the black man", said Marcia ingenuously.

Benjin went on buttering his bread unconcernedly, but Mrs. Benjin pricked up her ears. "With whom?" she asked, unable to keep a little sharp excitement out of her voice.

Suddenly there was an unaccountable tension around the table. A baffling obstinacy came into Marcia's eyes; Benjin looked up, puzzled; across from him his wife held herself in and repeated her question.

"Answer your mother, Marcia."

"I said it."

"Then say it again."

"No." Her answer was barely whispered.

"Of course, perhaps she cannot be expected to trust me", said Mrs. Benjin, looking distressed, clasping her hands at her breast, turning her wedding ring nervously.

"Answer your mother, Marcia", said Benjin in a sharp voice. "With whom were you playing?"

"With the black man."

"But there is no black man in town, surely", said Mrs. Benjin. "Not since—well, since long ago, when you were a little baby."

"When Mum was still here."

"Yes, dear."

They waited for Marcia to say more, but she did not. After she had been put to bed, Mrs. Benjin expressed some concern for her. But not so he; by that time he had more or less figured it out. It was perfectly natural that children should imagine playmates; he had done it himself as a boy. It was especially true of lonely children, and it could not be denied that all the other children of the neighbourhood were either in school or were too much under five to serve as adequate companions for Marcia.

"Still, a *black man*!" said Mrs. Benjin with an alarm which she pretended very hard to feel.

"Yes, I admit that *is* a strange coincidence, isn't it?"

"It's three years now", she said musingly. She remembered it very well because it was at the carnival that she had first caught a good look at John Benjin and determined to have him for her own, if something could be made to come between his wife and him. Something had come between them, but it was none of her doing; Mrs. Benjin's death had taken place only a little over a year afterwards, and she had had her way with John a year later.

She thought about what Marcia had said and saw in this too something she could utilize to widen a rift between the child and her father, and once she could turn Marcia towards her, she could mould her as she wished. She did not know quite what she wanted to do with the girl, but in her heart she wished devoutly the girl was not here so that she could be free of that feeling of being watched as if—as if from beyond; yes, that was it; it was as if the eyes of John Benjin's first wife looked at her out of the dark eyes of her daughter.

Two days later Marcia was late again.

"If this doesn't stop", said Benjin in his placid way, though there was no mistaking his determination, "you'll not be permitted to go over to that merry-go-round any more, Marcia."

Of this, plainly, Marcia was afraid. "Oh, no, please!" she cried.

"You *must* learn to come home on time. Anyway, I don't think it's good for you to be over there alone all the time. That machinery is getting old, and may be falling to pieces. You may get hurt."

"But I'm not . . ." She sealed her lips and shot a quick, contemplative glance at her stepmother.

"What, dear?" asked Mrs. Benjin, leaning towards her with a synthetic sweetness on her hard features.

"Nothing."

"Marcia!" said her father.

"Nothing, Mother", she said.

It enraged Mrs. Benjin that the child hesitated to call her "Mother." It had been so from the first, and every attempt to force her to obey her father's wishes in this only made it more obvious.

"I wish she would trust me", she said, biting her lip with such force as to bring tears to her eyes.

"Now, now, Nell—take it easy", he said, putting one hand on her arm, and looking at Marcia with tired indignation.

Once again there was that tension around the table. What stirred and further angered Mrs. Benjin was this; she was convinced with the deepest conviction that somehow the child knew what her stepmother was about; Marcia could not tell her father, she could not put her feeling into words, but somehow she *knew*; and it was a source of rage and humiliation that this five-year-old girl should so easily see through what was a mystery to Benjin. Perhaps Marcia had even guessed that her stepmother's quick hope had sprung up when Benjin had spoken of physical danger for her if the machinery fell apart.

"Now then", said Benjin, turning to his daughter, "whatever it was you were going to say, say it now; we've got to show your new mother that we trust her, haven't we?"

"Yes." She said this reluctantly.

"Well, then."

No answer.

"Come Marcia—please. Just pretend you're playing a game with us—with me, then."

She shook her head.

"It was the black man again, wasn't it?" Mrs. Benjin could not keep herself from making the guess.

Marcia looked at her blandly, saying nothing.

Overflowing with irritation, Benjin said angrily, "Answer your mother at once, Marcia, or take the consequences."

"Yes", said Marcia in a low voice.

"There, I knew it!" said Mrs. Benjin triumphantly. "And now I wonder, John—is it imagination, or is it just plain lying?"

"I don't tell lies", said Marcia scornfully. She was hurt.

"No, dear—I didn't mean that you meant to tell lies, but that perhaps you just couldn't help it."

The girl gazed at her without expression; what she thought and felt lay hidden behind her eyes, and this wall against her curiosity baffled and further infuriated Mrs. Benjin. It was inevitable, the woman knew, that soon now the child must be broken, and she must be broken to the woman's taste.

After that, Marcia was gone from the house more and more often. Perhaps she sensed the woman's waiting cruelty; perhaps the house in which once her own mother had created her world was too dark with this other woman's hatred and jealousy and angry suspicions; she sought her haven from dawn to sunset, and would have gone back of evenings if she had not been prevented from doing so. Seeing this, Mrs. Benjin set about to circumvent the girl as much as possible.

But Marcia quickly learned to develop a remarkable deviousness; she escaped her stepmother repeatedly; she began to assume a wiliness and shrewdness to match the woman's, and always managed, at times of crisis, to keep her father between them in such a way that there were times when it became impossible for the woman to conceal her exasperation, and Benjin had to remind her to be patient and understanding—"Let Marcia come to you, my dear; don't force yourself upon her."

"Ah, I try so hard!" Mrs. Benjin cried out, making her habitual gesture of twisting her wedding ring in agitation.

It was a touching scene, in which Marcia did not come off at all well. She was ultimately forbidden to go to the carnival grounds.

She disobeyed, and went anyway.

That was the result Mrs. Benjin desired.

She was curiously unable to face her husband that night at supper table, to which for once, knowing she had done wrong,

Marcia preceded her father. Mrs. Benjamin avoided his eyes in so telling a manner that he could not help noticing that something was wrong. Finally, he asked. She shook her head. He divined that it concerned Marcia, and finally sent the girl to her room.

"Oh, I don't want to say it", she said, distressed. "But Marcia ran away and spent the whole day over there."

"Then I will have to punish her", he said.

Punishment did not prevent her from running away.

"It's humiliating", said Mrs. Benjin on the second occasion. "I mean, it hurts me to know that she must dislike me so much that she wants to risk being punished by you—and she loves you; I can see that—by going over there. To that black man or who-ever it is she imagines plays with her there."

"Is she still talking about that?"

"Yes."

He shook his head. "She must learn to obey you, Nell. We can't go on like this. It will disrupt the household."

"I'm afraid it may."

"It can't be. You'll have to take her in hand."

"But I can't—I really can't." But inwardly she exulted; she had waited patiently for this. "How could I punish her?"

"I'm afraid you must; she must learn to respect you."

She played her part to perfection, so that in the end poor deluded John Benjin, who sincerely loved his daughter, actually felt sorrier for his wife than he did for Marcia at the thought of the girl being punished. He was a stern man, but not an unkind one; he was simple, and had no knowledge of complexity; his first wife had been similar to him, unmotivated by complex passions and frustrations, and he would have been honestly horri-fied if he could have seen into his second wife's mind.

Mrs. Benjin bided her time.

After Marcia had been lulled into a sense of false security, Mrs. Benjin asked about "the black man. Does he still play with you?"

Marcia admitted that he did. "He told me not to worry any more, he would watch over me. Over papa, too."

"Oh, he did, did he?" She could not keep the chillness from her voice. "Weren't you told not to tell lies, dear?"

She whipped her very thoroughly, and when he came home, Benjin found his wife in tears, which stood in her eyes in contrast to his daughter's white-lipped pain and indignation which could not hide a kind of sullen loathing for her stepmother. Thus victimized, Benjin was more than ordinarily sympathetic with his wife; he simply could not understand what had come over his daughter.

After Marcia had gone to bed, her father went to her room and sat beside her bed and talked to her. He was trying very hard to understand, and when he had softened his daughter sufficiently, she clung to him and sobbed. She was lonesome. Her stepmother hated her; why couldn't he understand? She was like the black man. He was lonesome, too. He had always been lonesome, all his life.

Benjin shook her. "Marcia! What are you talking about?"

She tried to explain, faltered before the look in his eyes, and was silent, retreating behind the wall of childhood into that world of her own, peopled with fantasies and strange beings sprung from her lonely imagination.

He made another attempt, trying to be patient. "How big is he—this black man?" he asked.

"Real big—bigger than you, Daddy. And he's so strong. He makes the merry-go-round go for me. I get a ride every day."

"Is he nice?"

"He's glad to see me whenever I come. He just stays there all the time, by the merry-go-round waiting for me. He's the nicest man I ever knew, except you, Daddy. And he's going to watch over me and you, too."

"Like your guardian angel?"

"Yes, except that he's black, and I guess my guardian angel's white."

It was not a very satisfying or illuminating conversation. He was very puzzled when he sought his own bed, fretting now lest his daughter's loneliness were affecting her mind.

Having made so auspicious a beginning, Mrs. Benjin could hardly contain herself until a second opportunity to punish Marcia was offered. But that initial whipping had betrayed the violence of her hatred to the child, and Marcia walked with care. She came home to supper on time night after night, and the summer deepened towards autumn. As day followed day without overt disobedience upon which Mrs. Benjin could seize as a pretext to work her angry way with her stepdaughter, she grew more irate and frustrated, and at last, one day, when she knew John Benjin would be remaining at his desk longer than usual, and so would not be home on time for supper, she took matters into her own

179

hands to force the issue, and peremptorily forbade Marcia to go again to the carnival grounds.

Marcia ran away. Mrs. Benjin had known she would.

She waited with an almost unholy anticipation for the day to end.

Promptly at a quarter to six Marcia came tripping across the street and into the house, humming a little melody. She stopped short at sight of her stepmother waiting in sultry triumph.

"You disobeyed me", said Mrs. Benjin coldly.

"What are you going to do to me?"

"I'm going to punish you. Your father said I must."

"No, please."

"Please what?"

"Please, Mother. Don't."

"Yes, it's for your own good."

Mrs. Benjin could not keep herself from prolonging the child's torture. She came slowly around the table, bringing the stout whip she had held behind her gradually into sight of the child's horrified eyes.

With a shrill cry of fear, Marcia turned and fled.

Across the street, through the hole in the fence, into the carnival grounds.

But Mrs. Benjin was not to be so easily thwarted. She went after her, crossing the road and working her way into the grounds through that small opening in the fence, being careful to bring the whip with her, and remembering how easily some of that machinery might collapse and fall or be brought to fall on some-one, a child who would know no better . . .

She saw the child readily enough, clinging to one of the weather-beaten horses of the carousel. But Marcia was no longer afraid; she sat there with a curiously dispassionate air, watching her come on with such a sense of security from her that for a moment Mrs. Benjin was nonplussed.

As she came up to the merry-go-round, she heard her step-daughter's voice come out at her.

"Don't! Don't touch me! Mr. Black Man won't let you. Mr. Black Man is watching over me."

Slowly, slowly, almost imperceptibly, the carousel began to move.

Mrs. Benjin, seeing only that somehow the child seemed to be escaping her, leaped forward. At the same time Marcia slipped from the back of the wooden horse, darted quickly across, and dropped off the other side of the carousel.

As Mrs. Benjin stepped up into the merry-go-round, something took hold of her.

There was one horrible scream, and then a succession of terrible sounds that mounted together with the grinding of the carousel going faster and faster. Into the gathering dusk curious oddments spun and flew from the merry-go-round, most of them spattering red upon the carousel and the earth beyond.

Marcia watched with interest and satisfaction.

When the carousel was still again, she walked around it towards the hole in the fence. There was nothing to be seen of her stepmother save some dark masses here and there. One of them lay between Marcia and her way of egress. She walked around it with almost savage detachment.

It was Mrs. Benjin's left hand, with the wedding ring still on one finger.

The Man With A Tail

Just imagine what life would be like if you had a tail. Useful, I suppose, if you enjoyed swinging through the trees, but a little inconvenient—not to mention potentially dangerous— when using public transport. Still, it would certainly bring variety into anyone's life as Esther Carlson shows in this story of a young man who does possess one and has to find his own special solution to the problem.

HEADS YOU WIN . . .

By Esther Carlson

Dr. Aesop Abercrombie, whose health column appears in 1,000 newspapers, received the following letter:

Dear Dr. Abercrombie,
   My problem is, I have a tail. It is long and bushy. It really has not bothered me much. I am used to it. Usually I wear my trousers hind to fore and keep my tail in my pocket. Now I have joined the Y.M.C.A. and all the fellows stare at me. Do you think I should have an operation and if so, who does this kind of operation?

Sincerely yours,
Perplexed.

Without hesitation, Dr. Abercrombie gave the syndicated help:

My dear Perplexed,
   Yours is a unique problem, but by no means unheard of in our animal kingdom. As I understand it, you wish to have your tail removed by surgical means; however I feel you would be making a grave mistake. My advice to you is: Be proud you are different! Make the most of your unique endowment! Forget your embarrassment and relax, content in the knowledge that you have more than your fellow man.

Dr. Aesop Abercrombie.

   P.S. Should you still be determined to go through with an operation, I advise consulting your local vet.

Roland Feeney read this encouraging answer in Tuesday's *Daily Forthright*. He hastened to his dingy furnished room, stripped, and looked at himself in the mirror of the sagging bureau. There it was, a red-gold shaggy tail, very much like a collie's. Roland tried to overcome the chagrin he always felt at

183

this sight for he had tried for several months now, to grow a moustache and was unable to raise even a scraggy row of hairs.

"There you are!" he said, addressing the tail, which dropped rather limply over the footboard of the bed.

Then, in a brighter tone: "Make the most of you!" And after musing over the special attributes of his extended vertebrae for several minutes, he clothed himself once more and took himself off to an establishment on 42nd Street.

"I'm a freak", he announced to the manager of Happy Harry's Horror House.

"Oh yeah?" the manager said, who was tiny, embittered and an albino. "Where's your other head?"

"No head", Roland answered. "A tail."

"Oh, yeah?" the manager said. "Let's see."

Obligingly, Roland drew his tail from his back pocket and the manager gazed at it for some time with his pink eyes. Then he said:

"Nah."

"No?" cried Roland. He had so built up his hopes. "Tell me why!"

The manager had turned away but some spark of human kindness still flared in his shrivelled chest.

"Listen, kid", he said. "Two heads, O.K. Three heads, nice. But a tail . . . nah. So what will the yokels say? 'Prove it grew on him,' they'll say. 'O.K.,' I say; 'take off your pants, Dog Boy,'. and then what happens? The cops close the joint. Lewd and lascivious."

Downcast, Roland departed and tried next a famous anthropological museum up the street.

"I", Roland said to the director, who was large and bald and blue-veined, "have a tail."

"Do you have it on you?" said the director.

"Yes", said Roland.

"Indeed!" said the director.

"Maybe I'm a missing link", Roland said hopefully.

"If you don't mind", said the director, calling in his colleagues. "Let's have a look at it."

Roland was laid on a marble slab under a fluorescent light while the experts poked, pried, measured, whispered, took notes, and ate sandwiches, for it was lunchtime.

Finally Roland was told to put on his clothes and take his

184

former chair in the director's office. This he did and waited there with bated breath, wondering what sort of fame and glory might be in store for him.

The director reappeared and dropped into his creaking swivel chair. He picked his nose and looked out of the window for some time without speaking. Then he said:

"Mr. Feeney, you are a great disappointment."

Roland's heart plunged to his garters.

"You", went on the director, scratching his stomach, "are no more of a missing link than I am. You are a perfectly normal young man with a tail."

"Oh", Roland cried. "Then I am of no use to you at all?"

"I wouldn't say that", said the director kindly, without suppressing a belch. "We could stuff you and put you with the minor curiosities in the east basement, but you would be distinctly minor. Distinctly."

"Not everyone has a tail", Roland said, with a feeble defiance ticking in his breast.

"That's so", said the director, chewing a fingernail. "Nor does everyone want one."

And with that the interview was concluded.

Luckily, Roland, in his other back pocket, had Dr. Abercrombie's inspiring letter. Now he drew it out, unfolded it and read once more: "Be proud you are different! Make the most of your unique endowment!" Roland read these two sentences over and over, folded the clipping neatly, put it once more in his pocket, and lifted his head high.

As a consequence of lifting his head high, his eyes fell upon the lettering on a third-storey window just off Times Square.

MASTER YOUR MUSCLES, PERFORM AMAZING FEATS. ASTOUND YOUR FRIENDS. TAJ MAHAL SCHOOL OF YOGI.

In no time Roland was up the flights of stairs and knocking on a soiled white door upon which the same legend was written in peeling gilt. Underneath was tacked a card: SWAMI RABINDRANATH VATRAKOSHINDAR, PROP. After an interval, an enormously fat fellow in diapers and a turban opened the door.

"Oh, sure", the fellow said. "Come right in."

Here at last was more of a warm greeting. Roland beamed and stepped into the tiny room which, he noticed, was without furniture but literally plastered with scatter rugs.

185

"Are you Swami Rabindranath Vatrakoshindar?" he asked shyly.

"Oh, sure", said the Swami.

"Then", said Roland, "you are just the man I want to see. I have a tail."

"Oh, sure", said the Swami.

"You know about it then!" Roland was positively enthralled. "You know what to do with tails. What can I do with mine?"

"You can switch it, that's what. Switch it."

"But that's just the trouble", Roland cried. "*I can't switch it.* I can't do a thing with it. It just hangs."

Swami suddenly squashed down upon the nearest rug and yawned.

"Oh, for heavens sake", he said, "lie down any old place and I'll see what I can do."

He scrabbled around under his rug and presently brought up a small pamphlet. This he opened and read aloud: "Remove clothing down to loin cloth."

"Shorts", said Roland virtuously. "They will have to do."

"Remove clothing down to shorts", Swami amended.

Roland did so.

"Sit", read Swami in a bored voice.

Roland sat.

"I think I know what to do now", Roland said. "I contemplate my navel."

There was a long, long silence from Swami Rabindranath Vatrakoshindar. Finally he said in an injured tone: "Well, if you've *read* this book . . ."

"Oh, I haven't", Roland said hastily.

"All right then", Swami went on. "Contemplate your . . . contemplate your . . . " He paused, then continued triumphantly: "Contemplate the end of your tail."

Roland's tail was lying in a straight line directly behind him. He wondered if the Swami meant to bring it around and look at it, then decided that the meaning of the phrase was to think of it inwardly, become conscious that he had a tail with an end to it. He thought about this very hard.

"By the way", the Swami said. "For navels it's 50 cents, tails it's $1."

But Roland was concentrating so very hard he didn't hear the Master's voice. "I will astound my friends!" he was thinking.

186

"When I get home." After an hour's intense application, Roland began to get a bit stiff. He looked over at his tutor.

Swami lay with one foot on his bent knee, eating a salami sandwich and reading a magazine.

"What do I do now?" said Roland.

Swami lay his magazine on the summit of his vast middle, picked up the pamphlet and read: "The mind is the seat of muscular control. Are you now aware that you have a blank?" he took another bite of his sandwich and gestured slowly in the air. "It's blank here, but I'll put in *tail*. Are you now aware that you have a tail?"

"Yes!" said Roland solemnly.

"Then switch it!"

Roland switched it. The act astounded him so that he was unable to do anything but gape.

"All right now", said the Swami. "Up, down; right, left; up down; right left; one two, one two . . ."

Flushed and bright-eyed, Roland performed his exercises, watching all the while, over his shoulder, his tail behave in a wonderful tail-like manner.

"Goodness", the Swami said, "you'll get a crick in your neck."

"What do I do now?" asked the breathless and happy young man.

"Belinda closed her eyes, her breast heaving, and as the monster slithered towards her over the slimy floor, choking shrieks of delight rose in her . . . oh." He stopped, put the magazine down, picked up the pamphlet. "End of Lesson I", he read. "One dollar, cash, before leaving."

"Well", said Roland, "I certainly thank you. You certainly have taught me a lot. When shall I come back?"

Together they made up a series of appointments, Roland jotting the dates down on the side of the clipping, the Swami writing them laboriously on the back of the pamphlet.

Needless to say, Roland was delirious with happiness. He wagged his tail all the way home and refused to let the fact that he almost caught it in a subway door dampen his spirits. He had to tell somebody about his progress, so he sat down and wrote to Dr. Aesop Abercrombie:

Dear Dr. Abercrombie:
    You sure were right! Thanks a lot for your advice. I met

the most wonderful fellow named Swami Rabindranath Vatrakoshindar and he is giving me exercises. Soon I will master my muscles and be able to perform astounding feats and amaze my friends.

Sincerely yours,
Formerly Perplexed.

My dear Formerly [answered the good doctor]:
Keep up the good work! Perseverance! Excelsior! Nothing can stop you now. I am overjoyed that my small encouragement has provided you with the courage you need.

Dr. Abercrombie.

When the next lesson period rolled around Roland was very early and paced the street in front of Swami's building, aquiver with eagerness. Finally it was time. He knocked on the soiled white door and when the Swami opened it he cried: "Here I am!"

"Oh, sure", said the Swami.

Once again the Swami put him through his paces which Roland performed pridefully. "What do I do now?" he asked.

Swami Rabindranath Vatrakoshindar turned a page in the pamphlet. "Hang from light cord by tail", he read.

"Right!"

Roland sprang to his feet, grasped the naked light bulb suspended from the ceiling, hoisted himself up, caused his tail to hook around the cord, and let go.

"Oops", said the Swami.

For Roland fell directly to the floor, landing on his head with a nasty crack. When he came to he noticed that the Swami was several pages along in his magazine and was sipping a chocolate malted.

"It didn't work", Roland said, a fear nagging at his heart.

"Oh, there you are", said the Swami.

"It didn't work", Roland repeated. "Tell me the truth. My tail goes only up and down and sideways, doesn't it? Not around things. I can never, never, never be a trapeze artist."

"End of Lesson II", read the Swami. "One dollar, cash, before leaving."

"I'm no good", said Roland. "I flunked." He stared before him at nothing.

188

In the street once more, Roland drooped in every part. All his high spirits of the morning had fled; he felt himself a failure. Almost without realizing it, he put his tail in his hind pocket. His self-confidence was gone. Only one thing remained, one small chance: he put an ad. in the paper as follows: —

Boy with tail wants job. Will do anything. Write Box 2563M.

He got an answer.

The good Dr. Abercrombie, always interested in those who wrote to him for advice, watched each day's mail closely for a third letter from *Perplexed*. Over his afternoon tea and pie, he wondered about the fate of the uniquely endowed young man.

"Have fame and fortune reached him?" he mused to his secretary. "Are his friends agape with astonishment and awe?"

In the end, Dr. Abercrombie's curiosity got the better of him and he, with some difficulty, sought out the learned Swami Rabindranath Vatrakoshindar and inquired after his patient.

Swami Rabindranath Vatrakoshindar, who was now proprietor of a billiard parlour, failed to remember Roland at first, but at last the doctor's skilful psychological questioning brought out that such a young man with a tail had, at one time, taken a series of lessons from him at $1 a throw.

"And then what happened?" Dr. Abercrombie asked gently.

"He left", said the Swami.

"He left", the doctor repeated. His keen mind reconstructed the scene and he saw that Roland could have done then only one thing . . .

Detective work came easily to this man to whom thousands confessed their aches and pains. He located at last the ad. in the *Forthright* files and continued on from there.

So it was that a distinguished-looking gentleman with white hair and kind brown eyes approached a certain counter in the basement of Saks Avenue A.

"Is there", he asked the clerk, a crone of uncertain years who was covered with warts, "a man with a tail working here?"

Several warts knocked together on her forehead when she frowned.

"At night", she said, "there's Ronald Feeney."

"I'll wait", said the doctor.

The store closed. The woman clutched her lizard handbag and

went home. When dusk fell a stooped and pale-faced fellow descended the narrow stairs. The doctor watched him as he pulled from his back pocket a gloriously tawny red-gold duster and commenced with it to flick the bric-a-brac and chinaware. He did not notice the distinguished-looking man standing in the gloom and was startled in the extreme when the doctor stepped forth from the shadows and announced himself.

"Are you happy?" the doctor asked earnestly.

"Yes", said Roland. "Happy Harry's Horror House was not for me. In the museum I should have become bored, and, as for being a famous trapeze artist in the circus . . . it was not my fate, since I am allergic to peanuts. Here I have found a place for my small talents in the workaday world. One day I shall climb my way up to Gimbel's basement. I am content."

With a light heart and a light step, Dr. Abercrombie left Saks Avenue A and continued on uptown for supper, glowing with the knowledge that once more he had helped his fellowman along life's thorny path.

The Platinum Girl

It is a fairly safe bet that the best shudder in a book of this kind would be provided by Robert Bloch, author of some of the most horrifying tales in the entire macabre genre. And this is undoubtedly the case with "Girl From Mars" which Bloch regards with affection as one of his own best stories. Maybe it will teach you, too, to beware of light skinned strangers ...

GIRL FROM MARS

By Robert Bloch

"The wild Man from Borneo—he eats 'em alive...he eats 'em alive—"

Ace Clawson leaned against the side of the platform and listened to Lou, the spieler. Somebody had to listen to him, and there was no crowd in this lousy drizzle.

The rain was letting up now as it got dark, but the afternoon storm had made mudpies in the Midway. Ace stared up the deserted carny street as the lights came on over the soggy tents and the drooping banners of the WORLD OF WONDER shows. He shivered. This was a stinking climate—no wonder these Georgia crackers got malaria.

Maybe it would stop raining soon. Maybe the marks would come down after supper. They'd better. Only two days left to play here and Ace wasn't off the nut yet. Well, that's the way some seasons went, just one bad break after another.

Ace scratched his chin. Better shave. Ah, phooey on that. And phooey for Lou, too—blatting his brains out for nothing up there. He looked at the gawky spieler on the platform and grinned. Punk kid, his first season out, and he needed practice. Ace cocked his head and called.

"Hey, Lou!"

"Yeah?"

"Shut up!"

Lou shut up and climbed down. He tossed his head and Ace ducked the spray of raindrops. "You damn' fool, barking at nobody! Stuff it. Go inside and take the gang over to Sweeney for chow. We won't see a sucker around here for an hour yet."

"Sure, Ace."

Lou went inside and rounded up the Strange People. They came out single file; Fat Phyllis waddling along with little Captain Atom, Hassan the fire-eater puffing on one of his rancid

192

shoe pegs, Joe the Alligator Boy wearing a raincoat, Eddie in his wild man outfit.

Ace stood behind the ticket stand. He didn't feel like talking to them. Somebody was bound to make a crack about Mitzie and Rajah. Nuts to that noise!

He watched them plod through the red clay of the Midway, then squinted up at the banners behind the platform. All the Strange People squinted back with their painted eyes—Phyllis, Captain Atom, the World's Smallest Man, the Mighty Hassan, the Alligator Boy, the Wild Man from Borneo, Rajah the Magician and the Girl from Mars.

Rajah the Magician, dressed in evening clothes and wearing a turban on his head, was sawing a woman in half. The Girl from Mars spread her batwings over the sky. Ace scowled at them and cursed.

They had to take a powder on him, did they? Had to run out —and together! That's what hurt. They ran off together. Rajah and Mitzie. It was probably her idea, the tramp. Just giving him the old double-X behind his back. Laughing at him. Bad weather, a poor take, and on top of it she had to run out on him too!

Ace bit into his lower lip. That was all the supper he needed. That and a drink.

He sat down on the edge of the platform and pulled out his pint. Almost full. He pulled out the cork and threw it away. It wouldn't be needed again for this bottle.

Tilting his head back, he swallowed. One swig for the rain. One swig for the lousy Georgia crackers. One swig for Rajah and Mitzie. Yes, and one swig for what he'd do to that broad if he ever caught up with her.

Out of the corner of his eye he noticed that the rain had stopped. And then, he saw the girl.

She came wandering up the Midway, walking very slow. She was wearing some kind of grey playsuit, but he could tell it was a girl all right, even from far away, because the lights showed off her blonde hair.

Blonde hell, she was platinum; as she got closer he saw the bush on her head was almost white. Her eyebrows, too. Like one of those—what did they call 'em—albinos. Only her eyes weren't pink. They were kind of platinum too. Starey eyes. She gawked at everything as she went past the pitches.

Ace watched her coming; he had nothing else to do. Besides,

193

she was worth watching. Even with that outfit on, he could see that she was really stacked. But built! Long legs, and plenty of meat on the torso. A disheroo.

He slicked back his hair. When she passed the tent he'd step out and walk over, sort of smiling. Then—

Ace hesitated. Because the girl wasn't passing the tent. She came up to the end of the platform and stopped. She looked up and began to read the banners, moving her lips. She stood kind of funny, swaying a little as if she had a load. Maybe she did, at that. Anyhow, she rocked on her heels and stared up. She kept looking at one banner and mumbling to herself.

Ace turned his head. She was staring at the Girl from Mars. Yes, and that's what she was mumbling out loud, too; he could hear it.

"The Girl from Mars", she kept saying. She had a kind of a foreign accent. Blondie. Maybe a Swede or something.

"Something I can do for you?"

Ace swung over and came up behind her. She jumped about a foot.

"*Teker—*"

Swede all right. But built. She didn't wear any makeup. She didn't need to. Ace smiled at her.

"I'm Ace Clawson. Own this show. What can I do for you, sister?"

She sized him up and then looked back at the banner.

"The Girl from Mars", she said. "Is that truth?"

"Truth?"

"There is such a one? Inside there?"

"Uh—no. Not now. She scrammed."

"*Kep?*" The girl swallowed quickly. "I mean—what do you say?"

"She ran away. What's the matter, you don't talk English so good, huh?"

"English? Oh. Speech. Yes, I talk it." She spoke slowly, frowning. At least her eyebrows frowned, but her forehead didn't wrinkle. Her skin was grey, like the playsuit. No buttons on the suit and she wasn't carrying a purse. Foreigner.

"She did not po—possess wings?"

Ace grinned. "No. Fakeroo." She was beginning her frown act again and he remembered she was probably drunk. "It was a gag, see? There is no Girl from Mars."

194

"But I am from *Rekk*."

"What?"

"I am from *Re*—from Mars."

She was lushed to the gills. Ace stepped back. "Oh, yeah. Sure. You're from Mars, huh?"

"I came today."

"Well, well. Just like that, huh? Pleasure or business?"

"*Kep?*"

"Skip it. I mean, what's on your mind? What can I do for you?"

"Hungry."

Not only a lush, but a mooch, yet. But she *was* built. And when Ace put his hand on her shoulder, she didn't move away. Her shoulder was warm. The heat just poured off her. Hot stuff. And she was hungry—

Ace glanced at the tent flap behind him. He was beginning to get an idea. It came to him when he put his hand on her shoulder. To hell with Mitzie. This was just what the doctor ordered. And the Midway was deserted. The gang wouldn't be back from Sweeney's for forty-five minutes yet.

"Hungry", the girl repeated.

"Sure. We'll get you something to eat. But let's talk first. Come on inside." Ace got another grip on her shoulder. Warm. Soft. Good stuff.

The lights inside were dim. Lou had switched off when he left. The flaps were down over the platforms against the tent walls, as they were during the grind when only one freak performed at a time. Ace led her over to the Girl from Mars platform. There was a cot inside and he could lower the flap. Take it easy first though.

She walked on her heels until he held her still and pushed her down on the steps on the side of the platform. Touching her made him want to hurry it up, even though he knew he had to be careful. The heat came off her in waves, and he was warm from the whisky.

"So you're from Mars", he said, huskily, bending over her but remembering to keep a grin on his face. "How did you get here?"

"*Ertells*. The—machine. With the others. *Hydron*, very swift. Until we land. Then this, we did not expect. In the atmosphere. Electric."

"The storm? Lightning?"

195

She nodded, expressionless. "You understand. The *kor*—the machine split. Broken. All *flerk*. All but I. I fell. And then I did not know. Because I had no orders. *Pre* was ended. You understand?"

Ace nodded. She was hot. God, she was hot. And built. He stepped back, still nodding. Let her finish. Maybe she'd sober up a little.

"So I walked. Nothing. Nobody. Dark. Then I saw light. This place. And the words. And you. I read the words."

"And here you are." Humour them. You got to humour them, dames and drunks. "How come you read English, and talk?"

"*Pre* did it. Education. Because he—planned we must come. Much I cannot know. I will understand. Now hungry."

There was no expression on her face. Lushes always twist their faces a lot. She didn't stagger, just walked on her heels was all. And there was no liquor smell from her. So—she wasn't drunk!

Ace stared.

He stared at the expressionless face, at the platinum hair and eyebrows. He stared at the sandals she wore, at the grey suit without any pockets, without any buttons. No buttons. That was it. *She didn't have all her buttons.*

Yeah. Sure. She was a whack. She came here this afternoon, all right. Busted out of the county nuthouse in the storm. No wonder she didn't carry a purse or anything. Just a lousy whack on the lam from the san.

Wouldn't that have to be the kind of break he got? A screwball with an empty gut and an empty noggin. That's all he needed. But she was *built*. And that's all he needed—

Why not?

Ace figured fast. Half an hour, maybe. Long enough. He'd hustle her out of here right away. Nobody would know. It was a dirty trick, maybe. What the hell, he'd been getting the dirty end long enough himself; rain, no take, that damned Mitzie running out on him, no woman. He needed a change of luck. And besides, it wouldn't hurt her, maybe do her good. Nobody would find out anything and even if they did, she was a whack. Didn't know what she was saying, even. Why not?

"Hungry."

"Wait a minute, sister. I got a great idea. Come on back here for a second."

He motioned her to her feet, led the way up the steps, and

196

lifted the flap. It was dark on the platform behind the canvas curtain. He groped for the couch, found it.

"Sit down here." He made his voice soft. She stood right next to him, not backing away, and when he pulled her down, pulled down all that heat and softness, she came without a sound.

He made himself wait, kept talking first.

"Yeah, I got a great idea. Why not? You're from Mars, ain'tcha?"

"Yes. From *Rekk*."

"Sure. And my Girl from Mars skipped. So the way I figure it, why don't you come along with the show? You can have the same setup, sixty a week and chow, travel around and see the country. Nobody to tell you what to do or when to do it, see? Your own boss. Free. Get it—free?"

He wanted it to sound good. Sort of subtle, about being free. Even if she was a whack, she had enough sense to bust out and probably knew she'd have to keep moving. Not that he'd let her tie up with the show, that was all con, but he wanted her to go for the deal. Then he could start.

"But that is not what you speak. Hungry—"

Ah, to hell with it! You don't waste your breath on a screwball. And here in the dark she wasn't a screwball. She was a disheroo, a tall blonde, hot, better than Mitzie, damn Mitzie anyhow, she was here and he could feel her, feel the warmth just busting out of her—

Ace put his hands on her shoulders.

"Hungry, huh? Well, don't you worry about that, sister. I'll take care of you. All you gotta do is co-operate."

Damn it! He heard the mumbling now, the gang was coming back, filing into the tent, climbing up on platforms and scraping chairs. He wouldn't have time.

But what the hell, he was behind the curtain, it was dark, he'd keep quiet and make her keep quiet and they could sneak out later. Besides, his hands were on her shoulders. Ace felt her lean against him, felt those curves, solid. Instead of drawing back, she kept coming in, she wasn't whacky, she knew what she was doing, this was all right.

Somebody in the outer tent flicked up the lights, and a thin glow filtereed through the canvas curtain. He grinned at her upturned face. Her eyes were wide, shining. He ran his hands down her back. She was strong, eager.

197

"Don't you worry about being hungry, baby", he whispered. "I'll take care of you."

The heat poured out of her as she pressed his shoulders. He bent his head to kiss her. She opened her mouth, wide, and in the dim light he saw her teeth. They were platinum-coloured, too.

Then he wanted to draw back, but something about the heat pouring off her made him feel dizzy. Besides, she held on to him so tight, and she kept whispering "hungry" over and over again, and now she was drawing him down on the cot and he saw the teeth coming at him. They were long and pointed. He couldn't move, she held him, the heat came out of her eyes to blind him, and the long, sharp teeth were coming closer and closer—

Ace hardly felt any pain. Everything turned to heat and whirled away. Somewhere in the distance a voice began to chant. It was Lou, standing outside, standing under the Girl from Mars banner and beginning his chant. That was the last thing Ace heard or knew. The chant, the spiel.

"The Wild Man From Borneo—he eats 'em alive—he eats 'em alive—"

The Monster

If Bloch's story contains the best shudder in this collection, Harry Harrison's tale runs it a close second. For here the ingenious mind of S.F. man Harrison has combined the old legend of Frankenstein with a sideshow setting and created a tale of chilling authenticity. If you ever wanted to know what it might be like as a freak—read on with caution.

AT LAST, THE TRUE STORY
OF FRANKENSTEIN

By Harry Harrison

"And here, before your very eyes, is the very same monster built by my much admired great-great grandfather, Victor Frankenstein, built by him from pieces of corpses out of dissecting rooms, stolen parts of bodies freshly buried in the grave, and even chunks of animals from the slaughterhouse. Now look—" The tall-coated man on the platform swung his arm out in a theatrical gesture and the heads of the closely packed crowd below swung to follow it. The dusty curtains flapped aside and the monster stood there, illuminated from above by a sickly green light. There was a concerted gasp from the crowd and a shiver of motion.

In the front row, pressed against the rope barrier, Dan Bream mopped his face with a soggy handkerchief and smiled. It wasn't such a bad monster, considering that this was a cheapjack carnival playing the smalltown circuit. It had a dead-white skin, undampened by sweat even in this steambath of a tent, glazed eyes, stitches and seams showing where the face had been patched together, and the two metal plugs projecting from the temples— just like in the movie.

"Raise your right arm!" Victor Frankenstein V commanded, his brusque German accent giving the words a Prussian air of authority. The monster's body did not move, but slowly—with the jerking motion of a badly operating machine—the creature's arm came up to shoulder height and stopped.

"This monster, built from pieces from the dead, cannot die, and if a piece gets too worn out I simply stitch on a new piece with the secret formula passed down from father to son from my great-great grandfather. It cannot die nor feel pain—as you see—"

This time the gasp was even louder and some of the audience turned away while others watched with eager eyes. The barker had taken a foot long and wickedly sharp needle, and had pushed it firmly through the monster's biceps until it protruded on both sides. No blood stained it and the creature made no motion, as though completely unaware that anything had been done to its flesh.

". . . impervious to pain, extremes of heat and cold, and possessing the strength of ten men . . ."

Behind him the voice droned on, but Dan Bream had had enough. He had seen the performance three times before, which was more than satisfactory for what he needed to know, and if he stayed in the tent another minute he would melt. The exit was close by and he pushed through the gaping, pallid audience and out into the humid dusk. It wasn't much cooler outside. Life borders on the unbearable along the shores of the Gulf of Mexico in August, and Panama City, Florida, was no exception. Dan headed for the nearest air conditioned beer joint and sighed with relief as the chill atmosphere closed in around his steaming garments. The beer bottle frosted instantly with condensation as did the heavy glass stein, cold from the freezer. The first big swallow cut a path straight down to his stomach. He took the beer over to one of the straight-backed wooden booths, wiped the table off with a handful of paper napkins and flopped on to the bench. From the inner pocket of his jacket he took some folded sheets of yellow copy paper, now slightly soggy, and spread them before him. After adding some lines to the scribbled notes he stuffed them back into his jacket and took a long pull on his beer.

Dan was halfway through his second bottle when the barker, who called himself Frankenstein the Fifth, came in. His stage personality had vanished along with the frock coat and monocle, and the Prussian haircut now looked like a common crew cut.

"You've got a great act", Dan called out cheerfully, and waved the man over. "Will you join me for a drink?"

"Don't mind if I do", Frankenstein answered in the pure nasal vowels of New York City, the German accent apparently having disappeared along with the monocle. "And see if they have a Schlitz or a Bud or anything beside the local swamp water."

He settled into the booth while Dan went for the beers, and groaned when he saw the labels on the bottles.

"At least it's cold", he said, shaking salt into his to make it foam, then half drained the stein in a long deep swallow. "I noticed you out there in front of the clems for most of the shows today. Do you like the act—or you a carny buff?"

"It's a good act. I'm a newsman, name's Dan Bream."

"Always pleased to meet the Press, Dan. Publicity is the life of show business, as the man said. I'm Stanley Arnold: call me Stan."

"Then Frankenstein is just your stage name?"

"What else? You act kinda dim for a reporter, are you sure—?" He waved away the Press card that Dan pulled from his breast pocket. "No, I believe you, Dan, but you gotta admit the question was a little on the rube side. I bet you even think that I have a real monster in there!"

"Well, you must admit that he looks authentic. The skin stitched together that way, those plugs in his head—"

"Held on with spirit gum and the embroidery is drawn on with eyebrow pencil. That's show business for you, all illusion. But I'm happy to hear that the act even looked real to an experienced reporter like yourself. What paper did you say you were with?"

"No paper, the news syndicate. I caught your act about six months ago and became interested. Did a little checking when I was in Washington, then followed you down here. You don't really want me to call you Stan, do you? Stein might be closer. After all—Victor Frankenstein *is* the name on your naturalization papers."

"Tell me more," Frankenstein said in a voice suddenly cold and emotionless.

Dan riffled through the yellow sheets. "Yes . . . here it is, from the official records. Frankenstein, Victor—born in Geneva, arrived in the U.S. in 1938, and more of the same."

"The next thing you'll be telling me is that my monster *is* real!" Frankenstein smiled, but only with his mouth.

"I'm betting that it is. No yogi training or hypnotism or such can make a man as indifferent to pain as that thing is—and as terribly strong. I want the whole story, the truth for a change!"

"Do you . . .?" Frankenstein asked in a cold voice and for a long moment the air filled with tension. Then he laughed and clapped the reporter on the arm. "All right, Dan—I'll give it to you. You are a persistent devil and a good reporter and it is the least you deserve. But first you must get us some more drinks, something a measurable degree stronger than this execrable beer." His New York accent had disappeared as easily as had his German one; he spoke English now with skill and perfection without any recognizable regional accent.

Dan gathered their empty glasses. "It'll have to be beer—this is a dry county."

"Nonsense! This is America, the land that raises its hands in horror at the foreign conception of double-think yet practises it with an efficiency that sets the Old World to shame. Bay County may be officially dry but the law has many itchy palms, and under that counter you will find a reasonable supply of a clear liquid that glories in the name of White Mule and is reputed to have a kick of the same magnitude as its cognate beast. If you are still in doubt you will see a framed federal liquor licence on the far wall, legitimatizing this endeavour in the eyes of the national government. Simply place a five dollar bank note on the bar, say Mountain Dew, and do not expect any change."

When they both had enjoyed their first sips of the corn likker Victor Frankenstein lapsed into a friendly mood.

"Call me Vic, Dan. I want us to be friends. I'm going to tell you a story that few have heard before, a story that is astounding but true. True—mark that word—not a hodge-podge of distortions and half-truths and outright ignorance like that vile book produced by Mary Godwin. Oh how my father ever regretted meeting that woman and, in a moment of weakness, confiding in her the secret of some of his original lines of research . . ."

"Just a minute", Dan broke in. "You mentioned the truth, but I can't swallow this guff. Mary Wollstonecraft Shelly wrote *Frankenstein*; or, *The Modern Prometheus* in 1818. Which would make you and your father so old . . ."

"Please, Dan—no interruptions. I mentioned my father's researches, in the plural you will note, all of them devoted to the secrets of life. The Monster, as it has come to be called, was just one of his works. Longevity was what he was interested in, and he did live to a very, very old age, as will I. I will not stretch your credulity any further at this moment by mentioning the year of my birth, but will press on. That Mary Godwin. She and the poet were living together at this period, they had not married as yet, and this permitted my father to hope that Mary might one day find him not unattractive, since he was quite taken by her. Well, you can easily imagine the end. She made notes of everything he told her—then discarded him and used the notes to construct her despicable book. Her errors are legion, listen . . ." He leaned

203

across the booth and once again clapped Dan on the shoulder in a hearty way. It was an intimate gesture that the reporter didn't particularly enjoy, but he didn't complain. Not as long as the other kept talking.

"Firstly she made papa a Swiss; he used to tear his hair out at the thought, since ours is a good old Bavarian family with a noble and ancient lineage. Then she had him attending the University of Ingolstadt in *Ingolstadt*—when every schoolboy knows that it was moved to Landshut in 1800. And father's personality, what crimes she committed there! In this libellous volume he is depicted as a weeping and ineffectual man, when in reality he was a tower of strength and determination. And if this isn't enough, she completely misunderstood the meaning of his experiments. Her jim-crack collection of cast off parts put together to make an artificial man is ludicrous. She was so carried away by the legends of Talos and the Golem that she misinterpreted my father's work and cast it into that ancient mould. Father did not construct an artificial man, he reactivated a *dead* man! That is the measure of his genius! He travelled for years in the darkest reaches of the African jungle, learning the lore of the creation of the zombie. He regularized the knowledge and improved upon it until he had surpassed all of his aboriginal teachers. Raise the dead, that is what he could do. That was his secret— and how can it be kept a secret in the future, Mr. Dan Bream?"

With these last words Victor Frankenstein's eyes opened wide and an unveiled light seemed to glow in their depths. Dan pulled back instinctively, then relaxed. He was in no danger here in this brightly lit room with men on all sides of them.

"Afraid, Dan? Don't be." Victor smiled and reached out and patted Dan on the shoulder once again.

"What was that?" Dan asked, startled at the tiny brief pain in his shoulder.

"Nothing—nothing but this," Frankenstein smiled again, but the smile had changed subtly and no longer contained any humour. He opened his hand to reveal a small hypodermic needle, its plunger pushed down and its barrel empty.

"Remain seated", he said quietly when Dan started to rise, and Dan's muscles relaxed and he sat back down, horrified.

"What have you done to me?"

"Very little—the injection is harmless. A simple little hypnotic drug, the effect of which wears off in a few hours. But until then

204

you will not have much will of your own. So you will sit and hear me out. Drink some beer though, we don't want you to be thirsty."

Horrified, Dan was a helpless onlooker, as, of its own volition, his hand raised and poured a measure of beer down his throat.

"Now concentrate, Dan, think of the significance of my statement. The so-called Frankenstein monster is no stitched up collection of scraps, but a good honest zombie. A dead man who can walk but not talk, obey but not think. Animate—but still dead. Poor old Charley is one, the creature whom you watched going through his act on the platform. But Charley is just about worn out. Since he is dead he cannot replace the body cells that are destroyed during the normal wear and tear of the day. Why the fellow is like an animated pincushion from the act, holes everywhere. His feet—terrible, not a toe left, keep breaking off when he walks too fast. I think it's time to retire Charley. He has had a long life, and a long death. Stand up, Dan."

In spite of his mind crying *No! No!* Dan rose slowly to his feet.

"Aren't you interested in what Charley used to do before he became a sideshow monster? You should be, Dan. Old Charley was a reporter—just like you. And he ran across what he thought was a good story. Like you, he didn't realize the importance of what he had discovered and talked to me about it. You reporters are a very inquisitive bunch. I must show you my scrapbook, it's simply filled with Press cards. Before you die of course. You wouldn't be able to appreciate it afterwards. Now come along."

Dan walked after him, into the hot night, screaming inside in a haze of terror, yet walking quietly and silently down the street.

Animal Freaks

Eric Frank Russell has a special place in the ranks of modern weird story writers and this tale, "Mutants For Sale" is one of those very rare stories which can stand re-reading and still come across fresh and full of wonder every time. There is probably a little shop just like the one here no more than a few yards from where you live, but whether you will have the courage to push into its musty depths after perusing the next few pages, I will not even hazard a guess.

MUTANTS FOR SALE

By Eric Frank Russell

The shop was small, dingy and halfway down a side street no
wider than an alley. One could pass it a thousand times without
giving it a thought. But above the green curtains across its window
was a small sign reading: *Mutants For Sale.*

Jensen popped his eyes and went in.

"I'll have six", he said.

"That's being greedy", reproved the little man behind the
counter. He had a white mane, watery eyes, a crimson nose and
a perpetual sniffle. If he had any brothers they were hanging around
Snow White.

"Look", invited Jensen, staring around. "Let's be serious, shall
we? Let's come down to earth."

"I'm there already." He stamped a foot to prove it.

"I should hope so", said Jensen. He leaned on the counter,
fastened the dwarf with his gaze. "These mutants, how do they
come?"

"Fat and thin", informed the other. "Also tall and short. Likewise loony and sane. If there are limits I've yet to find them."

"I know who's the loony", Jensen decided.

"You should", agreed the little man.

"I'm a newspaper columnist", Jensen offered.

"That proves it", said the other.

"Proves what?"

"Who's the loony."

"Snappy", opined Jensen. "I like people who come back at me
fast. Even when they're slightly cracked."

"For a pressman you're more than impolite", remarked the little
man. He wiped his eyes, blew his nose, blinked at his visitor.

"Attribute it to my especial status. At the moment I'm a pros-
pective customer. The customer is always right, isn't he?"

"Not necessarily."

"You'll see the point if you want to stay in biz", Jensen assured. He eyed the racks behind the counter. They were lined with all sorts of phials and queer looking jars. "About these mutants."

"Well?"

"What's the gag?"

"I sell them. Is that a gag?"

"Y'betcha!" said Jensen. "Know what a mutant is?"

"I ought to."

"Sure you ought—but *do* you?"

"Most decidedly."

"Then what is a mutant?"

"Hah!" The little man wriggled his nose. It went two shades richer in hue. "So you don't know yourself?"

"I raise them by the dozens. I'm a leading breeder."

"Really?" The little man registered polite incredulity. "What's your name?"

"Jensen, Albert Edward Malachi Jensen of the *Morning Call*."

"Never heard of you."

"You wouldn't—if you can't read." Jensen took a breath and went on. "A mutant is a freak of nature created by one chance in a million. A massive particle such as a cosmic ray wallops a gene and in due time Mom has got a circus exhibit on her hands. So let me tell—"

"Wrong!" snapped the little man. "A mutant is a radical change in psyche or physique that breeds true, regardless of whether naturally or artificially created. All my goods breed true to form, therefore they are mutants."

"So you can change the forms of things and guarantee that they'll perpetuate their new kind?"

"That is true."

"You must be God", said Jensen.

"Your blasphemy is unwarranted", said the little man, with much sharpness.

Ignoring that, Jensen studied the phials and jars a second time. "What are those?"

"Containers."

"I can see that much. What's in them—dissolved mutants?"

"Don't be absurd."

"I am never absurd", Jensen told him. "You sell mutants. You've got to stash them someplace."

"I do."

"So it says on the window. What's the gag?"

"I tell you there isn't any."

"All right. I'm a customer. Show me a few fashionable mutants. Something snazzy for evening wear."

"This isn't a dress shop", asserted the little man. "You want a low-cut gown. And you'd look like hell in it."

"Never mind about that. Hand me a mutant, that's all I ask."

"Any particular kind in mind?" asked the little man.

Jensen thought it over. "Yes. I want a pale blue rhinoceros seventeen inches long and weighing not more than nine pounds."

"Not a stock pattern. It would have to be made."

"I guessed as much. I had a funny feeling that there was something special about it."

"It might take a fortnight", warned the little man. "Or possibly three weeks."

"I don't doubt that. Months and years. A lifetime in fact."

"I could find you a pink elephant", offered the little man. "Roughly the same size."

"They're a drug on the market. I can find dozens of them in any saloon."

"Yes, they are rather commonplace." He smoothed his white hair, emitted a sigh. "It seems that I can do nothing for you."

Jensen said very loudly, "Show me a mutant. Any one. The cheapest you've got."

"Certainly". Wiping his eyes and snuffling a couple of times, the little man went through the doorway at the back.

Leaning over the counter, Jensen helped himself to a small, peculiarly shaped jar. It was transparent and half full of orange-coloured liquid. He uncapped it and sniffed. The odour suggested prime Scotch concentrated to quarter bulk. He stuck the jar back on the shelf, drooling as he did it.

The little man returned holding a white pup with a black patch around one eye. He dumped the pup on the counter.

"There you are. Bargain line."

"So I see", commented Jensen. "You ought to be sued."

"Why?"

"That's no mutant."

"Very well", said the little man, with offended dignity. "You're the authority." Grabbing the pup he bore it through the back door.

"Wise guy!" sneered the pup at Jensen just before it went from sight.

When the shopkeeper reappeared Jensen said, "I heard it talk. So does Charlie McCarthy and every other wooden dummy."

"Quite probably." He rattled the shelves with a sneeze.

"Any stage ventriloquist can do it better", Jensen persistently continued. "Being more polished and original."

"Quite probably", the little man repeated.

"I'm a stickler", Jensen went on. "When I find a newsworthy item I don't get pushed away. I stay right with it until something goes bang. That's me."

"I'm sure."

"All right, then. Look at it this way: you've got mutants for sale or so you say. That's news. There's a few lines in it—and a few lines here and there make a column."

"Indeed?" The little man raised white eyebrows. He seemed baffled by this information.

"Now", proceeded Jensen, looking sinister, "a good column by a competent columnist tells all sorts of interesting things. People read it. Sometimes it tells nice things, sometimes nasty ones. The cops read the nasty ones and feel grateful because I have drawn them to their attention. Usually, though, they're too late because the subject of my remarks has also read my piece and got out of town fast, see?"

"I don't see."

Jensen hammered the counter with an open palm. "You have just tried to sell me a pup. It said, 'Wise guy!' I heard it with my own two ears. That's false pretences. Obtaining money by means of a trick. Petty larceny."

"But I didn't obtain any money." The little man made a disparaging gesture. "Money, what good is it? I never accept money."

"You don't eh? Then what do you want for the gabby pup?"

The little man looked cautiously around, bent forward, whispered soft and low.

Jensen went popeyed and said, "Now I know you're cracked."

"I go mighty short of certain types of stuff", explained the little man apologetically. "Inorganic material is plentiful. Animal protoplasm isn't. Takes a lot of time and trouble to make it myself."

"I can imagine." Jensen glanced at his watch. "Show me one

genuine dyed-in-the-wool mutant and I'll do you proud in the Sunday edition. Otherwise—"

"I'm one myself", informed the little man, modestly.

"Is zat so? What can you do that the Navy can't?"

"I can make anything." He paused, added, "Well, almost anything. I'm restricted to what I can lift unaided. Nothing heavier."

Jensen tee-heed insultingly. "And you make other mutants?"

"Yes."

"Then go ahead and get making. I want a pale blue rhinoceros seventeen inches long. Not more than nine pounds."

"My powers don't function instantaneously. Manufacture takes time."

"So you said before. A good excuse is good enough for twice." Jensen scowled across the counter. "Could you make a first-water rose diamond the size of a bucket?"

"If it were of any use." The little man arshooed with violence, shoved a displaced jar back into position. "A gem that size would be valueless. And take time to produce."

"There you go again", Jensen threw a significant glance at the bottle-loaded shelves. "How much are they paying you?"

"Who?"

"The drug ring."

"I don't understand."

"Of course you don't." Pushing forward his face, Jensen displayed the cynicism of one familiar with life's seamiest side. "What it says in the window is a lot of guff. It doesn't mean what it appears to mean. A mutant is a key-word for a jar of joy-juice as your hop-headed customers well know."

"The jars contain reduction fluids", contradicted the little man.

"You bet they do", Jensen endorsed. "They've reduced many an addict's wad." He pointed to the jar at which he had sniffed. "How much for that one?"

"You may have it for nothing", said the little man, giving it to him. "But I want the empty back."

Taking it, Jensen again uncapped and smelled. He dipped a finger, sucked it cautiously. His expression became beatific.

"I take back all that drug talk. I get the idea now." He waved the jar, doing it gently lest he spill a drop. "Illegal liquor, ninety-six proof and no tax." Another finger-suck. "All the same, somebody really knows how to make it. Somebody is a revenue-dodging expert. Count me a customer—I'll be here regularly as from now."

211

With that he tried a mouthful. It was like a torchlight procession parading down his gullet.

"Youps!" He gained breath, eyed the jar with unconcealed respect. It was on the small side, holding no more than a fifth of a pint. That was a pity. He lifted it for another drink. "This one's on me. Here's to crime!"

"You have been very rude", remarked the little man. "Remember that!"

Grinning at him, Jensen tilted the jar and let the rest go down. Something exploded in his belly. The walls of the shop appeared to recede to an enormous distance and then shoot back. He teetered for five seconds while strength drained out of his legs, then bowed forward and permitted the floor to smack him in the face.

Aeons swung by, one after another, long, foggy, filled with dull sounds. They ended. Jensen emerged slowly as from a bad dream.

He was on all fours on a sheet of ice or something resembling ice. He was down like a dog, also rigid and muzzy-minded. His eyes were out of focus. He shook his head to revive his wits.

Thoughts gradually fought their way into his befuddled cranium. A drug depot. He'd found one and been too nosey. Somebody had pussied behind him. Somebody had handed him a large lump on the pate. What comes of talking out loud and asking too many questions.

"You've been very rude. Remember that!"

Rude nothing. Pretty soon, when he could pull himself together and regain his health and strength, he'd become downright vulgar. He would take the little man apart and strew the pieces around.

The eyes got working more or less, mostly less. They remained peculiarly and horribly short-sighted. His nose was functioning topnotch; it could smell umpteen things at once, including an overheated engine someplace fifty yards away. But the eyes remained poor.

All the same, he could see now that the ice was not ice. It was more like plate glass, thick and cold. There was another sheet of it far below him and another below that. Also a strong wire grille fronting the lot.

He tried to come erect but his back was stiff and refused to bend. His legs wouldn't obey his will. What a thumper he must

212

have caught! Still on all fours, he edged nearer the imprisoning grille, doing it with some sort of lethargic ponderousness. Voices sounded somewhere nearby but out of sight.

"She insists on a telepathic saluki and that's what it's got to be."

"It will take ten days", answered the little man's tones.

"Her birthday is Saturday week. Sure you can have it ready for then?"

"I'm positive."

"That's fine. Go ahead with it. I'll bring you a fat one when I come to collect."

Jensen screwed up his eyes and squinted myopically through the grille at a shiny surface opposite. More glass fronting another row of wired-in but empty shelves. There were vague, elusive shadow-pictures on it. Something like a distant window with words across. The words were reversed and took some time to spell them out: *Mutants For Sale*.

His gaze lowered to his own level, saw something else reflected a good deal more clearly. He moved to one side. It moved likewise. He shook his head. So did the other. He opened his mouth and the mirage opened with him.

Then he screamed bloody murder—but only a tiny snort came forth. The reflection also snorted.

It was pale blue, seventeen inches long and had a horn on its ugly nose.

The Horror Show

No fairground is ever complete without a horror show—and certainly this book would be incomplete without a story of one. By and large they are harmless enough—just a good spot for a few laughs and the opportunity to hold a girl tight when a spider, leaping from the dark, scares her almost out of her wits. The same cannot be said, however, for the next show. And the management here and now states that it will not be held responsible for any upset pulses or dry throats.

HORRER HOWCE

By Margaret St. Clair

Dickson-Hawes' face had turned a delicate pea-green. He closed
the shutter on the opening very quickly indeed. Nonetheless, he
said in nearly his usual voice, "I'm afraid it's a trifle literary,
Freeman. Reminds me of that thing of Yeats'—'What monstrous,
beast, Its time come, uh, round again, slouches towards Bethlehem
to be born?' But the people who go to a horror house for amusement aren't literary. It wouldn't affect them the way it did me."
He giggled nervously.

No answering emotion disturbed the normal sullenness of
Freeman's face. "I thought there was a nice feel to it", he said
obstinately. "I wouldn't have put so much time in on this stuff
unless I thought you'd be interested. Research is more in my line.
I could have made a lot more money working on one of the
government projects."

"You didn't have much choice, did you?" Dickson-Hawes
said pleasantly. "A political past is such a handicap, unless one's
willing to risk prosecution for perjury."

"I'm as loyal as anybody! For the last five years—eight, ten—
all I've wanted to do was make a little cash. The trouble is, I
always have such rotten luck."

"Um." Dickson-Hawes wiped his forehead unobtrusively.
"Well, about your little effort. There are some nice touches,
certainly. The idea of the monstrous womb, alone on the seashore,
slowly swelling, and . . ." In the folds of his handkerchief, he
stifled a sort of cough. "No, I'm afraid it's too poetic. I can't
use it, old chap."

The two men moved away from the shuttered opening. Freeman
said, "Then Spring Scene is the only one you're taking?"

"Of those of yours I've seen. It's horrid enough, but not too
horrid. Haven't you anything else?" Dickson-Hawes' voice was
eager, but eagerness seemed to be mixed with other things—
reluctance, perhaps, and the fear of being afraid.

Freeman fingered his lower lip. "There's the Well", he said after a moment. "It needs a little more work done on it, but—I guess you could look at it."

"I'd be delighted to", Dickson-Hawes agreed heartily. "I do hope you understand, old man, that there's quite a lot of money involved in this."

"Yeah. You've really got the capital lined up? Twice before, you were sure you had big money interested. But the deals always fell through. I got pretty tired of it."

"This time it's different. The money's already in escrow, not to mention what I'm putting in myself. We intend a coast-to-coast network of horror houses in every gayway, playland and amusement park."

"Yeah. Well, come along."

They went down the corridor to another door. Freeman unlocked it. "By the way", he said, "I'd appreciate it if you'd keep your voice down. Some of the machinery in this stuff's—delicate. Sensitive."

"By all means. Of course."

They entered. To their right was an old brick house, not quite in ruin. To the left, a clump of blackish trees cut off the sky. Just in front of them was the moss-covered coping of an old stone well. The ground around the well was slick with moisture.

Dickson-Hawes sniffed appreciatively. "I must say you've paid wonderful attention to detail. It's exactly like being out of doors. It even smells foggy and damp."

"Thanks," Freeman replied with a small, dour smile.

"What happens next?"

"Look down in the well."

Rather gingerly, Dickson-Hawes approached. He leaned over. From the well came a gurgling splash.

Dickson-Hawes drew back abruptly. Now his face was not quite greenish; it was white. "My word, what a monster! " he gasped. "What is it, anyway?"

"Clockwork", Freeman answered. "It'll writhe for thirty-six hours on one winding. I couldn't use batteries, you know, on account of the water. That greenish flash in the eyes comes from prisms. And the hair is the same thing you get on those expensive fur coats, only longer. I think they call it plasti-mink."

"What happens if I keep leaning over? Or if I drop pebbles down on it?"

216

"It'll come out at you."

Dickson-Hawes looked disappointed. "Anything else?"

"The sky gets darker and noises come out of the house. Isn't that enough?"

Dickson-Hawes coughed. "Well, of course we'd have to soup it up a bit. Put an electrified rail around the well coping and perhaps make the approach to the well slippery so the customers would have to grasp the handrail. Install a couple of air jets to blow the girls' dresses up. And naturally make it a good deal darker so couples can neck when the girl gets scared. But it's a nice little effort, Freeman, very nice indeed. I'm almost certain we can use it. Yes, we ought to have your well in our horror house."

Dickson-Hawes' voice had rung out strongly on the last few words. Now there came another watery splash from the well. Freeman seemed disturbed.

"I *told* you to keep your voice down", he complained. "The partitions are thin. When you talk that loud, you can be heard all over the place. It isn't good for the—machinery."

"Sorry."

"Don't let it happen again . . . I don't think the customers ought to neck in here. This isn't the place for it. If they've got to neck, let them do it outside. In the corridor."

"You have no idea, old chap, what people will do in a darkened corridor in a horror house. It seems to stimulate them. But you may be right. Letting them stay here to neck might spoil the illusion. We'll try to get them on out."

"Okay. How much are you paying me for this?"

"Our lawyer will have to discuss the details", said Dickson-Hawes. He gave Freeman a smile reeking with synthetic charm. "I assure you he can draw up a satisfactory contract. I can't be more definite until I know what the copyright or patent situation would be."

"I don't think my Well could be patented", Freeman said. "There are details in the machinery nobody understands but me. I'd have to install each unit in your horror house network myself. There ought to be a clause in the contract about my per diem expenses and a travelling allowance."

"I'm sure we can work out something mutually satisfactory."

"Uh . . . let's get out of here. This is an awfully damp place to do much talking in."

217

They went out into the hall again. Freeman locked the door. "Have you anything else?" Dickson-Hawes asked.

Freeman's eyes moved away. "No."

"Oh, come now, old chap. Don't be coy. As I told you before, there's *money* involved."

"What sort of thing do you want?"

"Well, horrid. Though not quite so poetically horrid as what you have behind the shutter. That's a little too much. Perhaps something with a trifle more action. With more customer participation. Both the Well and Spring Scene are on the static side."

"Uh."

They walked along the corridor. Freeman said slowly, "I've been working on something. There's action and customer participation in it, all right, but I don't know. It's full of bugs. I just haven't had time to work it out yet."

"Let's have it, old man, by all means! "

"Not so loud! You've got to keep your voice down. Otherwise I can't take you in." Freeman himself was speaking almost in a whisper. "All right. Here."

They had stopped before a much more substantial door than the one behind which the Well lay. There was a wide rubber flange all around it, and it was secured at top and bottom by two padlocked hasps. In the top of the door, three or four small holes had been bored, apparently to admit air.

"You must have something pretty hot locked up behind all that", Dickson-Hawes remarked.

"Yeah." Freeman got a key ring out of his pocket and began looking over it. Dickson-Hawes glanced around appraisingly.

"Somebody's been writing on your wall", he observed. "Rotten speller, I must say."

Freeman raised his eyes from the key ring and looked in the direction the other man indicated. On the wall opposite the door, just under the ceiling, somebody had written HORRER HOWCE in what looked like blackish ink.

The effect of the ill-spelled words on Freeman was remarkable. He dropped the key ring with a clatter, and when he straightened from picking it up, his hands were quivering.

"I've changed my mind", he said. He put the key ring back in his pocket. "I always did have the damnedest luck."

Dickson-Hawes leaned back against the wall and crossed his ankles. "How do you get your ideas, Freeman?"

"Oh, all sorts of ways. Things I read, things people tell me, things I see. All sorts of ways." Both men were speaking in low tones.

"They're amazing. And your mechanical effects—I really don't see how you get machinery to do the things you make it do."

Freeman smiled meagrely. "I've always been good at mechanics. Particularly radio and signalling devices. Relays. Communication problems, you might say. I can communicate with anything. Started when I was a kid."

There was a silence. Dickson-Hawes kept leaning against the wall. A close observer, Freeman noticed almost a tic, a fluttering of his left eyelid.

At last Freeman said, "How much are you paying for the Well?"

Dickson-Hawes closed his eyes and opened them again. He may have been reflecting that while a verbal contract is quite as binding as a written one, it is difficult to prove the existence of a verbal contract to which there are no witnesses.

He answered, "Five thousand in a lump sum, I think, and a pro-rated share of the net admissions for the first three years.

There was an even longer silence. Freeman's face relaxed at the mention of a definite sum. He said, "How are your nerves? I need money so damned bad."

Dickson-Hawes' face went so blank that it would seem the other man had touched a vulnerable spot. "Pretty good, I imagine", he said in a carefully modulated voice. "I saw a good deal of action during the war."

Cupidity and some other emotion contended in Freeman's eyes. He fished out the key ring again. "Look, you must not make a noise. No yelling or anything like that, no matter what you see. They're very—I mean the machinery's delicate. It's full of bugs I haven't got rid of yet. The whole thing will be a lot less ghastly later on. I'm going to keep the basic idea, make it just as exciting as it is now, but tone it down plenty."

"I understand."

Freeman looked at him with a frown. "Don't make a noise", he cautioned again. "Remember, none of this is real." He fitted the key into the first of the padlocks on the stoutly built door.

The second padlock was a little stiff. Freeman had to fidget with it. Finally he got the door open. The two men stepped through it. They were outside.

There is no other way of expressing it: They were outside. If the illusion had been good in the Well, here it was perfect. They stood in a sort of safety island on the edge of a broad freeway, where traffic poured by in an unending rush eight lanes wide. It was the time of day when, though visibility is really better than at noon, a nervous motorist or two has turned on his parking lights. Besides the two men, the safety island held a new, shiny, eggplant-coloured sedan.

Dickson-Hawes turned a bewildered face on his companion. "Freeman", he said in a whisper, "did you *make* all this?"

For the first time, Freeman grinned. "Pretty good, isn't it?" he replied, also in a whisper. He opened the car door and slid into the driver's seat. "Get in. We're going for a ride. Remember, no noise."

The other man obeyed. Freeman started the car—it had a very quiet motor—and watched until a lull in the traffic gave him a chance to swing out from the curb. He stepped on the accelerator. The landscape began to move by.

Cars passed them. They passed some cars. Dickson-Hawes looked for the speedometer on the dashboard and couldn't find it. A garage, a service station, a billboard went by. The sign on the garage read: WE FIX FLATTEDS. The service station had conical pumps, the tomatoes on the billboard were purple and green.

Dickson-Hawes was breathing shallowly. He said, "Freeman— where *are* we?"

Once more, the other man grinned. "You're getting just the effect I mean to give", he retorted in a pleased whisper. "At first the customer thinks he's on an ordinary freeway, with ordinary people hurrying home to their dinners. Then he begins to notice all sorts of subtle differences. Everything's a little off-key. It adds to the uneasiness."

"Yes, but—what's the object of all this? What are we trying to do?"

"Get home to our dinners, like everyone else."

"Where does the—well, difficulty come in?"

"Do you see that car in the outer lane?" They were still conversing in whispers. "Black, bullet-shaped, quite small, going very fast?"

"Yes."

"Keep your eye on it."

220

The black car *was* going very fast. It caught up with a blue sedan in front of it, cut in on it and began to crowd it over to the curb. The blue sedan tried to shake off the black car, but without success. If the driver didn't want to be wrecked, he had to get over.

For a while, the two cars ran parallel. The black car began to slow down and crowd more aggressively than ever. Suddenly it cut obliquely in front of the sedan and stopped.

There was a frenzied scream of brakes from the sedan. It stopped with its left fender almost against the black bullet-shaped car. The bodies were so close, there was no room for the sedan driver to open his door.

Freeman had let the car he was driving slow down, presumably so Dickson-Hawes could see everything.

For a moment, there was nothing to see. Only for a moment. Then two—or was it three?—long, blackish, extremely thin arms came out from the black car and fumbled with the glass in the window of the sedan. The glass was forced down. The arms entered the sedan.

From the sedan there came a wild burst of shrieking. It was like the flopping, horrified squawks of a chicken at the chopping block. The shrieks were still going on when the very thin arms came out with a—

The light hid nothing. The three very thin arms came out with a plucked-off human arm.

They threw it into the interior of the black car. The three arms invaded the sedan once more.

This time, Dickson-Hawes had turned neither white nor greenish, but a blotchy grey. His mouth had come open all around his teeth, in the shape of a rigid oblong with raised, corded edges. It was perfectly plain that if he was not screaming, it was solely because his throat was too paralyzed.

Freeman gave his passenger only a momentary glance. He was looking into the rear-view mirror. He began to frown anxiously.

The shrieking from the blue sedan had stopped. Dickson-Hawes covered his face with his hands while Freeman drove past it and the other car. When the group lay behind them, he asked in a shaking whisper, "Freeman, are there any more of them? The black cars, I mean?"

"Yeah. One of them's coming towards us now."

Dickson-Hawes' head swivelled around. Another of the black cars was hurtling towards them through the traffic, though it was a long way behind.

Dickson-Hawes licked his lips.

"Is it—after us?"

"I think so."

"But why? Why—us?"

"Part of the game. Wouldn't be horrid otherwise. Hold on. I'm going to try to shake it off."

Freeman stepped down on the accelerator. The eggplant-coloured sedan shot ahead. It was a very fast car and Freeman was evident an expert and nerveless driver. They slid through non-existent holes in the traffic, glanced off from fenders, slipped crazily from lane to lane, a shuttle in a pattern of speed and escape.

The black car gained on them. No gymnastics. A bulletlike directness. But it was nearer all the time.

Dickson-Hawes gave a sort of whimper.

"No noise", Freeman cautioned in a fierce whisper. "That'll bring them down for sure. *Now!*"

He pressed the accelerator all the way down. The eggplant-coloured car bounced and swayed. There was a tinkle of glass from the headlights of the car on the left as the sedan brushed it glancingly. Dickson-Hawes moaned, but realized they had gained the length of several cars. Momentarily, the black pursuer fell behind.

They went through two red lights in a row. So did the black bullet. It began to edge in on them. Closer and faster. Faster and faster.

Dickson-Hawes had slumped forward with his head on his chest. The black car cut towards them immediately.

Freeman snarled. Deliberately, he swung out into the path of the pursuer. For a second, it gave ground.

"Bastards", Freeman said grimly.

The black car cut in on them like the lash of a whip. The sedan slithered. Hub caps grated on concrete. The sedan swayed drunkenly. Brakes howled. Dickson-Hawes, opening his eyes involuntarily for the crash, saw that they were in a safety island. The same safety island, surely, from which they had started out?

The black car went streaking on by.

"I hate those things", Freeman said bitterly. "Damned Voom.

If I could— But never mind. We got away. We're safe. We're home."

Dickson-Hawes did not move. "I said we're safe", Freeman repeated. He opened the car door and pushed the other man out through it. Half-shoving, half-carrying, he led him to the door from which they had entered the freeway. It was still the time of day at which nervous motorists turn on their parking lights.

Freeman manoeuvred Dickson-Hawes through the door. He closed it behind them and fastened the padlocks in the hasps. They were out in the corridor again—the corridor on whose wall somebody had written HORRER HOWCE.

Freeman drew a deep breath. "Well. Worked better than I thought it would. I was afraid you'd yell. I thought you were the type that yells. But I guess the third time's the charm."

"What?"

"I mean I guess my goddam luck has turned at last. Yeah. What did you think of it?"

Dickson-Hawes swallowed, unable to answer.

Freeman regarded him. "Come along to my office and have a drink. You look like you need one. And then you can tell me what you think of this setup."

The office was in the front of the house, down a couple of steps. Dickson-Hawes sank into the chair Freeman pulled out for him. He gulped down Freeman's dubious reddish Bourbon gratefully.

After the second drink, he was restored enough to ask, "Freeman, was it real?"

"Certainly not", the other man said promptly.

"It looked awfully real", Dickson-Hawes objected. "That arm . . ." He shuddered.

"A dummy", Freeman answered promptly once more. "You didn't see any blood, did you? Of course not. It was a dummy arm."

"I hope so. I don't see how you could have *made* all the stuff we saw. There's a limit to what machinery can do. I'd like another drink."

Freeman poured. "What did you think of it?"

Colour was coming back to Dickson-Hawes' cheeks. "It was the most horrible experience I ever had in my life."

Freeman grinned. "Good. People like to be frightened. That's why roller-coaster rides are so popular."

223

"Not that much, people don't. Nobody would enjoy a roller-coaster ride if he saw cars crashing all around him and people getting killed. You'll have to tone it down a lot. An awful lot."

"But you liked it?"

"On the whole, yes. It's a unique idea. But you'll have to tone it down about seventy-five per cent."

Freeman grimaced. "It can be done. But I'll have to have a definite commitment from you before I undertake such extensive changes."

"Um."

"There are other places I could sell it, you know", Freeman said pugnaciously. "Jenkins of Amalgamated might be interested. Or Silberstein."

"Jenkins lit out with about six thousand of Amalgamated's dollars a couple of months ago. Nobody's seen him since. And they found Silberstein wandering on the streets last week in a sort of fit. Didn't you know? He's in a mental home. You won't be selling either of *them* much of anything."

Freeman sighed, but made no attempt to dispute these distressing facts. "I'll have to have a definite commitment from you before I make that many major changes", he repeated stubbornly.

"Well . . ." Fright and whisky may have made Dickson-Hawes a little less cautious than usual. "We could pay you fifty a week for a couple of months while you worked on it, as advance against royalties. If we didn't like the final results, you wouldn't have to give back the advance."

"It's robbery. Apprentice mechanics earn more than that. Make it sixty-five."

"I hate haggling. Tell you what. We'll make it sixty."

Freeman shrugged tiredly. "Let's get it down in black and white. I'll just draw up a brief statement of the terms and you can sign it."

"Well, okay."

Freeman stooped and began to rummage in a desk drawer. Once he halted and seemed to listen. He opened another drawer. "Thought I had some paper . . . Yeah, here it is." He turned on the desk light and began to write.

Dickson-Hawes leaned back in his chair and sipped at Freeman's whisky. He crossed his legs and recrossed them. He was humming "Lili Marlene" loudly and off pitch. His head rested against the wall.

Freeman's pen moved across the paper. "That's about it", he said at last. He was smiling. "Yeah. I—"

There was a splintering crash, the sound of lath and plaster breaking. Freeman looked up from the unsigned agreement to see the last of his entrepreneurs—the last, the indubitable last—being borne off in the long black arms of the Voom.

It was the first time they had gone through the partitions in search of a victim, but the partitions were thin and the unsuccessful chase on the highway had excited them more than Freeman had realized. There has to be a first time for any entity, even for Voom.

Ten full minutes passed. Dickson-Hawes' shrieks died away. The third episode had ended just as disastrously as the earlier two. There wasn't another entrepreneur in the entire U.S.A. from whom Freeman could hope to realize a cent for the contents of his horror house. He was sunk, finished, washed up.

Freeman remained sitting at his desk, motionless. All his resentment at the bad luck life had saddled him with—loyalty oaths, big deals that fell through, chisellers like Dickson-Hawes, types that yelled when Voom were after them—had coalesced into an immobilizing rage.

At last he drew a quavering sigh. He went over to the bookcase, took out a book, looked up something. He took out a second book, a third.

He nodded. A gleam of blind, intoxicated vindictiveness had come into his eyes. Just a few minor circuit changes, that was all. He knew the other, more powerful entities were there. It was only a question of changing his signalling devices to get in touch with them.

Freeman put the book back on the shelf. He hesitated. Then he started towards the door. He'd get busy on the circuit changes right away. And while he was making them, he'd be running over plans for the horror house he was going to use the new entities to help him build.

It would be dangerous. So what? Expensive . . . he'd get the money somewhere. But he'd fix them. He'd build a horror house for the beasts that would make them sorry they'd ever existed— Horrer Howce for the Voom.

The Future

The Freak Show, as we have seen, has been with us for a very long time, and I'm convinced that it has a future which stretches into the Space Age and beyond. Our next contributor, Harlan Ellison, would seem to be of this opinion, too, and in "Big Sam Was My Friend" he has created a unique and entertaining picture of a circus of the future. But things aren't quite as one might expect them to be . . .

BIG SAM WAS MY FRIEND

By Harlan Ellison

I guess working for a teeper circus ain't the quietest work in the Galaxy, but what the dickens, it's more than just a buck, and you see a lot of the settled worlds, and there's always enough quailette around to keep a guy happy, so why should I kick. By that I mean, so what if they *did* lynch my friend Big Sam out on Giuliu II? So what, you can always find another friend someplace around. But every time I start thinking that way, I kick myself mentally and say Johnny Lee, you got to stop passing Sam off like that. He was a good friend. He was a sick man, and he couldn't help what he did, but that's no call to be passin' him off so quick.

Then I'd start to remember the first time I'd ever seen Big Sam. That was outside Shreveport. Not the *old* Shreveport, but the one on Burris, with the green-sand hills just beyond in the dusk. We were featuring Dolly Blaze that time. She was a second stage pyrotic with a cute little trick of setting herself on fire, and what with her figure what it was, well, it wasn't much of a trick—even for a drum-banger like me—to kick up some pretty hot publicity about the circus.

It was the second show, and we'd packed the tent full—which wasn't odd, because two hundred Burrites, each as big as an elephant (and looking a little bit like elephants with those hose proboscises), crammed our pneumotent till there was hardly room for the hawkers to mill through—when I spotted him. It wasn't so strange to spot a Homebody from Earth on a Ridge world, what with the way we Earthmen move around, but there was something odd about *this* Homebody. Aside from the fact that he was close to seven feet tall.

It wasn't long till I spotted him as a teeper of some sort. At first I figured him for a clairvoyant, but I could tell from the way he watched the acrobats (they were a pair of Hungarian floaters called the Spindotties, and the only way they could have fallen was to lose their teep powers of anti-grav altogether), the way he tensed up when they were making a catch, that he couldn't read the future. Then I figured him for an empath, and that would have been useless for the circus; except in an administrative capacity of course. To tell us when one of the performers was sick, or unhappy, or a bad crowd, or like that. But right then credits were tight and we couldn't afford an empath, so I counted him off. But as I watched him sitting there in the stands, between two big-as-houses Burrites sucking up pink lemonade from squeeze-bulbs, I discounted the empath angle, too.

I didn't realize he was a teleport till Fritz Bravery came on with his animal pack.

In our circus, we clear both side rings for the central circle, when a speciality act goes on. Then the fluorobands are jockeyed into position over the centre ring, and the mini-tapes set their reaction music for all-bands. That way we draw attention to the big act only.

Fritz Bravery was an old-timer. He had been a lion-tamer in a German circus back Home, before teeping was understood, and the various types outlined. That was when Fritz had found out the reason he was so good with animals was that he was what the French had labelled *animaux-voyeur*. Which, in English, the way we accept it now, means he and the beasts think alike, and he suggests to them and like they just go through hoops if he thinks *jump through a hoop*.

But Fritz was also one of those harkeners after the old days. He thought show biz was dead, nothing but commercial and plebeian crap left. You know, one of those. And he had lost his wife Gert somewhere between Madison Square Plaza and Burris, and eventually the old joy juice had grabbed him.

That night old Fritz Bravery was juiced to the ears.

You could spot it the moment he got into the ring with the beasts. He was using three big Nubian lions and a puma and a dree and a slygor, those days. Plus one mean bitch of a black panther called Felice, the likes of which for downright cussedness I've never seen.

Old Fritz got with them, and he was shaky from the start. King Groth, who ran the show, looked at me, and I looked at him, and we both thought, *I hope to God Fritz can handle them tonight with his senses all fogged up like that.* But we didn't do anything, because Fritz always had his escape plate ready to lift him over their heads, if he got into trouble. And besides, it was *his* act, we had no right to cramp it before he'd shown his stuff.

But King murmured in my ear, "Better start looking around for a new cat man, Johnny. Fritz won't be good much longer." I nodded, and felt sort of sad, because Fritz was as good a cat man as we'd ever had with the circus.

The old man went around them, walking backwards, with his lectrowhip snapping and sparking sweetly, and for a while everything was fine. He even had the lions and the puma up in a tricky pyramid, with the black panther about to leap up the backs of the five lions, to take her place at the apex of the pyramid. He pulled off that number pretty well, though one of the lions stumbled as the pyramid was breaking up, and growled at him. We had grown to know the difference between a "show" growl—commanded mentally by Fritz—for fright effect in the act, and a real one. A real one free of Fritz's control. That was this last one. So we knew old Fritz was losing control.

We grew more alert as he herded the lions and the puma into the corner of the force-cage in which he performed his act. It was transparent around the four walls, but there nonetheless.

Then Fritz—ignoring Felice, who followed the other Earth-beasts—went to work on the dree. He got her to rotate on all sixteen, and hump, and then turn inside out, which is a pretty spectacular thing, considering a dree's technicolor innards. Then he got it to lift him on one appendage, and place him gently on another, all the way up the length of her body, from appendage to appendage.

Then he worked for a while with the slygor.

It was poisonous, so he donned gloves, and used the sonic-whistle on it alone, since electricity did not affect it in any way. Even his work with the slygor was fair that night, and for a while we thought he would make it fine. I kept tossing this seven-foot Homebody in the stands a look from time to time, trying to decide what sort of a teep he was, but he was just watching the act, and smiling, and not doing a thing.

Then Fritz went to work on Felice.

She had been invershipped from Earth not more than three weeks before, and the trip through inverspace, coupled with her natural instinctive nastiness, and more than likely allied with some temperament quirk aggravated by the warping of the ship and its occupants through inverspace, had left her a jangle-nerved heaped-up body of hate and fury. We had had several close calls with her nipping her feeder-robots, and I for one didn't like to see Old Fritz in there with her.

But he was determined to break her—showmanship and all that bushwah—so we let him go ahead. After all, he *did* have the escape plate there, which whisks him anti-gravitically over the heads of the animals, should there be trouble.

He picked up his lectrowhip, and moved in on Felice. She sat crouched back on her haunches, waiting him out. He stopped a foot from her, so close he could have stroked her sleek black fur. Then he did a double-movement crack-crack! with the lectro-whip, and caught her on the snout with a spark. Felice leaped.

At that precise instant, the most remarkable thing I've ever glommed in all my days as flack for a top, happened. I've never yet been able to figure it out—whether the beasts were actually in mental contact with one another, or it was just chance—but the puma got to its feet, and softly padded over to the escape plate . . . and sat down on it. The lions moved out, and positioned themselves around the force cage. Fritz was hemmed in completely. Then Felice began stalking him.

It was the most fascinating and horrifying thing I've ever seen. To witness that big cat, playing footsie with old Fritz. The tamer tried to control her, but even from where we were in the stands, we could see the sweat on his face, and the dark lines in the completely white of his face. He was scared; he had lost control of them completely. He knew he was dead.

Felice's eyes were two barbs, ready to impale poor old Fritz, and we were so stunned, it all happened so quickly, we just sat there and so help me God we just *watched*!

I felt like a Roman in the arena.

Felice crouched again, and the muscles in her black shoulders hunched and bunched and tensed, and she sprang full on old Fritz.

He fell down, and her crushing weight landed atop him, and her jaws opened wide, with yellow fangs straining yowpingly for Fritz Bravery's neck. Her head came up, and back, and her throat was stretched tight so the pulse of a blood vein could be seen, and then the head came down like the blade of a guillotine.

But Fritz wasn't there.

He was sitting up in the stands with the seven-foot Homebody. That was when I knew. Hell, *anybody'd* be able to tell, by then. He was a teleport. The best kind—an outgoing teleport.

He had teeped Fritz out of the jaws of the black panther.

I looked at King Groth, who was looking from Felice to Fritz and back, not knowing I had already tagged the Homebody as a teeper, and there was amazement on his face.

"We got us a new star act, King", I said, slipping out of my seat. I cocked a thumb at Fritz, who was talking bewilderedly to the seven-foot Homebody. I started threading my way between the elephant-big Burrites, towards Fritz and his saviour.

Behind me, I heard King Groth saying, "Go get 'im boy."

I got him.

Now I won't bother going into the year Big Sam spent with the circus. It was pretty routine. We covered the stardust route from Burris to Lyli A to Crown Colony to Peck's Orchard to Moulton X/11i11 (they have a treaty there with the natives, so long as they use both Homebody and native name for the planet) to Ringaling and right along the Ridge to the new cluster worlds of Dawnsa, Jowlak, Min, Thornwire and Giuliu II. That was where we lost Big Sam.

There on Giuliu II—where they lynched him.

But to understand what happened, *why* it happened, I'd better tell you about Big Sam. Not just that he was nearly seven feet tall, with a long, horsy face, and high cheekbones, and dark, sad blue eyes. But *about* him, what he was like.

And this is the best way to tell it:

Sam's act consisted of several parts. For instance, at the beginning, we turned off all the fluoro bands. Then three roustabouts clanked out carrying this big pole in their metal arms. They would kick off the cover plate of the hole we had sunk in the floor of the arena or tent, and insert the pole in it, then clamp it so it was rigid.

Then one of the roustabouts would switch on the torchfinger of his utility hand, and set fire to the pole. We had already doused it in oil, and the thing caught fire up its length, till there was a pillar of fire in the middle of the ring. It was a specially-treated pole, and didn't really burn—though the fire on it was real enough —so we used the same pole over and over.

Then the ringmaster would swoop in on his plate, and his sonic voice would boom out at the audience, "Laydeez and Gentil-menn! I ddrawww your attenshuuun to the centre rinnnng, where the Galaxy's most mystifying, most extraordinary artiste will perform for you. I am pppprowd to present: The Unbelievable Ugo!"

That was Sam.

Then the one spot would go on, like the eye of a god, and pick out Sam, striding across the plastidust (sawdust went out with the high cost of invershipping). He would be wearing skin-tight black clothing, that accentuated his slim build, and high-topped black boots, very soft and with two inch soles to make him seem even taller. And a black cape with a crimson lining.

He would advance to the centre of the ring, just beside the burning pole, and raise his arms. A girl wearing spangles and not much else (that was Beatrice, whom I had been dating, when she wasn't on her iron filing kick—but that's another story, for-tunately) would run out and take his cape, and Ugo, that's Sam, would turn and look at the pole for a long minute.

Then he would take a running leap, hit the pole and start to shinny up. Everyone would shriek. He was being burned to death. Then he was gone.

And a second later, he was at the top of the pole, on the little platform above the flames. Everyone was astonished. For some reason, they never realized he was a teleport. I guess there aren't many teleports around, and most people don't see them as flagrantly displaying their talents as Big Sam did. It's a recessive trait.

For a moment he would poise himself there on toetip, as the audios scirled their danger music on all bands, and then as the drums rolled, Sam would do a neat swan dive off the platform. The shrieking would get even bigger then.

He would turn a gainer, a flip, a half-gainer and then—just as it seemed he was about to smash full force into the ground—he disappeared . . .

. . . and reappeared standing lightly on the balls of his feet, in the same position he had been when he started—his arms wide-spread over his head, an enigmatic grin splitting his craggy features.

That was the first part of his act. The applause was always deafening. (And we never had to modify it by taped responses, either, isn't that beyond belief?)

To see an almost certain horrible death—you know how crowds all sit on the edges of their seats, *praying* subconsciously for a spectacular accident—and then to be whisked away from it so suddenly—brought to the edge of tragedy, and then to have their better natures win out, showing how much nicer they always *knew* they were—that was the supreme thrill.

But it was merely a beginning.

Then Ugo-Sam did juggling—magnificent high-flown juggling with hundreds of knives, and fireballs, and even thousand pound weights—all moving them by teleportation. Then he wrestled with the bear, slipping out of the most fearsome grips, as easily as a greased fish. Then came the tennis match he played with himself. (He beat himself in straight sets.)

His act was sensational. For on many of the outer Ridge worlds, they had had little or no truck with teleports. By the Service system for teeps, each of the categories had to send representative members to the Ridge world to serve tours, to spread Homebody technology and advantages around, but there were so few teleports, they had been rarely seen.

So Big Sam was a novelty. And as such, he dragged the credits for us. I played him big.

But there was more to Sam than just the tricks.

We used to sit alone at night under a saffron sky, or a mauve sky or an ebony sky, and talk. I liked talking to him, because he wasn't dumb, like most of the washed-up and used-up carny creeps we had with us. He had been an educated man, that was obvious, and there was a deep, infinite sadness about him that sometimes made me want to cry, just talking to him there.

I remember the night I found out how sick Big Sam really was. That was on Rorespokine I, a little plug of a world by all rights we should have avoided; but a combination of low money for pay cheques, repair work for the ships, and general all-round lethargy, had set us down on that whistle stop for a three-week set.

Mostly, we just puttered around and killed time resting up till the big six-month tour on Giuliu II.

That night, Big Sam and I lay back with our heads on grassy mounds, staring up at the night that was deep blue with the stars ticking away eternity over us. I looked over at the rough topography of his face, and asked him, "Sam, what the hell is a guy like you doing out on the fly like this?"

His face tightened all over. It was so odd, the way he looked. So tight, like my question had sucked all the life from him.

"I'm looking for a dead girl, JohnnyLee." He always pronounced my name as though it were one word only. His answer didn't sink in for a second.

I didn't want to push, but I felt somehow this was the first opening-up he had ever given me.

"Oh? How'd that happen?"

"She died a long time ago, Johnny. A long time ago."

His eyes closed. He no longer saw the stars.

"She was just a girl, Johnny. Just another girl, and I guess I was more in love with the idea of love, than with her."

I didn't say a word. For a long time, neither did he. Then, when I was starting to fall asleep, and thought he already had, he went on: "Her name was Claire. Nothing very pretentious about her, so simple and clean. I wanted very much to marry her, I don't know why, we were nothing alike. Then one day we were walking, and I don't know what it was—just something, you know—and I teleported away from her. Half a block away. I didn't know then, quite, what I could do. I had never teleported in front of Claire. I suppose it was a shock to her. She was a No-Talent, and it must have shocked her. I could see she was repulsed by the idea of it."

"I'd, I'd been . . . sleeping with her, Johnny, and I guess it was pretty foreign. Like finding out the guy you'd been making love to was an android or somesuch. She ran away. I was so shocked at her attitude, I just didn't follow her.

"Then I heard a screech and she screamed, and I teleported to the source of the scream, and she'd been hit by a truck, trying to cross the street. Oh, it wasn't my fault, nothing like that, and no guilt complex or anything, but—well, you know, I had to get away from things. So I took to the fly. Just like that."

He was finished. I said, "Just like that. You ever goin' back, Sam?"

He shook his head. "I don't suppose so. I'll find her someday."

I said, "Huh?"

He glanced over, and there was a hurt in his eyes. "Yeah, I suppose I never told you this, probably think it's a crazy idea; everyone else does. She's in Heaven."

"Nothing crazy about that, Sam," I said, big magnanimous that I was.

234

"Heaven is out here somewhere."

That stopped it. I was back to, "Huh?"

He nodded again. "Out here, on one of these, is Heaven. That's where she is. I'll find her." He waved at the stars overhead. I followed his arm. Up here? Heaven? On an alien world? I didn't say anything.

"Crazy?"

"No, I don't suppose it's any crazier than any other idea of Heaven or Hell," I replied soberly. It gave me the creeps, frankly.

"I'll find her," he reiterated.

"I sure hope so, Sam. I sure hope so."

He fell asleep before *I* did. Who could sleep with something like that to scare the crap out of you?

We hit Giuliu II on a Thursday, and by the following Friday week, we had a command performance scheduled for the Giuliun royalty. It was a wonderful deal; once we had performed and pleased the court, our success on Giuliu II was assured. Because they had a real Monarchy Plus set up on that world. And if the court liked us, the high glub-glub or whatever the hell they called the king, would send out a proclamation ordering *all* his subjects to attend or suffer some penalty. So we'd be all set.

We ran through the acts, in the palace, which was a great mansion, twice as big as our pneumotent, and I've got to admit, even washed-out Dolly Blaze and Fritz Bravery and the rest were magnificent. But, of course, Sam stole the show. They had never seen a teleport on Giuliu II, and Sam was at his sparklingest best. He was more daring and unusual than ever. There was even a trick with Felice that had everyone gasping and finally chuckling.

When it was over, the king and his court invited us to a huge banquet, and ceremonial party. It was the greatest. They had huge platters of fried and braised meats, bowls of planetary fruits, tankards of ales and liqueurs that were direct lineal descendants of ambrosia. It was the greatest.

Then they brought on the dancing girls, and they were even better. I spotted one smooth-limbed little number I decided to approach with dalliance in mind, after everyone had settled down a little. The Giuliuns were Homebody type right down to their navels, and I wasn't worried about picking up any alien equivalents of VD. Besides, she had the cutest little po-po I'd seen in months. Beatrice, the girl who assisted Sam, and who I had been shacking with, was eyeing me, and eyeing a handsome brute, all tanned and wearing bronze armour, who was guarding one of the big doors. I decided to let her cheat on me, thus leaving the road clear for the little dancer.

The party was well under way, when the king stood up and made some big deal announcement about us being just in time to see the Sacred Virgin Ceremony of Giuliu II, which occurred but once every twenty-five years. He even hinted it had been moved up a few weeks to accommodate us in this hour of circus triumph. We all applauded, and watched as they set up a high platform made of ever-smaller gold risers. It was quite a thrill.

We were all gathered around at the one end of the ceremonial hall, with the pyramid of risers at the other. We weren't interested in the least about this ceremony, but to be polite, we watched as they set up some sort of chopping block affair, and put two burning braziers beside the block.

It was getting more interesting by the moment. While most of the circus folk were still gorging themselves on the foods and fruits overflowing the table, Sam and I turned full around to watch this. I heard him mumble something about picturesque native ceremonies, and nodded my head.

The king signalled to one of his bully-boys, and the bully-boy swung a long-handled clapper at a tapestry hanging from floor to ceiling beside him. They must have a gong concealed behind it, because the sound almost deafened me.

Then the king—of his title I'm not sure, but his rank was obvious—spoke for a few minutes on the history and traditions of the Sacred Virgin Ceremony. We didn't really listen too closely, mainly because he was speaking in similes and the noise from the crowd around us drowned him half out.

But in a little while we got the impression this was very important stuff to the Giuliuns, and when the king clapped his hands, we turned to the gang, and tried to get them to shut up. Those slobs would rather eat than think.

They didn't shut up till the gong sounded again, but when the grey-hooded man with the gigantic meat cleaver brought the pretty blonde girl out on to the platform, they all signed off like we'd cut their vocal chords.

She was a magnificently beautiful creature. Her hair was long and blonde, and her body was full and straight. Her eyes the deepest and most lustrous brown I've ever seen.

The executioner—hell yes! that's what he was—helped her

236

over to the block, and her face was very calm. Calm, it seemed, the way someone's face would be if they were dying of cancer, and knew they could do nothing about it. But this young girl wasn't dying of cancer; she was about to have that grey-hooded man chop off her head.

It was apparent, that was what was about to happen.

A sacrificial ceremony.

The hooded man helped her to kneel before the block, and she lay her head in the notch. The executioner pulled her hair away from her neck, gently, and laid it over her left shoulder in a long blonde streamer.

Then he tested his hatchet's edge, and stepped back. He planted his feet wide apart, and swung the axe up. Everyone screamed, and it sounded like a million buzzsaws. Before anyone could do anything the executioner brought the axe down almost touching her neck, to get the proper placement for the real swing.

That was when I heard Sam's muted gurgle. He had been mumbling, there beside me, for over a minute, and I hadn't realized it, I was so engrossed in watching the tableau on the chopping block. Then I heard him mutter, "Claire!"

And I knew there was going to be trouble.

I saw him stand up, out of the corner of my eye, and as the executioner swung the axe up in a two-handed whirl, Sam disappeared from beside me, and the next instant, before the hatchet had a chance to fall on that lovely neck, he was there. His arm snaked around the grey-hooded man's neck, and his hand shot out to catch the descending shaft of the axe.

He wrenched the executing tool from the man's hand, and threw it with a spinning clatter to the floor of the chamber far below the pyramid. Then his fist came back and caught the hatchetman across his hidden face. The executioner stumbled, and Sam doubled him over with a belly-blow that made the grey-hood scream. Sam straightened him with a right to the tip of the jaw, and the hatchetman went caroming off the pyramid. He landed with a sick thump.

The king was on his feet, livid with rage, and the court was screaming, "Profanity! Outrage! Transgression!" The king clapped his hands, and a dozen of the tanned bully-boys (one of whom was the one Beatrice had been ogling) raced on to the pyramid and grabbed Sam around the waist, the neck, the legs . . .

237

. . . of course he teleported out of their grip. He was back beside me. The king was leaping up and down, screeching at the top of his lungs, to *get* that man. Sam stood impassively, waiting. Then King Groth walked over, and said, "Stand still, Sam. Let's find out how much damage you've done."

He went to talk to the other king. Groth was a sharp operator, and if anyone could pour oil on the waters, it was him. We watched as he talked to the king, who was getting more furious and apoplectic by the moment.

"Sam, Sam," I pleaded quietly, "why did you do it? For Christ's sake, *why*?"

He looked at me, and said, "This isn't much like Heaven, is it?"

Then I knew he had found Claire.

The blonde girl still kneeled beside the chopping block. She had not moved, except to raise her head from the notch.

King Groth came back, and his face was grey.

"Sam, they say you have to die."

Big Sam looked at him, and didn't say a word. I don't think he cared, really.

"Look, Sam, we're going to fight this. They can't do it to a Homebody. We can fight it, don't worry."

The king came rushing over, and started to screech something. "Listen," I piped in, just to stop him, "he is a sick man, he didn't know what he was doing. You have to remember he knows nothing of your local customs."

It didn't make a bit of difference. "He must die. That is the reward for interrupting the Sacred Virgin Ceremony."

We argued and hassled and made a big stink out of it, and I think the only reason we all didn't gallop out of there and pull up stakes was that we were afraid we'd *all* be held and executed. And Big Sam was the only teleport in the crowd. And there was something else; something I'm afraid and ashamed, even today, to say.

I think we were all afraid of losing the business.

That's right. Pretty disgusting, ain't it? We could have set Dolly Blaze to burning the joint, and we could have escaped. We could have done at least a hundred things to distract the Giuliuns. But we were afraid we'd lose the business, and we were almost willing to let the man die for that.

Finally, though, the king said: "We must leave it to the Sacred Virgin, then. Let her decision be the one."

238

That sat okay with us—we wanted a way out so bad then it didn't matter—and we all looked at Sam. Softly, the hurt came back into his eyes, and a softness surrounded his mouth, and he nodded. "That's fine," he said simply.

We all walked up to the pyramid, and looked at her. She was very clean and simple looking. Just the way I'd imagine Sam's Claire might have looked. We all stared at her, and with a sneer, she snarled, "Let him die!"

And that was that.

They took him up to the block, and they removed her, and they shoved Sam's head into the notch. Then someone made the motion that he be hung, because the block was reserved for the Sacred Virgin. So they strung up a fibre rope—right there in that beautiful hall—and they put it around Sam's neck, and ten men got on the other end of the rope that hung over a beam from above.

And we just watched. Can you understand that? We just stood there and watched as Sam was prepared for hanging. I tried to stop them, finally. I suppose I came out of my trance. "Wait, you can't do this!" But King Groth and two of the performers grabbed me by the arms, and held me.

"This is their world, Johnny, let them do what they have to do."

And Sam looked at me, and I could see in his eyes that it didn't matter to him. It was the same hurt, all over again. He had been wrong; he *did* have a hag riding him about Claire's death. This was one way to clear it off.

They yanked on the rope, and Sam went up.

He hardly twisted or kicked or twitched.

I couldn't watch.

Because there were a couple of things that made me ill way deep inside. The first was knowing that King Groth and the circus and even myself, had sacrificed this nice, quiet guy with a problem, for the sake of a credit. And the other thing, the thing that really stopped us from trying to help him, I think, was that Sam wanted to die. He could have teeped out of that noose at any moment, but he didn't. He let them lynch him. He had squared away with Claire.

We finished our tour on Giuliu II. Sam had been right: it wasn't much like Heaven.

239